SACRED TERRAIN

Veronica Mahara

With much love, I dedicate this book
to my daughters Star and Heidi.

Part One

Chapter One

Clermont City, California–August 1887

*S*tepping back from her latest painting with a tilt of her head, Jessica dabbed on a bit of green, then more purple. Had she forgotten that the minister's daughter's coat was more maroon? It didn't seem to matter anymore. For the last two hours, her thoughts had drifted away from her canvas and back again. It was stifling hot in her little art studio even though she'd propped up the small window as far as it could go. The door remained closed, however, since the grocer next door hadn't had his garbage removed in over a week. With the slightest breeze, the stench from rotting produce and animal fat wafted into the space, making her cover her nose with a handkerchief. Jessica would have to talk to Mr. Talbot, the gallery owner, about it again. She wasn't paying him rent to smell garbage all day. Needing air, she placed her brushes in the tin of mineral spirits, letting the liquid touch her fingers. After wiping her hands clean, she took off her apron and headed home.

The tidy, hard-packed, dirt streets of Clermont City were familiar to her now and she let her mind wander to Jacob, imagining a place where their love flourished and society accepted them. Keeping their relationship secret was a painful struggle, but they'd had no choice. Her aunt and uncle's adopted son was considered her cousin, and it would destroy their close-knit families. The daydreaming had become a bad habit, but she couldn't empty her heart of him and so many questions remained unanswered.

Their last rendezvous in June had left her with some hope. The love they expressed for each other went beyond lust. Jacob had willingly left his life on the trails to come to her, and they had promised to remain true to each other. Finding peace with that had been difficult, but some days were easier than others. Since he kissed her good-bye, the shine had been scrubbed off that hope. As always, her daydream ended with a thud. Jacob had not written to her.

The heat weighed down her clothing, making her petticoat cling to her sweaty legs, and the boned bodice of her dress was smothering her. She made her way to the gate of the white picket fence that surrounded the front of Aunt June and Uncle Burt's bungalow, painted a cheery yellow with white trim. Today, however, it reflected the sun like a hot beacon. Curly strands from her upswept, dark-brown hair stuck to her moist neck. Why hadn't she brought her parasol to shade her from the searing sunlight? More evidence of her distracted mind. She closed the gate behind her, ready to get into a less constricting day dress.

Sitting on the porch in one of the white rockers was Aunt June. A large pitcher of lemonade and two glasses sat on the wooden table beside her. Aunt June was a constant comfort, not only with food and drink, but with words of encouragement. Jessica smiled. "Hello, Auntie."

"There you are!" Her aunt's cherry-red cheeks swelled under her bright-green eyes. "I knew you'd be along soon enough. This heat is not fit for a lady locked in a small, stuffy room. I wish you would take our large shed for your art studio. A breeze comes through it."

Helping herself to a tall glass of lemonade, she listened to her aunt's chatter. The cool liquid had just the right amount of sour and sweet. "Yours is the best lemonade in the world!" Taking a long swallow, she came up for air. "Let me change into something lighter, and I'll sit with you for a while."

The larger guest bedroom with a flower-painted ceiling had become Jessica's own room now. The generous bed with its crisp, cotton linens called for her to luxuriate in it. A lazy evening in bed would be heaven. She had been standing most of the day in front of her easel. The window overlooking the hills, the trees, and her aunt's garden, gave her a feeling of security and gratitude, yet she was restless to be on her own. Her uncle's shed was tucked in back of the house shaded by large trees and surrounded by her aunt's touch of flowering shrubs and spring bulbs.

In the heat of day, the offer tempted her and she came to a decision. The bay of windows on the opposite side of the room opened to the street side, and she recalled a warm, early September afternoon when she watched Jacob come out of the house. Bringing to mind his tall, confident body and long, brown hair sent a wave of longing through her. He mounted his horse with ease and trotted off. She hitched a breath. That was the summer life changed, bringing her to where she was now. Another September was on the horizon, and she marveled at all she had been through in a year. How different she felt and how free she had become, yet the burden of her choices lay heavy on her heart—the pain of saying good-bye to Jacob, the courage to get a divorce and start life on her own, and mostly, the heartbreak of losing her unborn child, their unborn child. Was it not enough for Jacob to see her love and her strength to want him to stay and make a life in the city by the bay?

The windows were open, still the room was stifling. She stripped out of her sweaty clothes and changed into a light petticoat and simple dress. In the bathroom across the hall, she splashed her face with tepid water and patted it dry. With the day's work and the world's dust removed, she was ready to relax on the porch.

When Jessica returned, a plate of raspberry scones and a small bowl of clotted cream had joined the pitcher of lemonade. She smeared on the chilled cream and devoured the treat. She hadn't realized how hungry she'd been. Thinking of Jacob had given her an appetite. "I might take you up on your offer, Auntie. Mr. Talbot's little room is becoming so cramped with my larger canvases. He's been a dear to let me rent the space, and being right behind his art gallery has helped." Jessica thought aloud as she nibbled on her second scone.

"Well, it's settled then." Aunt June had a smile on her face.

Jessica felt a twinge of regret. The tiny studio was hers, even if she had outgrown it, not to mention the love she and Jacob had shared in it that June day only a few months ago. Her heart leapt in her chest at the thought. She reached over to her glass of cool lemonade.

"My, Jessica, you are thirsty."

Jessica grinned at Jacob's mother. "The heat." She turned her thoughts to her association with Mr. Talbot. Although he had raised the rent from nine dollars a month to ten, she showed a profit on her paintings. His small gallery sold most of her watercolor art. Depictions of the town's park, its homes, businesses, landscapes, flowers, and animals sold well.

Her canvases, thick with the heavy oil paints, were another matter. She painted scenes of the different lifestyles in San Francisco when she lived there with her husband, Frederick Moore. Her covert escapes from her stuffy, abusive life with him led her to places she had never dreamed existed—a place called the Tenderloin District, where the poor lived on the edge of society, Chinatown, where her experience was a mix of delight and horror, the wharves, Nob Hill, and the opulent Palace Hotel. She painted those scenes in stark reality to each other on every canvas. According to Mr. Talbot, they were too controversial to sell under her own name. She had let him talk her into selling those paintings under a pseudonym, J. Lingerhoph. Ridiculous, but her work sold in Oakland and San Francisco. Mr. Talbot told her the paintings were attracting an audience. City collectors accepted such art more readily than the small town she painted them in. She had heard that the mysterious J. Lingerhoph evoked thoughts one should not indulge in, and that was the reason he stayed away from the public eye. It made her laugh, yet she longed to expose the truth. But not now. Those paintings brought her a nice income.

Sitting back in the rocker, she let its gentle movement lull her into splendid relaxation. She wanted to drift off, but her aunt was having none of it. Her chatter kept on.

"We've cleared the shed of your uncle's hobby. He's too busy at the land company to do any more of his woodworking. As if he loved it," she said, then laughed. "I suppose he tried it, but you know, as a lawyer, he's much too ... how do I say it"—she searched the sky for the right word—practical. He's better suited to Dunbar's real estate business, and they so appreciate his legal help."

Jessica knew her aunt meant that her husband had been under foot since he retired from his law partnership with her father, Thomas Messing, back in Hartford, Connecticut. She smiled with half-closed eyes.

"Have you been sleeping well, my dear?" her aunt asked.

Suddenly self-conscious, she straightened her back. "Yes, of course," she replied. Was her daydreaming that obvious? Floating back to the sweet memory of making love with him in the small studio among her canvases and art supplies was too much to bear in the light of day. However, thinking of those times with him soothed her restless heart. Jacob had promised he and her brother, Will, would make good of their wild trading days and start a business in San Francisco. He would be nearer to her, if not completely hers to claim. Her innocent nature believed him, but her life experience gave her pause. Promises are only dreams until they become reality. Then she wondered how, at only twenty-three, she had become a cynic.

Turning her attention back to her aunt, who was onto a new recipe, Jessica tried to remain attentive. June loved experimenting in baking and cooking, and her skill for it was reknown among the family and beyond. She hoped to someday have the same expertise. Presenting Jacob with a plate of pear crisp or roasted chicken with lemon made her smile.

"So I feel we could do the whole thing with apples instead of blackberries. They're too juicy … the berries, that is," June said. "Jessica?"

"Yes, apples instead of blackberries." Barely listening, Jessica wondered with an eager heart where the man she gave her love to was. Would he ever return to Clermont City?

Chapter Two

August 1887

*J*acob Stanford took out the worn map from his pack and laid it on the blanket that covered the dew-dampened ground. He smoothed out the wrinkles. The cool morning was marked by patches of white fluff sailing along the sky. Their camp was outside of Medford, Oregon among the pines. Green pastures lay in front of them, glistening when the sun came from behind the clouds. Light and shadows played on the paper. "We'll be heading west to Jacksonville," he said.

"Where exactly is the location?" his cousin Will Messing asked. He sat on a stump with a cigarette hanging out of his mouth, his hair untied, strands of the brownish-blond mane dancing in the breeze. The dark shadow of his melancholy still hung around him. When Jacob met up with Will in Medford after his visit with Jessica last June, he came back to find his cousin in a hotel room in a state of pathetic drunkenness. Mi Lee, the woman carrying his child and the love of his life, had vanished. It took several days to get Will sober and several more days to get him back on his horse so they could continue their lives trading, stealing, and selling guns and ammunition. From what Jacob could gather from his cousin, Doc Middleman's nurse had taken up with a Chinese man

7

and they took the train up to Portland for her father's approval. Shortly thereafter, they were married.

Jacob scratched his chin whiskers. "Damn it, Will. Haven't you been paying attention? The post office is here, about ten miles away. The target is less than a mile from there. He pointed to where the next deal would be made. Looking up at Will, he tried again to ease his cousin's pain. "She just wasn't the one for you."

"I have a child in this world who may never know me."

Jacob huffed. "I know, but she's married now and her new husband will raise it. It's a fact you'll have to come to terms with. Maybe someday. ..." Jacob didn't want to give Will false hope. The chances of him seeing the child again were slim to none, and Will would have to face a court battle. Will had met Mi when, on that fateful day after selling guns and bullets to five men, a war broke out between the men and a band of Indians, and Will had been shot in the arm and side. Doc Middleman, as he was known in Medford, had stitched him up, and Mi had nursed him back to health. According to the doctor, Mi wrote to him, stating her new husband would adopt the baby once it was born, claiming the real father had abandoned her and the unborn child. It wasn't far from the truth, but Will had every intention of coming back for them once he was established in a real line of work.

"Damn those Indians!" Will lashed out.

"Indians? She's Chinese."

"If they hadn't stormed us after that trade, I wouldn't have gotten shot and I never would have met her. How does a woman's love turn just like that?" he asked, snapping his fingers.

"You have to move on, Will." Jacob waited for a sign to continue talking about their future. It was hard to see his cousin's easy going nature so dampened. After a while, Will forced a smile.

Once they solidified their plan, Jacob gathered the map and they broke camp. The men headed down the road to pick up the guns they would sell. Half the profit would go to Joe, the covert dealer at the post office. It wasn't the best trade they made, but deals were slim and they needed the cash.

Knowing Jessica waited for him, Jacob vowed to make enough money to fund his business. For now, he couldn't let himself think of her—not the shape of her tender lips, not her smooth, round hips, nor the eyes that held love for him. More so, he wouldn't let himself dwell on the fact that she might have found someone to take his place. He wouldn't blame her if she did. It was his lot in life ever since he decided his heart belonged to her.

Chapter Three

Clermont City–August 1887

$\mathcal{A}$fter another survey of the acreage he intended to call home, Caleb Cantrell mounted Lightfoot. "I could do a lot on this land," he said, patting Lightfoot's withers. "How'd you like to graze in that field, eh, boy?" The horse tossed his shiny, black mane. The rush of the Rail River, and the heady smells of sundried grass mingling with firs, spruce, and pine, were familiar to Caleb, but the peacefulness of this place was something he'd experienced only in his dreams. Yet here he stood, drinking it in. He imagined a home and barn, rows of vegetables, an orchard filled with oranges, lemons, and apples, and his own silversmith shop. His trail mates, Levi and Cork, had settled on Levi's family's farm. It wasn't too far away, and the silversmith business he hoped to work at was just a few miles from town. He mused how his guiding spirits had not abandoned him after all. He rubbed his arm. *Even after what I've done.*

It was his first purchase of land, and he wanted to do it properly. With his newly shortened, blond mane and tidy goatee, he was ready to present himself to the land company in Clermont City, California. Steering his horse down the narrow, winding, dirt road away from the land and onto the main street, he went over his finances again. He had been frugal with what he earned with J. Keaton and his company of gunrunners, along with his cut of the spoils from the Colorado shoot-out. There would be more than enough to get himself settled. At the thought of Colorado, his hand drifted to the scar on his left upper arm. He tried to abandon his memories of Colorado, but even as he moved toward a better life, the ghosts of three dead men in the shack in the hills haunted him. *You gave us no choice.*

The quaint town was quiet as he secured his horse to a black, wrought iron figure standing stiffly, holding a large ring. It was an odd site to Caleb, but then Clermont City wasn't just a backwoods village planted in the middle of nowhere. It was a proper town, with rows of houses and well-maintained, packed-dirt streets. Though the population marker just within the town's limits read three thousand, it felt more like a small city.

The town hall, courthouse, and post office were much grander than the town itself. From what Levi's parents had told him, Clermont City had been on track to become much larger and more important, but then the railroad plans were moved north to the city of Oakland. The grand buildings stood as a reminder of lost opportunities.

He approached the decorative, white structure with lace trim work and a sweeping porch. He checked the sign again—The Main Street Land Company. The reception area was hot and stuffy and smelled of cold, cooked meat. The oriental rug beneath his feet partly covered an uneven, planked floor. Beyond this room were two rows of desks. A large, gray-haired man rose from behind the second desk, wiping his mouth and hands with a square, white napkin. Caleb removed his hat.

"Good afternoon, sir. How may I help you today?" the man asked.

They shook hands. "Good afternoon. I'm looking to buy some of the land up along Rail River."

"Come on back, young man."

Caleb followed as the man crossed to a plat map pinned to the wall. "Let's take a look. Here's the river. I see this piece is for sale, and the field next to it as well. Which are you interested in?"

"I'd like to purchase both," Caleb said confidently. "How much acreage is that?"

"You're looking at about ten acres in all. What are you planning to do with it, if I may ask?"

"Farming and a workshop for silversmithing jewelry and small trinkets."

"Oh, so you're a silversmith?"

Caleb ran his hand through his shoulder-length hair. "I intend to be."

"It's a fine skill. Your field there is a good one for planting. Put the shop away from the banks of the river. You never know when a good rainfall will flood it over."

"I'll be sure to take that into account." Caleb took a seat in front of the man's desk at his invitation. His new clothes felt stiff. "I'll pay cash," he added.

"Superb," the man replied, visibly impressed by Caleb's prosperity. A twinge of deceit crept into his heart.

"Come on in tomorrow, and I'll take you up there myself. We can have a good look at the markers to make sure you're getting what you want. By the way, I'm Burt Stanford, and you are?"

"Caleb Cantrell, good to meet you," he said. "Are you the owner here?"

"No, that's Ray Dunbar. I'm the attorney for the business. Dunbar is out of town for a few days, but I can sure start the paperwork."

"I appreciate that, Mr. Stanford."

"You can call me Burt."

"And, it's Caleb."

"All right then, Caleb. Meet me here tomorrow at noon, and we'll take a ride up there."

Burt's carriage rocked from side to side as he steered over potholes and around small boulders along the five miles of rough road. Past the creaking, wooden bridge over the Rail River, the tall trees on either side gave way to an expanse of land littered with bushes and thin trees, almost two acres in size. To the west lay a meadow full of late-summer wildflowers, and to the east, an expansive field of low grass. A knoll dipped down to the private banks of the tributary. Beyond was the forest, leading into valleys, then mountains. To Caleb, it couldn't be more perfect.

As they walked the field, Burt commented. "Good thing you've got this clearing here. The rest of it is dense with trees." They followed its gentle slope to the pristine river. The sound of the water flowing freely was music to Caleb's ears. The river cut across the land, winding ever so gently past the field and into the lush forest. Its banks held small trees and a variety of grasses, with wildflowers dotted throughout. It gave one the feeling that Mother Nature had planted it with care, leaving a few openings for a cool dip on a hot summer's day.

It had the serenity Caleb longed for. He knew this is where he belonged. He removed his hat and turned in a slow circle. The town was just near enough for needed supplies and a bit of socializing now and then to get him out of his own head. But the uninhabited wilderness to the east appealed to him—being too close to civilization made him nervous. He welcomed the privacy.

They backtracked through the field and walked south toward more of the forest.

"The trees up here could supply the timber for your home," Burt suggested.

"You read my mind, Burt. I plan on building my home out of them," Caleb said, pointing to a stand of Douglas firs.

"That's mighty ambitious. Have you felled trees before?"

"I have." Caleb's thoughts rushed to the Klamath Reservation and his time helping the Klamath people cut and prepare the logs for the sawmill. His gaze went to the sweet meadow along the roadside. He'd take rest there, a good cup of coffee in hand and a trusty dog by his side.

"Over there is a side road for another homesteader to access the main one," Burt said. "I looked at the records, and a couple by the name of Benjamin Loggin and his wife, Sally, live there. They could be a good resource for you. I read their well went pretty deep, too."

"That's good to know, Burt."

Burt touched his chin. "Let's walk this area, though, and make sure you're getting what you want. Large, whitewashed stakes will indicate the corners of the property. The number will be on the stakes. It's 138."

Caleb nodded in agreement, and with that, they scouted out the landmarks. Over brush and around trees they searched, conversing as they went. Caleb had a feeling that Burt's

familiar, reserved manners and speech were not originally from the West. They reminded him of his childhood. Although relieved to be free from those societal confinements, he still mourned his parents and brother. He wondered briefly if his grandmother was still alive. "Where do you hail from, Burt?"

"Hartford, Connecticut." Burt pulled back his shoulders with pride.

Caleb's intuition was right. "I thought I had detected an accent. I'm from those parts myself, New York City to be exact. I left shortly after I finished my schooling."

"Did your family come all the way out here? That must have been quite a journey back then."

"No, I left on my own. Been traveling ever since. It's time I settled down." Caleb surveyed the beauty of the untouched wilderness around him.

"I'm sure there's a lot to your story, Caleb. I'd like to hear about it sometime. Matter of fact, my wife is the best cook in this county. Why not come for supper tonight, unless you have somewhere else to be?"

Chapter Four

$\mathcal{D}$elighted her husband had invited company for dinner, Jessica's aunt bustled about in preparation, then they headed for the garden. With a wide-brimmed hat and a straw basket in hand, Jessica followed June, who carried a tattered rug and gardening gloves. They stopped in front of a row, and her aunt dropped the rug and knelt on it.

"Burt gave the man good directions. He's staying at the boarding house," June said. "My goodness, I hope he isn't too rough. Apparently, he's been on his own since he was just out of school. Never the mind, we'll be happy to have him, won't we?" she chirped as Jessica extended the basket to receive the leeks her aunt harvested.

"Auntie, you are much too generous! He could be a scoundrel whose only intention is to take advantage of good-natured people like you and Uncle Burt." Jessica settled the basket on her hip. "I'd be very cautious if I were you. Leave the good silver locked away in the pantry cupboard."

June got up and handed over more of the leeks. Jessica placed them neatly in the basket and stood aside as her aunt moved to another row. She knelt back on her rug among the turnip greens. "Jessica, don't be silly. Your uncle Burt is a good judge of character." She became thoughtful. "It might be good if you get out

15

once in a while and socialize. You may find there's more to life than painting. I know it's given you solace over a rough patch, but my dearest, it's time to look for another husband. We never get younger, now, do we?"

Jessica adjusted her weight. "Another husband? I've just found my freedom. My paintings are not an escape, they're my living. Why, just last week Mrs. Harding bought one of my landscapes for ten dollars. Her daughter wants a still life and is willing to pay as much as twenty-five. And don't forget, the new gallery on Center Street wants to show my paintings in their next exhibit. That's a remarkable thing, don't you agree? All of their paintings are done by men." She continued to arrange the vegetables in her basket. "I can get along without a husband. Someday I'll earn enough to find my own place to live, but until then, I'm grateful for you putting up with me."

"Oh, Jessica, I didn't mean it like that," June said in mid-pull of a turnip. "We wouldn't think of it. We love having you here. It's good for us, and we are so pleased that your talent is being noticed." She shook the dirt off the cream-and-purple-colored bulb. "I was just saying that soon you will want to live otherwise. A man can provide a way of life more suited to you, though, heaven knows, Frederick didn't leave you with many choices." June sat back on her legs. "You know, Uncle Burt still can't figure out how he went so long deceiving the investors. Thank goodness you had none of that scandal, and now we hear he's doing land deals." She shook her head as she scooted to the carrot tops, dragging her rug with her. "I've heard rumors from some of the ladies in my club who frequent the city that his new wife is a real hen. And the woman he cheated on you with … well, where is she now?" She plucked each carrot, looking at the crop with satisfaction.

Jessica found it hard to hear anything about her ex-husband, although she did take satisfaction in knowing his domestic life was turbulent. "Have you heard any more from your father? Surely they've come to terms with the divorce by now."

Becoming somber, she took the carrot bunch from her aunt.

Talk of her parents never failed to stir up guilt. "I don't think they have. Father is still angry and wants me to come home," she replied with a sigh. "He doesn't trust that I can take care of myself."

"Your father has more pride than he needs, and you've inherited some of it, I'm afraid. He's just worried for his daughter. You can't hold that against him. Your mother writes they have no more to do with the Moore family. I suppose with them living in England, it makes it easier. What a shame. Your father was fond of Charles."

She thought of her ex-husband and the miserable life she had led under his thumb. "I know they weren't too pleased about his choice in a wife. When Frederick decided to move us out here, his father disowned him. I don't see how my father could be friends with a man like that."

June paused before resuming her chore. "Yes, I remember that horrible evening. We were all so shocked. San Francisco was a world away from Hartford. I'm just thankful my brother and his family were here. Were it not for them, your uncle and I would never be here and you would be. ..." Jessica caught her eye. "I'm sure you would be back home in Hartford."

She swung the laden basket to her other hip. The thought of going back to live under her parents' roof was unbearable. "Mother says it's difficult to talk to Father about any of this. I suppose he'd like to disown me."

"Don't speak such nonsense." Moving to another row, June looked over the wilted tops of the potatoes. "You know, I've been thinking ... we should encourage them to move out here."

Jessica kept quiet. She didn't share her aunt's enthusiasm. Her parents would be relentless in trying to run her affairs. Even writing to them about Will's and Jacob's unexpected visit last September had to be handled with diplomacy so as not to disappoint them further. The slightest mention of her divorcing Frederick had her mother writing back, *It would be too great of an embarrassment for both your father and me, and I'm sure I would have to withdraw from a few of my clubs.* As far as Hartford, Connecticut was concerned, she was still married to a successful finance attorney.

Although Jessica loved them dearly, she couldn't escape her parents' disapproval. She realized that her actions had made life difficult for them even with the great distance in miles between her and Hartford. She wrote less to them of her own situation and more of her aunt and uncle's lives.

"Well, you are the judge of your own life, Jessica. I'm just saying, don't wait too long to find a man. The life of a spinster is not for you, not with your beauty and lovely disposition. For now, get yourself ready and I'll finish up here." She tidied up the rows from the harvest.

Jessica rested the basket of vegetables on the ground and walked away, but her aunt's voice stopped her. "We will introduce you as Miss Messing to our guest, and nothing else need be said." Jessica agreed and left June to her garden.

After dressing for dinner, Jessica went to the porch while her aunt put the final touches on the meal. She sat in the rocker and wished Jacob were in the empty chair beside her. Closing her eyes and breathing in the delicious air filled with late-summer fragrances, she thought back to last year when they had talked together on this very porch after making love the night before. The bittersweet tension of that time coursed through her body. How foolish she and Jacob had been, with Fredrick due in the next day. Her body trembled at the memory of his almost feral passion, so unlike last June when he was gentle and his expression of love had satisfied her so completely. She fingered the beads at her neck and felt their smooth comfort. It was all she had of him right now while she continued to carve out her own future.

Despite what her aunt thought of her art, Jessica knew she was on the right path. Yet she also knew the road to success would be difficult. Each time she arrived at a new venue with her paintings, she had to endure the inevitable questions—"Are you married?"

"Who is your husband?" and the most irritating comment, "This is a wonderful hobby for a woman. Your husband must be so proud of you." She guarded herself against those who demanded more than her art. She showed her work in towns outside Clermont City and farther north in Oakland, but she had much bigger dreams. She wouldn't be satisfied until her paintings were available throughout the country, particularly in New York City and Chicago.

Her own ambitions threatened to overwhelm her and stop her progress, but once in front of her paper and canvases, her creativity seemed boundless. Peacefully rocking in the porch chair, her mood was broken by the thought that her aunt might be right—life without a husband was harder. She thought of the single women she had met and recalled that most of them were either widows or spinsters, resigned to their fates. They seemed content, but not fulfilled. Jessica's intellect and heart knew the difference, and she desired to have both love and career. Could she have both? The answer felt insurmountable. She reminded herself not to think too far ahead—a habit of hers she wished she could break.

A dog barked in the distance, ending her daydream. Her and Jacob's hopeless love, and the fact that he was far away on a trail, sat with her always. She wiped the sweat from her brow and went back inside. Lost in her own life, she hardly gave any thought to the stranger coming to visit.

"Do I pass inspection, Miss Messing?" Mr. Cantrell looked at her with the bluest eyes she ever saw.

Jessica broke her stare from the strikingly handsome man and dipped her chin to feign interest in her plate of food. His chuckle heated her cheeks. Finding her grace, she asked, "Are you a cowboy?"

Grinning, Caleb brought his napkin to his lips and gave a quick swipe before he told the threesome about some of his adventures after he left home—catching and eating rattlesnake, roasting salmon over a fire the way the Indians do with sticks put together like a ladder, the beauty of the Southwest and northern regions he had traveled. She could hear his stories were kept light for their benefit, and she wondered what hardships he hid behind his fair features and good manners.

After the meal, the women stood at the door, bidding him a good evening, while Burt accompanied him to his horse. "I have a good feeling about that land up there, Caleb," he said. "You will do well with it. Let's get the paperwork going. By the time Dunbar returns, it'll be ready for you to sign. I'm sure the city will approve of it."

"That sounds good, Burt, thank you. Let's talk sometime next week." The men shook hands. Caleb mounted his horse, and he and Burt waved good-bye. Jessica got the feeling they would be seeing a lot more of Mr. Cantrell.

Back at the boarding house, Caleb sat on the bunk bed and drew out the plans for his home. He would have to consult a professional on structural aspects and hire several men. His father, Henry Cantrell, had been a successful architect in New York City before his tragic death, and architecture had intrigued Caleb since he was a little boy. If Henry had lived, he would have passed his knowledge and experience to his son. Caleb's life would have turned out very differently. This house would be a tribute to his father.

His thoughts wandered to Burt's beautiful niece. He'd been more drawn to her personality, not to mention her big, brown eyes and full, pink lips as the dinner progressed. He let himself dwell on her for a short while, then came back to his own business, but the thought of their next encounter made it difficult to concentrate on the lines and measurements. *You've been in the wilderness too long, Cantrell.* The hardness of his life seemed to soften, if just a little.

He took his watch out of his pocket. It was getting late. Besides the land deal, he had a meeting the next day with Stewart Higgins, the silversmith. He turned down the light in the kerosene lamp. *This was a good day.* It had been a long time since he ended an evening with such a thought. He bunched the thin pillow behind his head and let himself drift off, sensing the approval of his Indian mentor, Soaring Feather. He was soon in a deep sleep.

Chapter Five

"*H*owdy!" a voice came from down the road. It was Burt, and Caleb was pleased to see him. He had been felling trees all day, and the September sun lie across his land in long, defined shadows.

"Hello, Burt!" Caleb shouted back.

"This looks like progress to me!" Burt joined Caleb in the clearing just north from the stand of Douglas firs.

"Getting there." Caleb wiped his brow. "I've hired men to help with the larger ones."

He walked Burt through the area where he planned to build his house and barn. It was good to have a rest, but he was eager to take advantage of the cooler evening air.

"I came to deliver your permits to you. You can build any time."

Caleb looked over the papers. As with the deed to his property, he felt a sense of pride in ownership. "Thank you, Burt. Your help has been a great service."

"Glad to do it. You'll be contributing to the town in your own way, so we're happy to have you here. Oh, before I forget, June told me to ask you to supper tonight. Accepting would save me a trip up here with her pot roast and potatoes." He grinned.

"Tell Mrs. Stanford I'd be very grateful for one of her meals." Caleb chuckled. "Someday I'll repay the kindness with a meal in my very own house."

"We'll hold you to it! So you're a cook *and* a carpenter and silversmith?"

Caleb laughed and scratched his cheek. "I may have to borrow some of Mrs. Stanford's recipes."

After Burt was out of sight, Caleb scanned the permit and let out a yelp. Having the go-ahead to build his dream gave him the energy he needed to continue, already tasting the pot roast and potatoes. It had been a few weeks since his first visit to Burt's home, but it seemed a whole lot longer. He turned his attention to the road. Burt's carriage rocked unevenly as it headed down the winding path. *I'll have to grade that soon*, Caleb thought, stroking his goatee. *His* road, the one that led up to his own home. A smile crossed his face as he lifted his axe, slung it over his shoulder, and headed back to the trees. One more before quitting time, he told himself and his stomach.

The night before, he'd met Levi and Cork at the Towne Saloon. He'd ordered the hash to quell his hunger and downed the meal with several watery whiskeys. His head had hurt this morning, and after several cups of coffee and the boarding house's stale bread pudding, he tackled the land. A small lunch of biscuits and Bertha's greasy meat spread, along with a few apples, was long gone.

He finished up his work, then stood in the middle of his field, satisfied with his labor. He shook his hair free from the thin piece of rope that had held it back. The aromatic breeze took it playfully, tossing it against his damp face and neck. The heady smell of the meadow caught his attention. He walked to the pretty area and picked a small bouquet as a token of appreciation to Burt and his family.

As he rode back into town, he looked forward to a cool bath at the boarding house, then

a rich meal while seated across the table from an attractive, young woman.

The wildflowers stood happily in the milky glass vase June set them in. "Jessica will do a marvelous job painting those flowers, Mr. Cantrell," she said. "Did you know she was just commissioned to do a few of her landscapes for the literary guild to auction off? I'm sure we'll see a pretty penny from it." June clearly took delight in boasting of Jessica's talents, making certain to add how gifted she was as a cook and homemaker. Jessica winced at the latter.

"Indeed," Caleb said with a wink to Jessica.

She smiled, and they exchanged an amused look.

"We are very proud of her," June continued. "Now, if we could get my son, Jacob, and her brother, Will, to settle here and make a business for themselves, I would be as happy as a lark."

Jessica's heart thumped with the mention of Jacob. Looking up at Mr. Cantrell, she noticed he had become serious and his brows were knitted. "Messing ... Stanford," he said almost to himself.

"Yes?" June tilted her head. "Do you know the names? I would think there's more than one family of Messing or Stanford, though I know only of us." Squinting her eyes, she searched her memory. "Only us," she concluded.

Caleb leaned back in his chair, staring at his food.

"Is everything all right, Mr. Cantrell?" June asked. "You look as if you've seen a ghost. Don't tell me if you have. They say the souls of the men who lost their lives in the Gold Rush haunt this part of the country." Her eyes were wide with fright.

He gave her a blank stare, then a short laugh. "I'm sure we're safe from any spirits, unless they love pot roast ... then, I don't know."

The forced grin on his face gave Jessica cause for concern. What did they know about this man? Then her uncle talked about the two families and the law firm he and her father had back East.

"Our sons would rather go into the wilderness in some trading business than follow in their fathers' footsteps. We tried to stop them, but they had their minds made up. By the way, you mentioned to me your father was an architect. What did he design?" Burt inquired.

"And what are the names of your family?" June asked.

Caleb took a sip of wine and cleared his throat. "My father, Henry, designed banks." He turned to June. "My mother's name was Georgina, and my brother was Johnathan."

June put a hand to her mouth. "Oh dear."

"Along with my father, they were killed in a carriage accident when I was fourteen."

"We are so sorry to hear that, Mr. Cantrell," Jessica said. A short pause followed. She couldn't imagine what he suffered. She missed her brother, Will.

"So your father built banks?" she asked. "How very interesting."

"He thought so."

"Yes, it's quite remarkable," June added.

The conversation was directed away from the tragedy of his youth, and Jessica could see he was relieved. When she looked into his eyes, she saw a veil had been drawn. He took a bite of his meal. "Some of those buildings are quite elaborate in their design. Did he contribute to the ones in New York City?" she asked.

"Yes, in part. They stand as a legacy to his artistry and talent."

"And is your house going to be similar in design?" It was meant to further lighten the mood. It worked. His smile was back.

"No, not at all. I don't have that kind of money, nor the skill. No, I'm hoping to build a comfortable home for myself, and one that can expand … for whatever the future may bring." His last words were spoken quieter.

"Our Jacob and Will do just fine," June suddenly interjected, glaring at Burt.

"Do just fine? Why, we haven't seen hide nor hair of them in a year. I hope they're doing fine."

Again, Jessica saw Mr. Cantrell's demeanor change, as if he had escaped into his own thoughts.

June placed another slice of roast on Caleb's plate, even as he tried to gesture he'd had enough. "They were rough, but travel always does that to a person. I found them to be well. They had to leave, however, to get back to their business." She glanced at her husband.

Jessica felt her cheeks redden from her aunt's and uncle's disagreement. She steered the conversation back to their company. "Have you had many careers in your time, Mr. Cantrell, or just a few?"

"I found work as I traveled and picked up many skills in my life, but one has intrigued me to no end. I became acquainted with a tribe up in Oregon and learned the art of silversmithing from an Indian there, mostly jewelry. I've been fortunate enough to find employment in Stewart Higgins' shop as an apprentice for now, but someday I hope to be good enough to be promoted to artisan."

"Ah, yes, I've heard of that business," Burt said. "The Higgins Company. I think June has a small trinket from one of his collections. Fine work. Good for you, young man."

"Indians?" June exclaimed, her mouth full. She quickly swallowed, then dabbed her lips with her napkin. "I've seen a few at a distance, but my, they frighten me."

"By my own experience, there are good and bad people in all cultures. I regard the people in this tribe as my adopted kin."

"Oh, well, yes, but still, we have to be careful around here. Some of the stories I've heard," she insisted. "Weren't you ever afraid?"

"At times."

"I'm so thankful Jacob's and Will's business is doing well," June said. "I'm sure they get to stay in decent hotels and eat well enough. Yes, as Mr. Stanford said, it's been some time since we've seen them. I know they will return successful." She patted Jessica's hand.

Jessica bit her lip. She couldn't tell them the truth. She couldn't tell them she saw their son in June. Her insides churned, the acids rising in her chest. She took a sip of water.

"They're traders, you say?" Mr. Cantrell asked. "What do they trade?"

"Selling mostly. Basic supplies to homesteaders who can't get to a nearby general store," Burt explained. "They buy goods and resell them for a profit. Isn't that how business works? They said it was lucrative, but I can't say it looked that way."

Caleb nodded. Jessica noticed his politeness couldn't cover the sadness in his eyes.

After supper was over and the apple pie had been enjoyed by all, June commented on the evening air. To Jessica's surprise, Caleb took the bait. "Would you like to take a short walk, Miss Messing?"

Chapter Six

"*Y*our aunt is a generous soul," Caleb said as they walked along a path across the street that was flanked by overgrown blackberry bushes and grasses. The air was pungent with the sweet smell of over-ripened berries.

"And so are you for putting it so nicely," she replied. "But she is a dear."

The conversation flowed easily, neither of them needing anything more than a simple walk on a fragrant, summer evening. Even the quiet moments fell naturally.

"We should walk on over there." Jessica pointed to the side of the road beyond the bushes. "It's more open."

"Your reputation is at stake with this '*cowboy*,'" he joked.

"Is it?" she asked, playfully.

"Maybe." She caught a roguish smile cross his lips. His self-deprecation amused her.

Walking alongside Caleb, Jessica attributed her light-headedness to the cooler air after a hot day. She hated to think his looks and confident demeanor could provoke such a girlish reaction. Yet, if she was honest with herself, he did give rise to certain feelings. The thought of woman of all ages swooning over him dampened those feelings, and she was glad of it. She had better things to do than chase after a handsome man. They walked along the roadside now, past the neighboring houses, the gap between them closing.

"This is a sweet, little town," Caleb said.

"It is, but. ..." She caught herself and wished she hadn't included the last word.

"It's not what you want?"

His blue eyes stared back at her, and the corners of his lips slightly curled up. She cleared her throat softly. "No, I just feel there's a bigger world out there." Catching a whiff of his scent, musky yet clean, took her attention. Unnerved by her arousal, she let the space between them widen.

"I think the world is too big," he said. "I've found myself a spot up there in the hills, and the world can get along just fine without me searching around in it."

Catching his meaning, she thought of her little studio and a small place she would someday call home. It gave her a warmth that wrapped around her heart. "Yes, you're right. It might be just fine to take a piece of it for ourselves and be happy with that. I suppose I was wanting for art's sake." She wondered if his experiences had rounded the rough edges of his pride, this tall, fair man walking so calmly beside her, his confident masculinity tempered. Had Jacob come to that place?

"Are you happy, Miss Messing?"

Caught off guard by his questions, she hesitated before replying. "I am happy. Not in every aspect of life, but who is?"

"May I ask why you haven't married?"

"You are bold, Mr. Cantrell. Do I look like a spinster to you?"

"Not in the least bit, but your uncle worries at your lack of interest in marriage." He nervously adjusted his bolo tie. "I'm sorry, it's none of my business."

"I've taken no offense. Truly. I do enjoy my singlehood for now. My art keeps me occupied a good deal of the time. I desire for my work to go out into the world and be a part of what I may never get a chance to see."

"May I see your paintings sometime?"

Jessica stopped. "Shall we head back? I wouldn't want my aunt and uncle to worry."

"Of course."

They walked in silence, but for a comment about the roses in one yard or the finely trimmed hedge in another. As they approached the front gate, Jessica sensed his question in the air and wanted to blow it away. If she hurried inside, he wouldn't ask her again, but it was too late. He touched her arm. "Miss Messing, this has been a lovely evening. Thank you for your company. I sense your hesitation in letting me see your work. I understand. The process can be a private one."

She relaxed and nodded her head with a smile. They went inside. He thanked her aunt and uncle for dinner, then he was gone.

Chapter Seven

*Q*uiet and uncomfortably warm, even at nightfall, the room's soft, white curtains billowed from the open window. Jessica stretched her body on the bed and pushed the down-filled pillow under her head, her cotton shift raised up to her thighs to allow the breeze to touch her legs.

Looking up at the flower-painted ceiling, she thought of Mr. Cantrell, how different he was from what she had imagined. No one else she had met in the small town of Clermont City had made her feel so alive. Dark-haired and stout, Mitch Simons came to call just last week at the request of her aunt. He'd asked Jessica to the theatre, and she'd politely declined. It was an awkward moment, yet she felt she couldn't bear to spend an entire evening with someone so boring and ill-suited to her. Then there was John Mansfield, tall, lanky, and handsome in his own right, who followed her around the general store where he worked whenever she came in, too shy to talk directly to her. She felt nothing for either man and hadn't expected to. She was in love with and devoted to Jacob.

Fluffing her pillow, she tried to quiet her thoughts, but she tossed and turned most of the night.

In the morning, she dragged herself out of bed. Downstairs, she found her aunt and uncle

discussing something in hushed tones. They fell silent as she entered the kitchen. She yawned and accepted the cup of hot tea from her aunt. "Good morning, thank you." Taking a seat at the small kitchen table, she looked at one then the other. "What is it?"

Her aunt answered. "We've received a letter from Hannah Rolland asking if we need her services. Are she and her husband still employed by Frederick? I'm sure they are both miserable there, what with the circumstances of his new wife competing for his affection over that English import he cheated on you with. The whole house must be feeling the upheaval of it."

Jessica took a sip of tea before asking to see the letter. "English import?" she asked.

"Well, yes," her aunt replied. "He brought her over here, didn't he? From Liverpool?"

Taking a moment to reply, she looked at her uncle. The large, gentle man drank his coffee in silence.

"His life doesn't concern me in the least." Jessica leaned forward to grab a biscuit. "But the Rollands do."

June handed the letter to Jessica. "When your uncle was in the city last week, he ran into Mr. Frederick Moore," she began, practically spitting out the man's name. "He says he wants to make peace and offered Burt an investment deal on some land." Her aunt glared at her uncle with indignation. "As if my husband would have anything to do with him! Proper Englishman, indeed!"

"My dear June, you need not get yourself worked up over this again," her uncle said.

"Isn't it just awful though, Jessica?"

"June, that's quite enough."

"Then I won't tell you what message he wanted your uncle to relay to you." Her aunt turned away from the table.

"Auntie, whatever Frederick has to say will not bother me." Jessica lied.

Her uncle put down his cup of coffee. "He wanted me to wish you well, and let you know that he is doing fine, though I did catch in the wind that his wife is quite a handful. And ... well, he hasn't been the model husband. There are several mistresses now."

Shaking her head in disgust, Jessica read Hannah's letter, and indeed, the woman, nearly the same age as herself, gave accounts of abuse and misconduct toward the household staff. She folded the letter and placed it back into the envelope. Her heart thumped in her chest at the thought of Frederick abusing his power over Hannah. "This sounds dreadful, but where could they go if they leave Frederick's employ?"

"Back to England, I suppose," her uncle offered, "though who knows if his family will take them in after what Frederick did by coming out here. My Lord, how does a son take all of his inheritance right out from underneath his father's nose?" Burt drained his cup.

"He's proven to be a scoundrel!" June exclaimed.

Jessica nibbled on the biscuit and sipped her tea while she thought of how she could help Kevin and Hannah. "Poor Mr. and Mrs. Moore. They came across the Atlantic to our wedding with their gift of servants and left in a blaze of disbelief and anger. I traveled across this country with Kevin and Hannah. Servants or not, they were my companions. Frederick always said not to get attached to the help, but it hurts me to see them in such bad circumstances. How can we help them, Uncle?"

Her uncle thought a moment. "I think Frederick may want to keep Kevin on. We'll have Hannah stay with us until I can figure out what to do."

"Do you mean that?" Jessica looked from her uncle then to her aunt.

"I could use the help," her aunt said. "What with you busy with your art and me getting on in age. She could have the small room next to the laundry. A far cry from what she had in the city, but we can't have Frederick ruin their lives as well."

Jessica tilted her head toward her aunt. "My life isn't ruined, Auntie, but he could ruin Hannah's and I won't have that. As for myself, he has no power over me."

"My dear, I'm sorry, but the truth is what it is. His actions forced you to be husbandless."

Giving a short puff of air, she responded, "He no longer has *me* as his wife. He ruined it for himself."

"Yes, I suppose that is also true." She patted Jessica's hand. "I will say it again. I am very proud of your strength and courage."

"Thank you, Auntie." They exchanged a knowing look.

Then June was up in a flash. "Oh! How could I forget?" She came back from the parlor with a small envelope in her hand. "This came for you this morning."

As Jessica read its contents, she figured by her aunt's broad smile, June already knew who it was from—Mr. Cantrell. She pocketed the note. "He's invited us to visit him on his land today."

Burt rose. "I've got to get to Dunbar's," he said as he left the room. "You ladies go without me. I have too much work to do."

"I can manage the buggy, Uncle," Jessica said after him. She tempered her excitement at Caleb's invitation as June continued to smile. "A pie, Auntie?"

"Of course!" June clapped her hands.

Chapter Eight

$\mathscr{B}$ y the end of September, the mornings began chilly before giving way to the day's heat. Jessica and her aunt rode to Caleb's land, which he named Rail River Acres, with a warm rhubarb pie in hand. In her rusty-red-colored day ensemble with the simple, turned-down collar and green-plaid waistcoat, Jessica felt she had dressed appropriately for an outing in the hills. She was glad for her chemise and petticoat, as the chill of the morning had not left the land they climbed. She pulled her thick, brown shawl around her shoulders as she maneuvered the horse and carriage over the rough road.

Shortly after they arrived, June excused herself. Lifting her skirts, she walked through the makings of a path in the wildflower-filled meadow. Jessica was onto June's plan, and she sensed Caleb was as well. As they conversed in the awkward space between them, she felt as if every word weighed a hundred pounds.

Jessica gazed out onto the field. "Your land is beautiful, Mr. Cantrell."

"Thank you. Would you mind calling me Caleb?"

"Not at all, Caleb." Speaking his name gave her a chill. She hoped he didn't notice her nerves. Perhaps this wasn't a good idea. The sun was heating up, but she drew her shawl tighter.

"I'm happy you and your aunt ventured over that road to come up here."

"Yes, it was a challenge. Will you be grading it?"

"All in good time."

Chiding herself for asking such a silly question, she recovered with, "It's a lovely road, no less, and your land is beautiful."

"Yes, so you said." He chuckled and moved a step closer. "I love it here, and I'm glad you think it's beautiful."

She studied his finely chiseled profile as he spoke. A strand of his long hair escaped from the tied-back mane and danced along his cheekbone. His gentle gaze was on her and she became guarded. "You were saying something about a workshop?"

June returned, uncharacteristically silent, and handed each of them a blossom. Jessica placed the delicate, blue larkspur in her hair. Caleb brought his flower next to hers, making sure it would stay. His hand brushed her cheek, sending a tingle up her spine. Her cheeks burned. Praying for a breeze to cool her, she heard Caleb ask if they would like to see the inside.

They walked through the timber frame of his home, and he pointed out the future rooms and their uses. "It will have three bedrooms and a proper outdoor privy," he boasted.

Although Jessica politely approved, the skeleton frame offered little to the imagination. "I'd love to see how it progresses." She ran her hand over one of the sanded poles. His work shirt hung from a nail. The smell of newly milled wood mixed with the aroma of a man hard at work was intoxicating. She wanted to inhale the heady mixture and take it with her.

"You may visit any time you like, Miss Messing. You also, Mrs. Stanford."

"Oh, I would love that," her aunt replied. "We wouldn't want to bother you, though."

He looked around and sheepishly offered each of them a stool. "I'm sorry this is all I have. I made these and that table." The pie sat on the small, rustic table. "I brought up some cider from the boarding house. Let me get some cups."

"Oh, now don't go making a fuss," June insisted.

"No fuss," he said as he sat the cups and jug of cider on the table. "I'm pleased to be able to show you what I've done so far. Thank you for coming."

After the refreshment, they strolled about his land and came to the knoll. Jessica was taken with the river and how much she wanted to sit by it on a hot summer's day. She let the thought pass. This was not her land, and talk of future visits made her uneasy.

"Auntie, we should get back."

Walking back to the carriage, Jessica assisted her aunt, whose breathing had become labored. "This is more exercise than I've done in ages!" her aunt announced.

Caleb helped Jessica's aunt into the front of the buggy, then he came around to assist Jessica. His strong hand guided her up and she took the reins confidently, the weight of his touch lingering on her arm. Looking down, she saw in his face a kind and gentle soul, yet something else—something a little dangerous. "Do you ride?" he asked.

"Yes, but I've had little opportunity to do so." She adjusted the reins.

"Would you like to join me sometime? I've created a riding path along the river."

Jessica paused. It was a simple request, and she hadn't had a good ride in a long time. "That would be nice." Her heart thudded.

"Good, I'll look forward to it." He turned his attention to her aunt. "Good day, Mrs. Stanford, and thank you for the pie."

Faced in the opposite direction to let them have a moment to themselves, June came around with a wide grin. "Thank you, Mr. Cantrell, for letting us intrude. Jessica practically made the pie all by herself, and I'm sure she won't need a chaperone for your outing. Good day."

Jessica rolled her eyes away from her aunt's notice, and she and Caleb shared a quiet chuckle.

"Be careful on the way down. It's a bit tricky," he said.

"Thank you, I will," Jessica answered.

"Good day, Miss Messing."

"Good day ... Caleb."

The road leading away from his land took all her attention. The grade made the buggy lopsided. She didn't remember it being so bad on the way up. Taking charge of the horse, she soon had the buggy straight again. Her heart was beating wildly, yet there was little cause for it. Growing up in Connecticut, she had ridden horses that threatened to buck her off, and she'd driven buggies and carriages in various types of weather and terrain, much to the chagrin of her parents. Why should this flare her nerves?

"My goodness!" June gripped the side of the carriage with one hand and held tight to the lap blanket with the other. "I do hope he does something with this road."

Jessica concentrated on getting them down the hill. The ground leveled out, and her mind went back up the road. She felt an unsettling pull. Deciding to keep Caleb Cantrell as nothing more than a friendly acquaintance, she shook the reins, and steered the horse to trot along the more civilized street back to town.

Chapter Nine

*T*he open window let in the perfume of eucalyptus, pine, and roses, inviting Jessica to throw caution to the wind. The day would be warm and sunny. *No harm in a friendly horseback ride.* "Of course there isn't," she said aloud. She rose and stood by the window. "Where are you, Jacob?" She wanted the wind to carry her question to him and bring back an answer that would ease her mind. As much as she tried to hold on to the wanting and waiting, it was out of reach today. It concerned her. A ride in the country was exactly what she needed.

Dressed in a cream-colored shirt tucked into a brown, cotton riding skirt, she was ready for the day. Putting on her fitted, tweed jacket, she adjusted the shirt sleeves and buttoned the high, lace collar, arranging Jacob's beads along the neckline. She pranced down the stairs aware of her mood. Her riding boots were waiting for her near the back door. Grabbing them, she headed to the stables. The smell of the hay and the horses ignited her excitement for the day ahead. Uncle Burt agreed to let her take out his well-mannered chestnut, Morgan. "It's time we went for a ride, Georgia," she said and saddled her up.

The going was easier with Georgia than it had been with the horse and buggy. She was able to watch the road for potholes and rocks. Taking an inhale of the fresh air, she was drawn to her surroundings. Caleb was on his horse when she arrived, and he led them to the path he told her about. They found a gentle pace along the edge of the winding Rail River. Tall grasses swayed naturally, and the variety of trees in the distant forest radiated earthy, cool scents. Jessica couldn't remember the last time she felt so calm and content, her mind unburdened and her heart free. Caleb looked back and smiled. The sun played hide-and-seek between the trees. The river flowed tranquilly, and the smells of clean water, grass, and wildflowers of poppies, lavender, and iris were heavenly to her senses. *What magic was in this place?*

Caleb led them to an opening up from the river's edge. The exposed clearing was green and warm. He stopped his horse and dismounted, but Jessica remained on Georgia. Caleb came around. "I thought we could have a picnic here." That beautiful face, those soulful, blue eyes. Her mind fought to stay out of reach, but she *was* getting hungry and the place he had chosen was so pretty. Though she needed no assistance, she let him help her dismount.

From his pack, he brought out a blanket and a burlap sack. After he laid the blanket down, he revealed the contents of the sack. He had packed a hearty lunch of cheese, crusty bread, apples, and cured meat. She couldn't help but clap her hands in delight. "Caleb, this is a feast!" A laugh burst from deep within.

"I hope it's not too rough," he said as he laid out the food on a piece of linen cloth.

"No, this is wonderful. I'm ravenous." Her hand went to Jacob's beads, a nervous habit. Yet today, she felt as calm and as natural as the forest around her.

Caleb took out a knife from the small pocket on the side of his boot. He unsheathed it and sliced the cheese, hard meat, and apples. He arranged the meal. It made a lovely still life. She would keep the picture in her mind and sketch it when she returned home. They said very little as they ate but agreed on how delicious a simple meal could taste. Taking another slice of cheese, she swallowed the sharp, salty bite and drank from her canteen. The sun warmed her and she removed her riding coat and laid it to one side.

When she looked at Caleb, she saw he was examining her necklace with a furrowed brow.

"Those beads must have a story behind them."

"They do, but the short of it is, my cousin Jacob gave them to me." Her hand went to the smoothness of the blue stones. "We're very close, and it pains me every day not knowing where he and my brother are." He leaned in for a closer inspection.

"Caleb?"

Crossing his legs, Caleb sat back, eating a piece of apple off his knife. "Your cousin must think you're very special. These are finely made. They mean strength and protection from illness."

"He didn't tell me what they represented. Thank you." Her thoughts went to the personal meaning of the beads. She had never thought they meant anything more than a token of his love. Caleb's clear, smooth voice took her out of her thoughts.

"I'm sorry your family causes you such worry. Knowing something about men, I would guess your cousin and brother are caught up in their own lives, but I'm sure they think of you often."

"Yes, you could be right. I know I can't be in the forefront of their minds. Still, it would be nice to hear they are safe."

"There's no guarantee of that, I'm afraid."

Dumbstruck by his honesty, her emotions were stirred and she couldn't respond.

"I'm sorry, Miss Messing. I've upset you. Please, don't take my cynicism to heart."

She changed her position on the blanket. Her legs were beginning to go numb. "You might know better than the rest of us what life is truly about. Away from society, that is."

"I'm sure they're well, and as I said, caught up in their lives." He reached for the burlap sack. "It's too pleasant a day for worry or pain." This time, he presented an item wrapped in paper. The

41

parchment crackled as he revealed the chocolate inside and offered it to her.

Recovering her lighter mood, she picked up a piece of the dark confection. "You thought of everything." It had slightly melted, and she licked her fingers once it was consumed. "Oh dear." Laughing, she wiped her chin.

"Let me." Caleb swiped a finger over the corner of her mouth. Their eyes locked and he moved in closer. She turned her head away and brushed her chin.

"We should be going." She reached for her coat and put it on, then swept a hand over her bun.

He patted her arm. "Help me clean up lunch, and we'll get you back to safety, my lady."

His humor broke the tension, and she was glad for it.

In the days and nights that followed, Jessica struggled with her unsettling euphoria. She admonished herself for having such feelings. Or had she forgotten how to be happy? Moving her art studio into her uncle's shed helped to keep her mind off Caleb. It was a good ten feet by sixteen feet, and the windows allowed the light to pour through in magical and inspiring ways. It felt like a palace compared to the tiny, concrete back room at Talbot's Gallery. The walls could hold her larger paintings, and the shelves provided more space than she needed for all her supplies. The windows were tall, and the exposed wood beam ceiling added to its airiness.

On this evening, shafts of amber and gold reached into her space, and the shadows changed as the sun slid behind the hills. She threw herself into her latest painting, letting the light guide the last touches on another landscape of Clermont City. She stood back and huffed. The hues of the sky weren't right, and the bell tower was leaning. What was happening to her? This new distraction had to end.

After dinner, she retired to her room to write another letter to Jacob. It would join the growing stack of letters she knew not where to send. Her small writing table by the window comforted her, and it encouraged her to write of her life to him. However, tonight was different. She couldn't tell Jacob about her afternoon with Caleb. Or that he'd tried to kiss her. She held her pen away from the precious paper she had purchased with her own money. Caleb had no place in her letters—or in her life.

Setting aside their brief flirtation, she decided to write in her journal about her own feelings and worries. Yes, that would help her figure out what to do about Caleb Cantrell. As she loaded her pen, a sense of unease rose up inside her. What was she doing expending such energy on this man? She laid her pen aside and capped her ink well, her heart beating faster.

Chapter Ten

The saloon in Clermont City was more civilized than any Caleb had been in. It doubled as a meeting place for folks to discuss the town's concerns before bringing their agendas to City Hall. On entering, the smell of tobacco and alcohol filled his nose revealing, after all, that this was a tavern. Taking a seat at the table already occupied by Levi and Cork, he waved for the barmaid. Although busy with his land, he still found time to socialize with his former gang members. In minutes a pitcher of ale and a tall mug sat in front of him. Caleb poured the dark amber and took a sip. Then he told them about Will and Jacob being related to his new friends, the Stanfords. It brought a spray of beer out from Levi's nose and a laugh heard throughout the saloon. Cork sat wide-eyed. "How in hell did fate come up with this?" Caleb didn't have any answers and was as astonished as they were. Jessica may be the reason, yet he didn't dare to think of her joining his life. He tucked any further thoughts of her away for tonight. Levi's invitation held more than a friendly round of beer.

Licking the froth from his lip, Caleb bent his head and spoke in a low voice. "Where did you get your information?"

Levi followed Caleb's lead and kept his voice hushed. "I was in Lamont a few days back and read this." He handed Caleb an article ripped out of a newspaper.

Sacred Terrain

Marshal Jason Lewis reopens investigation into gunrunners caught and killed in Colorado Springs in April of 1886.

Suspected outlaw Harper Davis, said to be the only surviving member of the group, confessed earlier this week that he knew of five more members of the illegal traders who had escaped the raid. In a plea deal to exchange information for a shortened sentence, Mr. Davis gave Marshal Lewis enough to go on. The marshal has enlisted several deputies to track down the outlaws within his jurisdiction, but he fears they have long since left Colorado. A scout has been hired to take the search beyond the Colorado borders. Surrounding states have been given a description of the remaining group members. Extradition to Colorado is strongly advised.

Folding the piece of paper, Caleb handed it back to Levi. Lost in thought, he sat back in his chair. "Christ."

"I knew that damn Harper was a bad penny when he ran from me that night with nothing but a 'See ya.' He owed me more than that, and now to betray us all like this? Damn. It ain't right," Cork lamented.

"What do you make of it, Caleb?" Levi asked their former boss.

Placing his elbows on the table, Caleb clasped his hands to his mouth. "We live our lives as we have been, but from now on, we keep our eyes and ears open for anyone new coming into town and questioning folks. They'd likely come in here first. As far as posters with our likeness, let's just hope Harper's memories are as confused as his ability to tell one place of trade from another."

"Yeah, he was a bit on the stupid side, but he knows how we look."

Caleb didn't want to give credence to this news since his life was finally taking a turn for the better. His hope of being with Jessica faded. How could he tell her about his past and Will's and Jacob's involvement? Levi's voice cut into his worried mind.

"Sounds good to me. We just keep our heads low and on our work. So, on that note, how's the land coming, Caleb? Last I saw, those timbers were ready for walls."

45

"Yep, I'm getting there. How goes things on the farm?"

Caleb couldn't get her out of his mind, as the mundane talk between the men barely held his attention. He drained his mug and was ready to return to his peaceful homestead. Cork gave him a nudge. "What about the Stanfords?"

Many nights, Caleb had stayed awake thinking about Burt and June Stanford and their son, Jacob, along with Jessica's brother, Will. Shaking his head, Caleb sat back. "They're good people, and they don't need to know anything about my past that I don't want them to know. And I'm sure as hell not going to tell them the truth about their son and nephew." He gave a stern look to both men.

"All right, then, 'nough said."

"Their unwed niece is quite a looker." Levi elbowed Caleb. "She turn your head yet?"

"That's none of your business." A smile crept over Caleb's face, revealing the answer.

Levi let out a small whoop. "You better hope Jacob and Will stay away. They'd skin your hide if they found out you been seeing their kin."

"No one has any say over who I set my eye on, Levi. You know me better. Now, if you'll excuse me, gentlemen, I'll get back to work on my house and land. Thanks for the info, Levi. Be sure to keep me informed." Placing his hat on his head, Caleb bid his friends good day.

A cool breeze had Jessica bringing up her collar with one hand while she laid on the reins with the other. The carriage gave a lurch as the horse moved down the road at a brisker pace. Mr. Talbot had sold most of her small paintings, and she was bringing more to him today.

As she brought the crate of framed art from the back of the

carriage, she spied Caleb's horse across the street. Her nerves flew into a state of alertness. Mr. Talbot came around and helped her with the crate. "Good, good, my dear," he said as he came closer to her. "There are a few women in there right this minute whom I know will like these. We could have several sales already." He pulled back the sheet and looked over the paintings. "My, these are good. Frank did a great job in framing them. I dare say, he'll take his cut by the end of this month, but don't you worry. I can get a good sum for these."

Jessica smiled. "Thank you, Mr. Talbot. That would be wonderful." She let him take her artwork, then decided to see if the dressmaker across the street had any new bonnets on display.

Strolling along the wooden sidewalk, she wondered what brought Caleb into town. She knew he had quit the boarding house and was living in his unfinished house. More supplies for his home, perhaps, or a bit of lunch at Midge's Café? Before she could think on it further, he stepped out of the saloon. *Oh ... of course.*

Wanting to get near enough to call to him without sounding obvious, she walked in his direction. "Hello, Mr. Cantrell."

Caleb reeled around. "Jessica ... um ... Miss Messing. Hello. What a nice surprise."

"Yes, it is. I was dropping some of my paintings off at the gallery."

He nodded his head and took off his hat. "I took a peek inside Talbot's a few days ago. I love the one with the bell tower. It reminds me of a place I visited with my parents in Upstate New York. I'll have to commission a painting from you for my home."

The thought of a painting of hers hanging in his home gladdened her heart. "I would be honored. Are you still coming for Sunday supper?"

"I wouldn't miss it for the world, but for now, I must be on my way. It was a pleasure to see you again, Miss Messing."

"A pleasure. Good day." Sensing he was in a hurry, Jessica turned before he could take his leave. Why she felt compelled to have the upper hand with him today, she couldn't explain. Perhaps it was his cool demeanor. It didn't matter. He was his own man, hardly her concern. She was suddenly anxious about Sunday. Would he ask her to take a walk with him after dessert as he had done the last time he came for Sunday supper ... and the time before that?

Chapter Eleven

*W*ith the Sunday supper underway, June finally sat down and began to eat. "I must say, the weather is changing, even for here. I almost had Mr. Stanford start a fire in the fireplace last night, Caleb. And how is your home coming along? I hear the stove is in and the walls are nearly covered."

Swallowing, Caleb answered that indeed his home would be warm and snug by Christmas. Jessica smiled at him, and he gave her a wink. She blushed and returned to her meal.

As June cleared the table, she gave strict instructions for Caleb and Jessica to take a walk. "Or you might want to show him your art shop, Jessica. She is too modest, Caleb."

Jessica pursed her lips. "Thank you, Auntie, but it's not modesty that keeps me from showing him my work. The studio is a mess right now." She turned to Caleb. "It's always the case after I've painted for days."

"I'll see it when you're ready," Caleb said. "A walk sounds good."

Taking her shawl off the hook in the foyer, Jessica wrapped herself in it as they headed outside. Feeling a bit silly for not showing off her art studio, she led Caleb around the side of the house and down a narrow lane. At the end stood a neat structure, a small version of the bungalow home—yellow with cream-colored trim. The tidy landscape around the entrance added to its charm.

When Jessica opened the door, the smell of oil paints and mineral spirits met them head- on. "I'm sorry about the odor." She went to the two small windows and lifted each one before turning to get Caleb's reaction to her creative space. In the corner under her easel was the stained rug, the table beside the easel was filled with tubes of paint, a wood palette contained smeared colors, a tin of mineral spirits held several brushes, a few paint-crusted rags lay on the rug next to the table, and her dirty apron was draped over the stool. The easel held the beginnings of a portrait of a young girl and her dog. Her watercolor table was just as messy. Color-dotted rags, a jar of dirty water, an open palette of paints, and discarded attempts at seaside scenes strewn the floor. On the walls hung many of her rough paintings and drawings for reference.

No one came into her studio. Her aunt couldn't take the odor, and her uncle would never dream of walking in unless invited, and she hadn't yet invited him. This was her space to be who she wanted to be and express herself without the concerns of the outside world. In fact, she had hung the portrait of her and Jacob on the wall without hesitation. It was the painting she had done that fateful day back in Hartford after Jacob told her he was leaving town. The lovers in the scene were not so clearly recognizable, but they held a familiarity that may cause some raised eyebrows if the rest of the family saw it. Here she was free to display her heart. Some of her more abstract art was even darker than she would have liked. At times, she let only emotions guide her inner creative self. Not sellable, she kept them as a reminder of her deep self-expression. Now it was all on display for Caleb to see and judge. A twinge of regret pricked her stomach.

"An artist at work. You inspire me, Jessica," he said as he leaned in to examine a painted canvas.

With a wide grin, she accepted his comment. Now more at ease, she explained a few of her works in progress. When she came to the wall of hanging art, Caleb eyes lingered on the one of her and Jacob. She gave no mind to his attention of it.

He came away and looked at her with a furrowed brow. "Is this you?" He chuckled.

Bringing a hand to her mouth, she laughed, trying to conceal her nerves.

"It's a very intimate scene. I think I'm even jealous. The man ... who is he?"

Tongue-tied, Jessica walked to her easel and steadied her nerves. She turned to him. "I'm an artist. I have an imagination."

"I see you do." He came closer. The light coming into the room lit his face, and she saw the tension in his neck. Surprisingly, she ached to her very loins to see beyond to his collarbone, to his chest, his stomach. "Jessica, I feel I should be honest with you."

Calming her unruly thoughts, she focused on his serious expression. "Honesty is always welcome in a budding friendship, but please don't put yourself out of your way. We are just getting to know one another." A distance needed to be established, and she would be the one to do it.

He tilted his head and gave a slanted grin. "Only friends?"

"Only friends." The words "for now" were so close to her lips, she rubbed her mouth to remove them.

"Then I won't worry so much about making a great impression on you."

The atmosphere became extremely awkward. How could she bring back the pleasantness of the evening? "I think we should return to the house. The days are getting shorter. You wouldn't want to ride home in the dark."

The daylight was nearly extinguished when Caleb brought his horse into the pole shed that served as a temporary barn. Entering his home, he sat in the middle of the room on the one chair he had built out of scrap lumber. The scent of the new wood permeated the inside, and it gave him renewed purpose. Tomorrow he would finish the walls and make this his retreat, which offered him a normal life. The thought of a wife and children entered his mind.

Normality seemed to escape him, yet he remained hopeful despite what fate had in mind.

The newspaper clipping Levi showed him disturbed his dream, and there it was again—no retreat, no peace. The trails of his past loomed in the distance as if calling him to escape into their fold, hiding him from the law. Canada perhaps. He let his fear take hold and saw Jacob and Will buckling under the pressure of the marshal or an unscrupulous scout. Dead or alive was not mentioned in the article, but most scouts got paid no matter what condition their prey was in. Shuddering, he got up and poured himself a stiff drink. The odds were in his favor, he had to remind himself. Clermont City was a good choice. The small town drew little attention to itself.

Sleep threatened to take hold as Caleb lie on a palette of wool blankets near the potbellied stove, yet his thoughts drifted to Jessica and her studio. He felt his heart had engaged with hers as he took in the artistic space. Then her words crashed into him. How could he be mere friends with a woman so lovely and so full of life, with an independence that attracted him like no other? The painting of her under the tree with a man sparked his interest. Did the man resemble Jacob Stanford, her cousin, or was it his own wild imagining? Shaking the thought from his head, he concluded he would have to court Jessica differently. Patiently.

Chapter Twelve

Clermont City–December 1887

"Another Christmas is upon us." Hannah sighed. "I have to say it feels right to be here with you and your kin, Mum. If only my Kevin were closer." The round-faced English maid tucked Jessica's undergarments in the chest of drawers, while Jessica looked through her closet for a gown to wear to tonight's formal dance at City Hall.

"I'm sorry we couldn't find work for Kevin in town, but he has good employment with Mr. Moore for now. We will find a way to have him here, someday." She wanted Kevin out of Frederick's employ just as badly as Hannah, but for very different reasons. For as long as Kevin Rolland was there, Jessica would have a connection with her ex-husband, a fact she loathed.

She stood at her bed, surveying each of the three gowns she'd laid out. "Would you mind helping me pick out a dress for tonight, Hannah? I can't seem to settle on any one I've chosen. I want you to accompany me to the dance. Mrs. Stanford has a fine dress for you to wear tonight."

Hannah looked down at her feet, uncomfortable with the request. "Are you sure, Mum?"

"Yes, of course. Please, Hannah, call me Jessica."

"Oh!" Hannah placed her hand on top of her head. "First the invitation, now this?"

"Don't look so shocked. Tonight, we are both free women." Hannah silently folded another silky camisole. Jessica saw the sadness behind her resignation. "Hannah, I'm so sorry. I know it pains you to be without Kevin. I promise we will do all it takes to reunite you."

"Thank you, Mum, Jessica." A smile lit up her face. "Do you think Mr. Cantrell will be there? He's so handsome. I'll bet he'll turn all the ladies' heads. I mean, except yours. Seems that one has already turned his way." Her eyes gleamed.

Jessica couldn't deny her growing fondness for Caleb. He visited her often, and she and her aunt had gone to see the property on several occasions. He'd been so eager to show her the progress of his home, and when she last visited with June, she was truly impressed. The rustic, three-bedroom house had all its interior walls, and with the help of his neighbor, Ben Loggin, and some men hired from town, it was beginning to resemble a real home. The road had much improved, its smoother ride tempting her to visit him more often.

Standing in front of her full-length mirror, she held one of the gowns up to her body. With a contented sigh, she recalled the visit to Rail River Acres. Then her guilt rose. Where was the man she promised to love, and who promised to love her? Still no letter from Jacob, and now life was taking her in a direction that widened the gap between them. She tossed the gown on the bed and opened her wardrobe doors wide. She would wear a plainer dress this evening. The Winter Ball was an event at which to be seen in one's finest, and yet she wished only to be seen as herself— an artist. Though why was her heart fluttering at the thought of seeing Caleb at the social event of the season? Would he actually come down from his hill to be there?

Hannah pulled back Jessica's hair in a tidy chignon, without the usual tendrils around her face. Jessica bent her head as Hannah secured the last hairpin into place. "I feel old."

The English woman peered at her in the mirror. "If you are feeling old, Jessica, then I should feel very old!"

"I suppose I'm being dramatic." Hannah laced up her corset, then helped her into the emerald-green gown. It was formal but had no lace. Instead, the wide, ruffled collar draped over her shoulders. The taffeta was soft and elegant. Hannah's nimble fingers worked the line of covered buttons up the back. Turning, she looked over her shoulder at her reflection, making sure the back flounce was just right. "I think this will do. Now go get dressed yourself. My aunt is downstairs pressing your gown."

"Oh! I should be the one pressing the gown!" Hannah rushed out of the room.

Jessica appraised herself in the mirror. The rounded neckline exposed Jacob's beads on her silky, white neck. She pursed her lips. Perhaps she'd leave them home tonight.

Having never become fully acquainted with all the nuances of formal dancing, Caleb wondered what he had gotten himself into. Thinking back to his boyhood, he saw his mother looking down on him as she led him around the parlor in a waltz, his feet balanced on hers, her gay laughter and loving eyes exclusively trained on him. He felt adored, and when she died on a snowy night, she took the gentility of art, music, and dance with her. His grandmother had him schooled in a more rigid fashion. Although she paraded him around society, she also told him that he was not to consider himself above others. "It's unbecoming for a man to show his vanity," she told him. Since his departure from her house, the only dancing he had done was the occasional drunken attempts on a barroom floor to the tune of a mouth harp, which he could barely remember the following morning.

Looking in the long mirror, which he'd propped up against a wall in the bedroom of his new home, he pulled back his hair, securing it with a string of brown ribbon. It had grown long again, blond with lighter, sun-bleached streaks. He kept his slightly darker goatee trimmed. His tanned body showed the results of working on his home and barn. Tucking a crisp, white shirt into his new, heavy, black wool pants, he then adjusted the stiff collar, making sure his tie was in the proper place. His overcoat cut a striking line, accentuating his tall figure. Then his courage waned. He wouldn't be doing such a foolhardy thing, in such a costume, if it weren't for the possibility of seeing Burt's niece.

She was unlike any woman he ever met. Besides being drawn to her beauty, he felt a sense of truth from her that spoke to his heart. His desire to be close to her was growing, and like the land he had decided to live on, he'd also decided to be with her. Despite his better judgment begging him not to get involved with this family, he couldn't let her go. The fact that his old gunrunning days were behind him didn't stop the flashbacks coming to him from the shoot-out in Colorado, Jacob standing above a dead man, a trail of thin smoke coming from his gun. *I have no business being involved with you, Jessica.* The blood rushed to his chest. "Damn!"

Walking out of his house, he stood on his new, cedar-planked porch, wishing he had his gun belt around him. He chuckled to himself. *It would do you no good tonight, Cantrell.*

The lights above the expansive hall hung with an uncommon formality. Figures in black-and-white attire led swaying ball gowns around the floor. The music flowed out to the dancers, and they responded with a seamless fluidity. Caleb looked down from the upper tier and took in the swirling, vivid scene. His legs felt weighted as he slowly descended the staircase and gazed out among the crowd for signs of a familiar face. He caught June waving her arm wildly and Burt slowly bringing it to her side. Caleb joined them.

"Good evening, Caleb," the couple said in unison.

"Good evening, Burt, Mrs. Stanford."

Then June's other niece, Sophie, appeared out of nowhere like a whirling dervish. "Oh my, I can't remember a more beautiful affair!" She was nearly out of breath. "Hello, Mr. Cantrell. Aren't you striking tonight! You must save a dance for me and make all the other women envious."

Caleb met the rest of Jessica's family in September—June's brother, Austin, his wife, Laura, their daughter, Sophie, her husband, Carl, and their two lively sons, who had asked Caleb all kinds of silly questions about Indians. He was amused and, at the same time, hoped he wouldn't have to endure too many visits with them. He shied away from Sophie's exuberance and turned to Burt. "Has Miss Messing joined you tonight?"

"Yes, yes, she's right over there," Sophie interrupted. "You'll have to wait a while before you get a turn with her. Well, I must go find my husband. Some of us will always have a dance partner." She left as dramatically as she had appeared, the sound of her billowing dress like a sharp wind through dry leaves. June excused herself, and soon they had both disappeared into the crowd.

Feeling a bit sheepish, Caleb turned to Burt. "I have a confession to make. I don't know how to dance."

"Why, a young, handsome man like yourself, never learning how to dance? I'm sure there's been more than one lady who persuaded you out on the floor." Burt chuckled.

Caleb didn't want to think back to the "ladies" he had known. This crowd would be less than welcoming to him if they knew the man he truly was. He pulled at his collar. "Nope, I guess I haven't led that life since leaving home. I'm afraid my memory will fail me, though I would love to take a turn with your niece."

"She's coming this way. You'd better polish your dancing shoes." And with that, Burt stood aside.

"Hello, Miss Messing." Caleb felt his heart pounding in his chest. She was radiant. Her complexion glowed under the many gas lamps and candles, her lips and cheeks flushed from dancing, and her skin softly glistened on her open neckline, which rose and fell with every breath. He stood still, captivated by her.

"Hello, Mr. Cantrell. You know our housemaid and friend, Mrs. Rolland."

He came out of his daze. "Yes, hello, Mrs. Rolland. You look well tonight. I mean, both of you ladies look exceptional."

For all the ease he had come to know with her over the past many months, Caleb stumbled in his efforts to remain calm and nonchalant in this most formal, pressure-filled moment. His throat tightened. He reminded himself of the many times he had looked death in the face and had come out victorious. *Why is this so difficult?* But it was, and he was about to get in deeper. He stood even straighter and extended his hand. "Would you like to dance, Miss Messing?"

Chapter Thirteen

*J*essica found Caleb's awkwardness charming. She curtsied and he bowed as the music prepared the dancers for a waltz. It wasn't the most fluid waltz, but it was somewhat graceful. He held her petite hand with confidence, and his long arm bent to accommodate hers. They went around and around the dance floor as if they were one. She found the courage to look up at him and caught his seductive eyes looking back at her. He drew her closer, and her hand slipped over his shoulder and toward his neck. Warning herself not to feel anything for him, she couldn't help but be swept up in his closeness. A swirl of her skirt, a tilt of her head, the room spun. *Oh, Jacob, why have you left me in such a vulnerable state?*

All too soon, the music ended. Jessica curtsied as he bowed. He led her off the dance floor to where another man stood, eager to take his place. Jessica found herself once again being swept about the ballroom, but not to the elevated state she had just been taken to. The music ended, and her partner escorted her off the floor and to her uncle. He wasn't alone. Caleb stood beside him. She sensed his eagerness. It touched her heart in a delicious and exciting way. She blamed her state of emotions on the atmosphere and mood in the hall, festive and light, buzzing with conversation, a touch of romance filling the expansiveness. Caleb came closer to her and she froze.

"Would you like to join me, Miss Messing, for some fresh air?"

His playful formality amused her and she relaxed. Nevertheless, she felt cautious. Catching her uncle's eye, she asked him if he would join them.

"No, no. You two go along without me. My bones don't care for the cool night."

She accepted Caleb's arm, and they weaved through the crowd. The noise receded and the light changed. Winding paths led to various gardens on the grounds of City Hall. Benches sat among the greenery. In summertime, it was a burst of reds, pinks, and purples, but on this December night, the light of the full moon created reflections and shadows. Caleb gestured to a bench away from the other couples. Jessica sat, arranged her gown, and then looked up to admire the sky. She dared not move as she brought her gaze back to the bench. Caleb was as close as the material spread over the seat would allow.

"I enjoyed our dance, but I prefer this." He took her hand in his, the surreal light catching his fair features. The warmth of his touch sent goose bumps over her flesh. He leaned in closer. "May I kiss you?"

She pulled away. "Excuse me, I feel chilled." The layers of her green taffeta swished and swayed as she hurried back to the hall.

Coming to the entrance, she brushed away a tear. How did she let it get this far? The noise of the crowd accosted her, and she held back from entering. Suddenly, Caleb was there, taking her arm. "I'm sorry, Mr. Cantrell, but. ..." Her uncle rushed up beside them, cutting her short.

"Jessica, there's been an accident." Burt's face was flushed.

"What is it? What's happened?" Jessica braced herself for his answer.

"It's Kevin Rolland." Burt struggled to get the words out. "He got caught in a shoot-out somewhere on the city docks. He's been killed."

Stunned, Jessica could not move. His words made no sense.

"Let me take you to Mrs. Rolland," Caleb said. He steered her through the crowd.

The interfering throng of noisy people made their search difficult, but they finally glimpsed Hannah outside, on her knees, with Sam, Frederick's driver, crouched beside her. Jessica turned to Caleb when a group of curious onlookers blocked their way. June, Sophie, and her husband, Carl, were now alongside them as they all pushed their way to the front. To Jessica's relief, once they reached Hannah, Caleb helped them to Burt's carriage. Before she entered the cab, Jessica looked back at him. He acknowledged her and she returned a meek smile, then her attentions were on the shocked widow.

Chapter Fourteen

Clermont City Cemetery–December 1887

*K*evin Rolland's body lay in state at the Dupree Funeral Home in Clermont City. The mortuary owner himself had prepared the body. It wasn't an easy task. Clothing could hide neither the marks on his face and hands from the horse that had trampled him, nor the bruises and knife marks from the thugs who had robbed him. The owner of the funeral home, and his staff, did their best but eventually suggested a closed casket ceremony.

Frederick Moore paid for the casket, it's transportation to Clermont City, and the burial plot in the small cemetery beside the church. It seemed as suitable a place as any. Hannah had always believed she and Kevin would be buried in England, but the expense was great and the thought of him being so far away changed her mind.

Hannah was resigned to it. "I should be grateful to Mr. Moore. After all, it's not the poorman's cemetery. I can hold my head high when I visit him."

On the day of the funeral, Caleb volunteered to accompany Jessica and Hannah. Jessica was happy to have him there. His presence calmed her. He helped June into the carriage first, then Hannah, and lastly, Jessica. She felt his hand squeeze hers. She caught his eyes, understanding and compassionate. Once Caleb secured the door, the women waited for him to join Burt at the reins. The carriage jerked, and the spoked wheels kicked up the pebbles in the circular drive as Burt steered the double-horse carriage toward the church. Hannah sat very still, a blank look in her puffy, red-rimmed eyes. Jessica felt helpless in consoling her. A winter chill raised the hair on her arms. She brought her shawl tighter around her dark waistcoat, then placed her hand over Hannah's. "Are you warm enough?" Hannah returned an empty stare. Jessica brought the blanket on Hannah's lap closer to her waist. She looked at her aunt, who shook her head and sighed.

"Life has such travails, my dear. I pray that your heart will be able to carry this burden." June's sentiment lingered in the cool, damp air as their bodies moved with the rocking motion of the carriage. Although it was a solemn moment, Jessica could still feel Caleb's deliberate touch. Her hand slid over her glove, and a flutter went through her stomach. She brought her attention back to Hannah. This wasn't the time to indulge in such thoughts or feelings.

Sam stood stoically, but for wringing his cap in his hands. Hannah threw a handful of dirt onto her husband's casket as the bright sun lit up her tear-filled eyes. Her round shoulders heaved under a black, woolen overcoat. Jessica held on to her, and the two women wept as they watched Kevin being lowered to his final resting place. From the church gravesite, Jessica spied Frederick's carriage parked away from the others, yet the man was nowhere in sight. She inhaled a ragged breath. Perhaps he would watch from a distance.

The priest recited another blessing, they said another prayer, then the small group slowly walked back to the poorly lit rectory, where a meager offering of cheese, bread, and wine waited on an old table. Hannah sat down on one of the few chairs, her head lowered. The heaviness of the room weighed on Jessica, with its stained-glass windows giving somber light through thick, dusty, green-and-red panes, the smell of frankincense clouding the air. She stayed close to Hannah, ready to comfort her in any way she could. The rest of the group gathered uneasily, allowing themselves a bit of wine, but no one touched the food. The priest entered from a narrow door at the end of the room. He offered Hannah a small Bible, then whispered a prayer above her. He left as quietly as he had appeared. Jessica shivered at the sight of his black robe disappearing behind the door that led back into the church.

Her eyes roamed around the room. They were a mournful group. Sam stood by the door fidgeting, his attention on the entrance. Nervous about who he might be expecting, she took a step in his direction, but before she could ask him, a sharp ray of daylight pierced the room as the door opened, revealing two figures. Frederick Moore stood with his wife, Annabelle, just behind him. They entered, and the door slammed shut. Jessica closed her eyes briefly. Guarded, she watched her ex-husband approach the young widow. "I'm sorry for your loss, Hannah," he said, his English accent as regal as ever.

Hannah raised her head. "Thank you, Mr. Moore." He reached into his overcoat and gave her an envelope. "May I? It's a small amount, and I know it doesn't make up for your circumstances, but I would like you to have it." He took her hand and placed the thick envelope into it.

"Thank you, sir. Thank you for taking care of my Kevin, with the casket and all." She clasped the envelope and bowed her head, staring at the floor. Frederick stood up.

It was the first time Jessica laid eyes on the man since their dramatic meeting when she had made a deal with him for his silence about her relationship with Jacob, when he had nearly raped her. She pressed her hand to her cheek and steadied her breath as she relived the memory of him seething with revenge, his hands all over her, his breath marked by alcohol, and her fear of him taking his anger to a horrible conclusion. She shook her head to unhinge the memory. *You are safe.* His hazel eyes and handsome face, crowned by wavy hair and a trimmed beard, lacked the formidable presence she once feared. His cologne filled the air with a pungent scent of bayberry and lime. At one time, this larger-than-life figure would have ruled over her, but now she wondered why she hadn't left him sooner. It made the day even more unreal.

His new wife, Annabelle, stood at the door, her purse clasped in both hands in front of her full skirt. Jessica looked at her and received a squinty-eyed glare. When she was married to Frederick and visited him in his office at the bank, she would first have to greet Annabelle. She came to think of the receptionist as a rather plain-looking woman with mousy-brown hair and eyes that held a lack of curiosity about the world around her. Today, however, she looked quite elegant, dressed in a rich, deep-blue dress covered by a long, matching, cutaway coat made of the fabric one sees in the finer shops in New York City. Her hair was swept under a round-brimmed hat adorned with pearls and peacock feathers. Every inch of her stated she was the wife of a wealthy man. *I wonder how she's being treated beyond all that frippery?* The thought vanished as Frederick extended his hand to her.

Receiving his hand took effort. Barely touching his fingers, she swiftly withdrew.

"My condolences, Jessica."

She acknowledged him with a slight nod. The room suddenly felt very crowded, and she sorely wanted to leave.

"Hello, Frederick," said Burt. "It was kind of you to arrange things, although June and I would have taken it on if asked."

"I felt it was my duty, Burt. Kevin was a dutiful and valuable servant, not to mention a decent man." Frederick's well-polished politeness made Jessica queasy, and Hannah gave an audible sob.

"Well, it was mighty good of you." Burt turned away and poured himself a small glass of wine.

When Frederick turned to greet her aunt, Jessica silently willed June to hold her views of him in check.

"Mrs. Stanford," he said with a slight bow.

Looking up at the tall man and directly into his eyes, her aunt said in a low, strong voice, "I'm biting my tongue, Mr. Moore."

"Thank you, June," Frederick said without apology. He turned to Caleb. "I don't believe we've met. I'm Frederick Moore, Jessica's former husband."

Jessica closed her eyes for a moment, wishing she could disappear. She turned her attentions to Hannah. "Let's go home." Taking Hannah's arm, she helped her up and they walked to the door.

The others soon followed, her uncle arranging the seating. "Caleb, I feel the ladies may need your comfort. June doesn't mind riding alongside me." Jessica furrowed her brow. What was he up to? Once inside the carriage, she held Hannah's hand while she peered out of the open door. To her chagrin, she saw that Frederick had pulled Caleb aside. Their conversation looked pleasant enough, but dread soon filled her when Caleb's face showed concern.

"You're hurting my hand, Jessica," she heard Hannah say in a faint voice. Jessica quickly loosened her grip and apologized. Then, as the two men parted, she heard Frederick say in a very clear voice, "I would be very careful if I were you." Caleb's brows turned in, and there were no friendly departing words or a handshake between the two men.

The ride back to the house was quiet. Jessica gave Caleb a smile. He returned it with a stare. What poison had Frederick unleashed? She came forward. "Mr. Moore and you seemed to be having a nice conversation. I can't imagine what he would have to say to you. Perhaps another one of his investment ventures? I suppose he—"

"Nothing I want to share at the moment." His sharp reply raised her suspicions.

Resting back in her seat, she searched his eyes. "I see. Perhaps after dinner?"

"No, I'm afraid I must be getting home. There's still enough light of day to work in."

She turned to the window. This melancholy day just got darker.

Caleb sat on his front porch and lit a cigarette, stunned by Frederick's comments. He reeled at the thought of having to give Jessica up after these many weeks of courting. He had warned himself not to get involved with her. Now his intuition had been validated. Recalling his conversations with Jacob couldn't bring to memory any talk about a particular woman. He had thought of Jacob as a man who had lost love, rather than one who hadn't found it yet.

So, Jessica and Jacob ... together. Was it the imaginings of a vengeful husband? He would have to find the truth. He bent head. How was he going to reconcile his own love for her with this knowledge? He told himself to wait patiently for the rest of the story to unfold.

Walking to his unfinished barn, he tried to make good on his statement to work before nightfall. When that failed, he walked down to the river. He watched the ducks by the cold water's edge, diving for food. A wind rushed the tall grasses, and they came alive with sound. Nature embraced him, and his peace was upon him at last. Closing his eyes, he thanked the spirits for the land he was fortunate enough to borrow.

When his thoughts veered back to Jessica, he lost his ground and felt adrift. How did he let a woman get under his skin like this? For years, he had dodged all sorts of affairs and never once had he let himself feel anything beyond the satisfaction of a soft, warm body or the company of a woman's mind and opinions. Why her? He pulled back his shoulders. He'd have to stay detached, as was his custom. His mind told him to walk away and avoid heartache.

Chapter Fifteen

*C*ursing Frederick, Jessica was determined her ex-husband would not intrude in her life. Had he broken their deal? His deviousness was out of her control. Looking out her bedroom window, she contemplated why it mattered whether Caleb knew about her and Jacob. He was just a friend, and she was confident he would keep such a revelation to himself. Then suddenly, a sadness came over her. Not the usual feelings in her longing for Jacob. This was different. Ever since she took that first walk with Caleb, she fought to deny any emotions other than friendship toward him. Today, the thought of never seeing him again made her anxious, and truly sad. Changing into her riding clothes, she hurried to the stables and saddled up Georgia. Without disturbing the household, she rode up to Rail River Acres.

As Caleb's sturdy home came into sight, she slowed. "We'll just have to be brave, girl," she said to Georgia as she stopped just yards from the timber-framed home. Dismounting, she secured the reins to a nearby tree. His own horse was out to pasture. She stepped on the front porch, the smell of cedar sharp in her nostrils. A gust of wind and the door came ajar, she peeked inside.

"Hello?" she asked meekly. She opened it farther. "Caleb?"

There was no answer. She retreated to the wooden bench on the porch and waited for several minutes. A chill wrapped her body, and she brought her arms to her chest. The warmth she felt escaping from his home tempted her. Looking out onto his land, she appreciated how beautiful it was, even in the winter. A misty, gray fog hovered over the field. The sloping land that led to the river felt open and free. Her heart wanted the same.

She grew even colder and entered the house, like a thief in the night. The small vestibule had a wooden bench with pegs above it. A gray, flannel shirt hung on one of them, and she resisted the temptation to bring it to her nose. A narrow door opened into a spacious room where a large, handwoven rug lay beneath two chairs, one covered in leather, the other in a red, paisley fabric, each with its own side table and kerosene lamp. The last time she was here, he had barely furnished the place. The chairs faced the stone hearth, which surrounded a large, potbellied stove that sat on new bricks.

"Hello?" she called out again, and again she received no answer. She continued in, drawn to the warmth radiating from the stove. Caleb couldn't be far. She told herself to wait outside, yet she stood in the middle of the room, too curious to leave. To the left of the stove was a doorway. Upon entering, she was pleased with the sight of a rustic yet well-appointed kitchen. The sink had a pump for running water. His well was a success. There was plenty of space for making pies and breads, and a thick, wooden table with two sturdy chairs sat off to the side. The pine cupboards gave a sweet aroma to the charming room. The window above the sink looked out over the vast field. A soft ray of low sunlight, cutting through the fog, transformed it into a magical land. Their ride on a warm day filled her with nostalgia. She swallowed the emotion, thick in her throat, and continued her self-guided tour.

Returning to the main room, she saw a closed door to her left and two doors ahead. The first opened to a small, empty room. The second room was the same. Three bedrooms as he promised. Passing by the stove, she went to the third door. She reached for the doorknob.

"Jessica!"

Clutching her chest, she jumped up and back. "Caleb! You startled me!"

"What are you doing here?" he demanded, fists on his hips.

"I came to talk to you." Heat rushed to her face. Her legs felt weak, and she sorely regretted her temerity.

"What about?" He stood still and unwelcoming.

This was a side of him she hadn't seen. He wasn't giving her an inch. Straightening her back, she folded her leather-gloved hands in front of her. "I want to talk to you about what Frederick said. You seemed distant in the carriage, and … well … I can't defend myself if I don't know what I'm accused of."

"And who has accused you?"

"I know Frederick."

He extended his arm to the paisley chair, inviting her to sit. She sat on its edge, ridged and alert. He sat on the leather chair, leaning forward with arms on his thighs and his hands clasped. A whole minute had passed, and she felt as if the silence was about to consume her when he spoke. "He claims that you're in love and devoted to someone else. Is this true?"

When she lowered her eyes to escape his blinding stare, she felt her head tremble and she lifted a hand to her warm cheek. His frankness gave her no place to hide. Still, she faltered in telling the truth for she had never let the words land on her lips. She would give another story—she and Jacob were close relations and nothing more. Frederick was a jealous, evil man. As she was about to speak, she looked into his eyes. What she saw was an honest man looking for the truth. Her guts churned, and she was instantly ashamed that she could think of lying to him. The fear of his rejection overwhelmed her. She wanted his respect, his affection. With her heart pounding in her chest, she asked, "May I assume I can trust your discretion?"

"Please, say what you have to say. I only ask, Jessica, that it be the truth. I want to know where I stand. You may think of us as only friends, and I wish that as well, but my feelings run deeper than that. I cannot be with someone who hides the truth from me."

She cleared her throat. She wouldn't lie, but she didn't need to reveal her lover's name. This might not be as dire as she first thought. "It happened over the course of several years. When he went away to school, I missed him greatly. I thought my feelings were a simple distraction from life, nothing more." Rubbing the back of her neck, she continued. "Each time I saw him, my feelings grew stronger." She looked down at her gloves and tugged on each one, bringing them farther up her wrists. "And then I found out he felt the same as me. Yes, we fell in love with each other. Our relationship had to be kept a secret for important reasons." She lifted her chin in defense of her pride. What had she to be proud of? Yet, there it was. The confession did not lift the years of wanting, and she felt heavy with loss. Clearing her throat again, she hoped to remove the heartache. She placed a hand below her chest and took in a deep breath. "He's far away, and as much as we love one another, it can never be possible. It's over now, and I'm completely resigned to it. I desire to give my love where it will be received and honored." Except for the part about being completely resigned to it, she felt she had delivered the truth and had nothing more to hide.

"It's more complicated than that, isn't it?" He sat back, arms folded across his chest.

Without shrinking from his stare, she held her ground. "What did Frederick tell you, Caleb?"

"Do Burt and June know about this?"

Jessica unhooked the top buttons on the high collar of her riding coat. The warmth from the stove was no longer welcoming, but smothering. She had revealed too much of her deep, inner secret, and Caleb wasn't sparing her from discomfort. "Of course not. You're the only one I've ever told." What had she done? "It's not something we could tell our family, as you could well imagine."

"I can imagine a lot of things, but I'd rather not." His reply was flat and lacked the compassion she sorely sought.

"He's adopted, if that eases your concern."

"It doesn't." Caleb's hooded eyes brought her a wave of embarrassment.

She stood, ready to have this over and their friendship broken, but he asked her to stay. Slowly, she sat back down.

Needing a drink, Caleb rose and went to the small bar in the corner of the room. He offered her one, but the flush on her cheeks grew more red. She asked for water instead. He watched her drink, her body quivering. He was in love with her, but his rational mind told him to send her away and never see her again. He had good cause, yet he found it easier to think than act.

More memories about Jacob came flooding back. He thought of their rivalry and what had caused them to compete over trades and gun deals. Was it the future impeding on the present as they sat in the rain and cold, waiting for their split of the spoils, or the hardship and danger they shared as they both worked for money and the respect from everyone in the camp? He had a difficult time figuring out what would motivate Jacob to risk a relationship with his own cousin. Jessica's beautiful face and slight figure gave him part of the answer, and he instantly felt jealousy stinging his gut. He thought again, as he had done too many times, of Jacob standing over him, having just saved his life by taking another. He wished he'd never met the man.

Her voice brought him back to the room. "If you feel you can no longer be my friend, then I will go and it will be over." He saw a proud woman rise from her seat and walk to the door. Something in his heart couldn't let this be the end of them.

"Don't make it too easy for me, Jessica." Her back was to him now. "It won't do well for us if we want a future together. I admire your strength, and you'll need it if we decide to continue." He stood with a drink in his hand. "I believe you when you say you're resigned to it, but I know that these things don't just leave a person easily. Love is a powerful force."

Jessica turned around. His words had given her pause. He

realized he had made them a couple by acknowledging a struggle had risen between them. Waiting anxiously for her reaction—or rather her rejection—he saw instead an open and sincere look on her face. "Have you done anything in your life that would change my mind and heart about us?" she asked.

After a hard swallow of liquor, he looked into his empty glass. "I suppose I have. He knew too well that if his past were revealed to her, he would be the one defending himself. They stood looking at one another, each in a quiet battle for self-preservation. "Tell me I can trust you, and I will," he said. "I can't possess you, but I need some assurance that I'm making the right decision."

She went to the door. "You presume too much of my feelings toward you. And ... I don't know if I can trust myself."

The ride home was filled with anguished tears. She yearned to gallop wildly through an open field. She made the turn into town.

Uncle Burt met her at the door. "My dear, where have you been?"

"We were worried, Jessica," her aunt said from the parlor. "Your uncle was about to take the carriage and go looking for you."

"I had to take a ride. I'm sorry I didn't tell you first. Excuse me, I need to rest." Jessica went to her room, leaving her aunt and uncle to themselves. She had no desire to hear her aunt's chatter. Quiet sobs rose from the downstairs room Hannah called home. Jessica shed her own tears. The world was too big today.

Chapter Sixteen

January 1888

*T*he days moved slowly as Jessica spent her time painting, helping her aunt, and caring for Hannah. A month had passed since the funeral, and she daydreamed of her horseback ride and walks with Caleb and how he tried to kiss her at the Winter Ball, the touch of his hand squeezing hers, then the abrupt intrusion of her reality—Kevin's death and Frederick revealing her secret to Caleb. She had not seen him since that day. Without meaning to give her heart to another man, she now felt cut off and alone.

This morning was shaping up to be another day of the same. After making her bed, she got dressed. A knock on the front door brought her to the bedroom window. Peering down onto the drive, she saw the messenger boy's horse. At this time of day? Jacob and Will? She flew down the stairs. Her aunt's smile softened the thunderous wave of fear that struck her. "It's for you." She took the telegram and calmed herself. The first line read, *May I see you?*

Light-headed from the scare, Jessica slowly climbed the stairs to her room, her aunt asking if she wanted breakfast. "Not now, Auntie, thank you." Sitting on the bed, she stared at the telegram. Caleb wanted her to come to his home this afternoon. This was one of those moments in her life that she would look back on as a turning point. First, she had to be honest with herself. She was falling in love with this man. Where it would lead only time could tell. She hoped it would be toward a good and happy life. With her feelings for Jacob safely tucked away, she let her mind wander to Caleb and his homestead. Could she live there with him? Then she came to the possibility that he might be wanting a proper good-bye. He was a gentleman even with his rough past.

The winter day was damp with more showers to come. Her aunt was fretting at the thought of her riding up to Rail River Acres in such weather. Uncle Burt tried to reason with her. "Not only are the roads bad, but you cannot go to his home unchaperoned again. My sister, your mother, would have a great deal to say about this."

"I understand your concern, Uncle. My mother would be aghast at my life as it is. I'm sure meeting Caleb at his land would send her to an early grave, but she isn't here and neither is my father. I've had your trust before. I ask that you trust me now. I must see him. We had a disagreement and it was left unfinished." Jessica turned to her aunt. "It was a silly squabble, but I feel we need to resolve it. In private."

"Caleb is a good man. You haven't been yourself these many weeks," June said. "Go and settle this. Your uncle will have the stableman prepare the buggy. And for goodness sake, Jessica, be careful on that road. Wear a good bonnet, too, and don't forget your riding gloves."

"Yes, Auntie."

Her uncle scratched his head. "I can see there's no use in reasoning with either one of you." He headed outside.

Feeling a twinge of guilt for worrying her elders, Jessica turned to preparing herself for the confrontation with Caleb. Her nerves were on pins and needles.

The warmth of the stove gave welcome relief from the cold, five-mile ride to Caleb's homestead. Standing in front of the blazing fire, having removed her boots in the vestibule, she still wore her winter coat, hat, and gloves. She rubbed her hands together. Quietly, Caleb went into the kitchen, and when he returned, a steaming cup of liquid was before her. She smelled the aroma of the Earl Grey tea. "Thank you." Wrapping her hands around the mug, she sipped the dark brew. It went down her throat with hot sparks and she coughed. When she had arrived a short while ago, Caleb was standing on his porch, waiting for her. He came off the last step and helped her down. As she looked up into his eyes, she braced herself, but she couldn't let him say good-bye. She commented about her ride up the hill, the weather—anything to stop him from saying what she dreaded to hear.

He stood in front of her now, close enough for her to smell his clean musk. It fixed itself to her inner being and she welcomed it freely.

"You can trust me." The words rushed out of her, followed by a wave of trepidation. Caleb took the cup from her hand and set it on the table. He tugged at her gloves with a smile. She unbuttoned each one and he slid them off her hands, tossing them on the chair behind her. Then she removed her hat letting it fall to the floor.

Taking both her hands in his, he spoke with confidence and she braced herself. "I've thought long and hard about my future. It would be empty and miserable without you in it."

Easing her tense shoulders, she gave a shy smile and nodded in agreement.

"There's one door you didn't get to open, Jessica." Giving an apologetic look, she followed him to the closed door. When he opened it, she saw a pretty room with a large bed, big enough for two. It had a simple, wood frame, covered in unadorned, white linens, clean and fresh. A heavy, patchwork quilt lay across the end of the bed. The dim winter light filled the space, its coldness staved off by a small wood burner. The room was comforting and peaceful, inviting one to enter its restfulness. It made her smile inside. In fact, she judged the entire home to be very pleasant. She found herself caught in a world she desired to be in. His voice came to her ear, soft and inviting. "Would you be comfortable living here with me?"

She took a step back from the frame of the door where they stood. Anticipation was written on his face. "Yes," she answered. Although it felt right, the word came too easily.

Bringing his lips down to touch hers, he moved his hands to her waist and she was up against his strong body. His kiss was full of self-assuredness, and it was alluring to her. He undid the buttons on her coat, slid it from her arms, and slung it onto the leather chair. With the pressure of his hands on her hips, a sensual weakness overcame her and she met him willingly. How new this helpless desire felt. How strange. She had not expected this. His passion was measured and controlled, and she was possessed by it.

Caleb took her hand and led her into his bedroom. He slowly unbuttoned her blouse. With a wave of embarrassment, followed by a flush of courage, she dropped her skirt and the woolen material pool at her stocking feet. Stepping out, she stood only in her white camisole and cotton pantaloons. Her hand reached to his shirt. Undoing the wooden buttons gave her a rush of lusty adrenaline. He stood back and undressed himself without ceremony, his body a marvel of well-defined muscles on a tall, slender figure. She caught a glimpse of his manhood, firm and upright against his belly. Barely able to stand for the heaviness between her legs, she sat on the bed. Caleb was like no one she had ever met. She looked up at his smooth chest and his strong arms. Then she saw the reddish, knurled scar on his left arm. "How did ...?"

He laid her on the bed, caressing her breast. "Later," he said in a hoarse whisper. Slowly unlacing her camisole, he pulled it from her body, along with the remains of her modesty. She fought back emotional tears as he continued to explore her with tenderness. His tongue played in her mouth and she tugged at it. He grunted, and she wanted more. Escaping her demand, he kissed her neck and finally sucked her hard nipples. He brought down her pantaloons and went down farther. Before she knew it, his tongue was teasing her in a place that aroused her beyond all reason. She lay still, abashed at his knowledge and skill. Her climax was earthshakingly sharp, and she couldn't suppress a high-pitched whimper. He slid inside her, her body so ready for him. Hearing herself moan, she was long gone into a different realm. There was only now, the wetness of their bodies, the unison of their movements, the smooth hardness of him filling her so completely, rendering her breathless.

"I want to stay in you forever," he whispered into her ear. His hand pressed her arm against the sheets as he reeled up and cried out. Then silence. Their bodies entangled together, both of them catching their breaths. When he plunged his fingers into her loosened mane, she caught a roguish grin move across his face. It wasn't unpleasant, and it added to her blissfulness. His warm lips kissed her cheek. Time didn't exist until he pushed himself up on one elbow and said, "Forgive me, my lady."

Jessica lay helpless, almost giddy. He had opened a door and let loose a playful spirit. "As you should beg for my forgiveness," she retorted with a curl of her lip. "Why, I've never been so—"

"You've never been so … what?" His one brow raised, and a smirk was on his face.

She was about to continue their banter when her heart swelled and her spirits dropped. Wiping a tear from her face, she shook her head. His thumb brushed her cheek, and then she was in his arms and he cradled her. "I've fallen in love with you," he breathed.

The pounding of her heart drummed in her ears. She knew he could feel it against his chest.

"Are you free, Jessica?"

She rolled over on her back. "I didn't expect this. I didn't expect to fall in love with you." She rose to sit, but he pulled her back to him and kissed her sweetly. Her heart lightened. Something odd was happening. For the first time in her life, she felt the freedom she had longed for since childhood. Spirited, she asked, "Are you going to keep me here forever, sir? I must return home ... some time."

Feeling his warm breath touch the top of her head, she heard his muffled reply. "You *are* home."

Chapter Seventeen

October 6, 1888

*O*n a sunny fall afternoon in the green field above Rail River, Caleb stood under a tall arch of branches intertwined with flowers of yellow and orange. He waited nervously for his bride. He looked as striking as ever in a white, cotton shirt accented with a silver, bolo tie of his own making, inlaid with turquoise he'd received from Soaring Feather's son, Strong Bow. His formal black pants and long, woolen coat contrasted with his blond, loose hair. The Reverend Tandy would perform the ceremony in front of a small group of friends and family gathered to honor the young couple.

Excitement filled Ben and Sally Loggin's home. Caleb acquainted himself with his neighbors, and they had become good friends. Burt was right in assuming they would be helpful. Ben was indeed a knowledgeable resource. The Loggins had been on their land for nearly seven years. Jessica had made friends with Ben and Sally through several supper invitations to her and Caleb. Sally was a generous, sweet woman, and Jessica liked her very much. Their private chats, while the men did what men do after a hearty meal, proved to Jessica that Sally would make a good neighbor. A little older, the Loggins were kind, reasonable people—he, stout with flared, brown hair, and she, petite and blue-eyed with her dark-blonde hair usually drawn into a bun under a plaid kerchief.

Today, the Loggins welcomed Jessica with Hannah into their home where Sally and Hannah helped the bride prepare for her wedding. Hannah fussed over the dress and brushed away a tear as she attended to Jessica. "The ribbon's bow might go in the middle," she suggested. "That way, you can tuck your pretty handkerchief to the side."

The simple, off-white, cotton wedding dress, a gift from her aunt and uncle, was adorned with a bit of lace at the ends of the long sleeves, matching the lace on the rounded collar. The hem was embroidered in small flowers with white thread, and the band of silk around the waist was a soft, blue satin. Hannah placed a small rosette of fresh flowers where strands of her hair came together in the back of her head, the remaining dark waves fell over her shoulders. Jessica looked down at her shoes. The beige, buttoned, low boots were without lace or adornments and she liked how they flattered her small feet.

Studying herself in the mirror, she felt certain she was doing the right thing. Being a few years older than she was at her first wedding, she knew her own mind better. She liked what she saw, not the trembling calf going to the slaughter, wrapped in yards of silk and satin as she was on the day she married Frederick. They were married in a church in front of God, her family, the whole city of Hartford, and Jacob. This time only her closest acquaintances and family would witness this wedding. Her parents, back East in their stately home and pompous society, would just have to accept her choice—when she decided to tell them. Jacob would also have to accept her choice. Yet, just yesterday morning, as with every morning since they parted, Jessica waited for the mailman to bring her the letter she longed for.

Throughout her courtship with Caleb, she still waited, hoping. Yet a word from Jacob to let her know he still loved her and they would be able to work out a future together would be a mixed blessing. Now she loved two men—one who waited for her with an open heart, and one whose love felt like a ghost from the past. She entered into a future with Caleb with Jacob still in her heart. As she thought about the long courtship with Caleb, from December to now, she realized he had been testing her love. For her, that love had only grown stronger with time. The spring and summer had brought many rides together on his land with dips in the refreshing Rail River. She helped him plant a garden, and he encouraged her when she complained of her latest work going poorly. His admiration and respect for her art spurred her passion for it even further. Their lovemaking stopped time, and a whole day could drift from light to dark without them hardly taking a bite of food or a sip of a drink. His toiling on the land and building his skill as a silversmith gave her insight into the man he was—strong-minded and determined to succeed.

Sally was speaking and Jessica came out of her thoughts. "It will be so good to have you close by," she said. "As you know, the next homestead is more than two miles away, and did I mention the wife is quite elderly? I believe they're both in their seventies!" Sally looked at the reflection of Jessica in the mirror. "You make a beautiful bride."

With a smile, Jessica thanked her. She felt beautiful inside and out. A flutter in her chest made her laugh. "And you look fine yourself, Sally."

A knock on the bedroom door alerted them to the time. From the other side came Ben's voice. "Everyone awaits, ladies."

Another look, and Jessica turned to the others. "I'm ready."

Walking down the grassy aisle accompanied by no one, Jessica couldn't help notice June's sister-in-law, Laura, trying unsuccessfully to hide her disapproval of a wedding held outdoors in a field, not in a church. Her daughter, Sophie, stood wide-eyed, overtaken by the romance of it. At the end of the path formed by the standing guests waited her betrothed. His face glowed, and she felt a deepening of her love. She could hardly compose her joy.

⚜

Caleb's heart swelled to nearly bursting at the sight of Jessica walking toward him in her white gown and loose hair, the slight breeze catching a few strands. Her beauty shone, and he felt himself bathed in her light.

He had reconciled his feelings of apprehension about marrying into her family, and now he stood ready to make his life with her. It was one of the bravest things he had ever done. Many nights he had lain awake thinking of Jacob and Jessica, forcing himself to take charge of his jealousy. She was marrying him. Jacob was in the past for both of them, or so he hoped.

An eagle flew overhead and a raven cawed loudly. Caleb took it as a good sign. The eagle was his trust and strength while the raven represented his transformation. He recited his vows with courage and love.

After the ceremony, they gathered around the food-laden table near the house, where Caleb announced, "I have a gift for my bride!"

Jessica stepped forward, smiling with anticipation. After disappearing into the house, Caleb soon emerged with a small ball of fur tucked under his arm. The scared, golden-haired pup whimpered as it dug its head into Caleb's armpit. The crowd sighed as one. Jessica took the puppy in her arms and cuddled it to her neck as he squirmed and licked her face. She reached up to her husband and kissed him lovingly, causing more applause.

"Thank you, Caleb." He saw in her the mother of his children and it touched him, but for now, a puppy would be plenty to take care of. "I'm glad you like him ... wife." His smile was wide and full of satisfaction.

With a small burst of sparks, the photographer captured the moment forever. He arranged the family for a portrait, and Jessica was once again a married woman—this time with her parents' certain disapproval and her brother and cousin nowhere to be found.

Chapter Eighteen

Six weeks passed. To Jessica's surprise, her aunt June had allowed her and Caleb time to themselves. She had seen her aunt and uncle only briefly since the wedding. Today, she came down from the hills in their open, second-hand carriage for a proper visit.

"My Lord, we thought you two had perished up there," her aunt said as she hugged her.

Jessica sat down in front of the pot of tea and baked goods. "I'm sorry I kept you in the dark, but, oh, the work needed to run our land!" She grabbed a muffin, bit into it, and shook her head. "It's wonderful, though, and I love it," she said, her mouth full. She caught a crumb on her lips and continued. "We've already planted a kitchen garden. I'll have fresh vegetables like you, Auntie." Scrunching her nose, she remarked on her other duty. "I'm not used to cleaning an outhouse, or using one, for that matter. It came as rather a shock, I have to admit. Caleb said that one day, we'll afford to hook up the well to an indoor privy he'll add on to the house."

"My, you have been productive," her aunt responded, bringing one of Jessica's hands closer for inspection. "I will give you the recipe for my grandmother's soap. It'll get the dirt out of every pore. That jar of jelly I have will soothe those rough hands. You can work hard, dear, but you don't need to look as if you do."

Jessica retrieved her hand and touched her mouth with the linen napkin, then took another sip of tea. "Yes, Auntie, thank you. I want your recipe for these muffins. I know Caleb would love them in his lunch."

"Another thing, my dear, don't forget to wear a hat," her aunt fussed, making up for lost time. "I know being out of society has made you a bit lax, but you are still a lady. I like the one you wore today. Very attractive on you. How is Caleb's work at the silversmith's getting along?"

Leaning back, Jessica fingered the silver wedding band Caleb had made for her, a smaller version of the one he made for himself. "He's frustrated with his progress, but I think it's marvelous what he can fashion. He's starting the plans for his own shop."

Her aunt drew up a finger, leapt from her seat, and hurried to the parlor. She came back with letters in her hand. "This one is from your mother, and the other looks like Jacob's handwriting, but it doesn't have a return address."

Jessica's blood pumped faster. Finally, news from Jacob. Her hand trembled as she received the letters from her aunt. The first one she knew held her mother's disapproval inside the gracefully addressed envelope. The other she could barely look at. It, too, held words she knew would alter her happy mood.

"Well?" Her aunt leaned forward in her chair.

"Yes, this one is from Mother, but the other I'm sure is from a friend back home. I'll read it later."

June sat back with a huff. "I was so hoping to hear from my son."

"I'm sorry." A jab of guilt hit her heart as she pocketed the other letter. With a deep breath, she opened the one from her mother. To her surprise, it was not at all what she had expected. "Oh."

"What is it?" June leaned in closer.

"Father and Mother are coming here for a visit."

June gasped. "That's wonderful news! Oh, my goodness! I have so much to do! When do they say they'll be arriving?" June looked around frantically.

Disbelief surrounded Jessica as she read the letter aloud, her aunt pacing in front of her.

My Dear Jessica,

Your father and I have decided that we need to see your present situation firsthand. I'm certain that your aunt and uncle have been well-meaning in guiding you, but we are very concerned with this new turn of events.

We will arrive on December 15th. I am fearful of the trip at this time of year, but how can I stay put with my anxiety? Why were we not informed earlier?

We hope you will keep an open mind. Do not rule out the possibility of coming back with us. We will endure what we have to in making this right.

We look forward to seeing you all. Give my regards to your aunt and uncle.

Love,
Mother

Jessica folded the page and placed it back into the envelope with downcast eyes.

"You don't look very pleased," her aunt commented, having settled her excitement. "This is good news, though it was such a short note. Bethany must have been in a state. Oh, I can't wait to see her and have her see us here. We'll have Christmas together! I know they will love the town and want to be here themselves. Mark my words!"

"I …" Her voice quivered. "I didn't expect them to approve, but I wasn't expecting them to come all the way out here to express their disappointment." The thought that she would consider going back with them was laughable, though she knew her mother was serious.

Her aunt's embrace lifted her spirits, yet she yearned for her mother's embrace most of all—her mother's embracing of her new life, of her art. She felt her aunt take her by the shoulders, and through her tears, she looked into the older woman's gentle, green eyes.

"I would never go against what your parents have in mind for you, dear. I will say this, however. I have seen you grow into a responsible and respectable woman, and I am sure that is what they will see as well. Their disapproval will soon turn into pride."

Jessica wiped her cheeks. Her dread was lessened. "I hope you're right, Auntie. I'm sure they won't be as open-minded as you. I don't think they ever were. I love Caleb and our life together, and they must see that."

"We'll make them see it." June winked.

When Jessica left for home, her spirits were dampened. Taking charge of the horse and carriage, she hastened up the hill. Caleb would still be at work until later that day, giving her time to be alone as she read Jacob's letter.

Once she secured the horse and carriage in the barn, Jessica settled at the kitchen table with a glass of brandy. She rarely drank in the daytime, but her hands were shaking and a simple cup of tea would not do. After a drink of liquor, she was ready to retrieve his letter from its waiting place.

"Why now, of all times?" Her frustration and anger rose. Had he sensed her happiness without him? Cursing, she swallowed more brandy and went to the bar to refill her glass. Wincing from the harshness of the liquor hitting her throat, she stared at the letter. It stared back, daring to be read. If he wanted her attention, he now had it. She read the pouring out of his heart to her.

"*I can't stop thinking about our time together that beautiful day in June when we shared our love for one another*" ... "*I miss you*" ... "*I barely saw the woman you've become, and I miss her so much*" ... "*I fear no one will ever fill my heart the way you do*" ... "*My life is a never-ending circle of trading and selling weapons"* ... *"I hope you can forgive me for not writing, but I couldn't put you through the anguish of hearing my troubles."*

Stopping, she drained her glass, coughed on the harsh liquor, then returned to reading. When she came to the part concerning her brother, her heart was filled with sorrow for him. His fiancée, Mi, had married a Chinese man, and her new husband adopted the child—Will's child.

"Oh, Will. I'm so sorry." She read on.

"I know you expected more of me, as I surely did from myself. Someday, I will prove my worth to you."

As she came to the end, a lump in her throat grew thick.

"Be free, Jessica, and know I will always love you."

She bowed her head over the letter and inhaled, letting out a trembling breath. Her tears dropped onto the hard surface of the table. Slowly, she raised her head and tucked his letter back into its envelope. He was letting her go, and she felt an emptiness no amount of liquor could ease.

She had nowhere to send a reply. Examination of the worn postmark didn't help. It came from somewhere in Oregon, but she couldn't make out the name of the town. On rising, the room tilted and she grabbed the edge of the table, catching herself from falling. After a few gulps of water, she went to the small room she used as her studio. His letter would be placed in the box that also held his beaded necklace, the rolled-up picture she had painted of them by Mary's Pond, and the letter she received a few years back that gave her hope for their relationship and the courage to divorce Frederick. She brought the envelope to her nose, inhaling the scent of him, and then she clutched it to her chest before placing it firmly on top of the other letter. With a troubled heart and foggy head, she closed the lid and left the room to begin dinner.

Resuming her day, she would let his words wash over her. She was a married woman and in love with her husband. Her job to light the kitchen stove and keep the flames at the right temperature was another challenge Jessica hadn't counted on. Caleb had taught her the proper way to place the kindling at the bottom of the stove and coax the flame. It took her so long to get a good fire started that she began supper soon after her noon meal. Jacob's letter had dug into that precious time. Opening the heavy, metal door, she laid the sticks inside, then reached for the matches. After several strokes of the matchstick, she brought the flame to the thinner pieces of wood and they ignited. Blowing gently, she encouraged the small fire, but it petered out and she tried again, and again. Finally, the flames were roaring. She stood up, frustrated but victorious.

She pumped water into a tub and washed her blackened hands. Would she ever get used to this? There had always been a housekeeper and cook in her life. Aunt June had been helpful, but being alone in the kitchen was very different. So far, she had burned flapjacks, baked biscuits until they were hard as tack, and over-boiled eggs to a rubbery consistency. Although Caleb hadn't complained, it didn't take a detective to tell her he was getting meals on the side. Taking a bit of lard from the pantry, she rubbed it on her hand to release the stickiness from the wood's pitch. The top of the stove was getting hot, so she placed a pot of water on it to begin the stew.

Struggling to stay on task, she chopped the short, fat carrots plucked from the garden this morning, then cut up the potatoes she had dug up and placed in the root cellar under the house and a large rutabaga she had purchased at the general store today. Next, she unwrapped the piece of venison Caleb bought from Ben. She turned her head away from the sharp, metallic odor. Quickly cubing the meat, she tossed it into the pot with the vegetables and a few heaping tablespoons of lard. After a good amount of beef broth, salt, and seasoning, she placed the lid on. All the while, she couldn't get Jacob's letter out of her mind. His words sat in the small box as if it were him, waiting for her.

The steam coming from the large, bubbling pot clouded the kitchen window as the evening's meal cooked and thickened. The crimson sky cast pink light into her home. She lit several large kerosene lamps, and the outside went black as the kitchen became aglow with amber light. With the meal stewing, and a small bowl of chopped apples tossed with sugar for dessert, she wiped her hands on a towel and walked back into her art room where she reread his letter. This time, her focus went to their awful lives, and it made her feel better about her own. "If this is what you have to offer me, then I am content not to be with you!" She pushed the letter into the box again, slammed down the lid, then wiped a tear from her cheek. The heaviness of loving him fought with her convictions.

Back in the kitchen, she splashed water on her face, then checked the stew. Their chubby puppy waited on the porch each evening for his master to come home. They had named him Boones after Caleb's grandfather's old hound dog. She heard him bark, heralding the arrival of her husband at the end of a long workday. When she came out of the kitchen, she noticed the fire in the parlor's stove had gotten low, and she cursed Jacob for his intrusion. It was too late now. Removing her stained apron, she waited at the entry as Caleb played with the pup before he came in.

"Ah ... it's good to be home, sweetheart." He swept her up in his arms, lavishing kisses on her neck. The puppy tried desperately to get between them, his little tail hitting the floor with a steady beat.

"Boones, go lay down," Caleb commanded, and the pup reluctantly obeyed. He chucked Jessica under the chin. "I didn't get a chance for lunch today. I'm starving."

Her heart was glad to see him, and her mind prayed the stew would be tasty.

He took a step back. "Have you been drinking?"

Jessica bit her bottom lip. "Just a little. I was feeling tense. I'll tell you about it later." He was easily distracted by her kiss and wanted more. "Caleb, stop." She giggled. "Supper will burn, then you'll be without both meals!"

Chapter Nineteen

 $\mathcal{C}$ aleb pulled away from his wife with a groan and let her return to the kitchen. Sitting on the bench in the vestibule, he removed his boots and entered the parlor. After stuffing his pipe with aromatic tobacco, he stooped down in front of the stove where he kept a silver container full of thin sticks to light his pipe. He looked at the roughly made piece and laughed to himself at one of his earlier attempts at silversmithing. Noticing the fire was all but warmed ashes, he reached for the poker. "I thought I showed her how to keep this going all day," he commented under his breath. Placing more wood in the stove, he quickly got the flames blazing.

He sat in his leather chair and rested in the peacefulness of his home. With his wife in the kitchen and his dog by his side, he felt as if he was still dreaming his future, but this was real and he could finally put his days on the trails behind him. Levi's news was disquieting, and he searched for a solution that would dissolve his past once and for all. None came to mind. Since finding out about the scout looking for him and the others, there had been no signs for concern. He found himself relaxing in the thought that nothing had come of it. Some days, he reminded himself not to get comfortable in thinking he had escaped the law completely, but his life was full and he refused to dwell on it.

The smell of the stew was making his stomach talk when Jessica came out and announced supper was ready.

Taking Caleb by the hand, Jessica led her husband to the kitchen table. It was set as she had done for the past several weeks, with a flower-printed tablecloth, a gift from Austin and Laura, china place settings, each with a glass stemware for wine, and a cup and saucer for tea and coffee. The silverware they received as a wedding present from Caleb's boss was a touch of elegance in its hand-crafted simplicity. The spices of nutmeg and cinnamon she purchased in town mingled with their homegrown rosemary and sage, permeating the whole house with heady scents. For once, she felt as if she had made a decent meal. Then she saw Caleb looking for something and her heart sunk. She had forgotten to pick up bread from the baker's shop. Not having mastered the skill of bread making, she resorted to purchasing a loaf.

"Sorry about the bread, and I didn't have time to make biscuits."

"That's fine. This looks and smells remarkable. I'll have to thank June for teaching you how to cook." He ate with enthusiasm.

At the end of the meal, he sat back with his glass of deep-red wine. "Thank you, Jess. Not bad. You're getting better, and it was just what I needed. Now what is this about you being tense?"

"As you know, I visited Aunt June this afternoon and—"

"I suppose she gave you hell for not coming sooner."

"She was very happy to see me. She sends her love. I invited them for supper in a few days. She said she'd bring the main meal." Caleb's face lit up, and she gave him a smirk.

"It's good of you to invite them over." He got up and started for the living room.

"Caleb, my parents will be here in a few weeks."

"Is that so? Traveling at this time of year? They must want to see you very badly. You must be pleased." Everything Jessica had spoken about her parents gave her the impression that her opinionated, conservative, albeit well-meaning parents were people he could do without meeting. He seemed unconcerned.

"Pleased?" She crossed her arms. "I can't say it will be all that pleasant, especially after they see where and how we live. This isn't something they're used to, but I will not let them impose themselves on us! And they can't say a wrong word about you or I'll. ...'"

"Humph! I can handle myself, sweetheart. I don't see why you need to be so upset about this. You have your own life, independent of them. Besides, they're coming a long way to see you. They must love you very much. I don't think marrying me is what they had in mind for you, and I couldn't give a donkey's ass about that, but they're still your parents and your love and respect is important to them."

Placing her fists on her hips, she bit her bottom lip. She was hoping he'd be more upset by this obvious intrusion. They could lament over it together, forming a formidable wall of resistance against her parents' onslaught of vocalized judgments, but instead, she got a lecture.

"You don't know how they are." Following him into the main room where he bent down in front of the stove, she continued to enlighten him. "They have strict rules, society rules. Don't you care if they make me feel as if I've made a bad choice in you and our way of life?"

He looked up, and the warmth of his smile eased the tension in her body. Laying down the steel poker, he rose slowly. "Come here. I think whatever you've been drinking has clouded your judgement."

Releasing her rigid stance, she walked into his arms. He was over a foot taller, and she fight nicely into his body. He held her and kissed the top of her head. She inhaled his smell of spiced sweat and burning wood, and she lingered in his warm embrace on this cool night.

"You're the only one whose opinion of me matters," she heard him say.

She squeezed him, then threw her head back for him to kiss her. Losing her balance, he caught her by the waist.

"I think you need to lay down." He chuckled.

"Maybe I do." She took his hand and led him to the bedroom.

They made love in a rush of passion, and afterward, Caleb looked all but spent. Jessica rolled over and placed her head on his chest. The time floated by in her contentment. The evening was dark and she could have stayed like this until dawn, but her body became alert with the thought of her parents' visit. "Are you sleeping?" she asked.

"Yes," he said in a low grunt.

Her head felt light and her tongue was loose. "No, you have no idea what they can do, how they can make you feel. I love them, surely, but I don't want to feel inferior."

Caleb's chest rose and fell under her head. "Don't let them make you feel anything other than what you feel normally." He sat up and winced.

"Caleb? Is it your arm?"

"It's a damn weather barometer. Every time the weather cools, it hurts."

"Do you want me to rub on the salve you got from the doctor?"

"Stop being so fussy with me. I can bear the discomfort. I already have."

"Fine." She plopped her head on the pillow. "Will you ever tell me how it happened?"

Caleb laid back and placed his good arm over his face. "It's a boring story, nothing to talk about. Just a careless accident. Slipped on an old, slick log and met with a sharp stick that cut pretty deep. Happened a long time ago."

"Then why not tell me sooner? When you asked me about the scar it left, I told you about the time I fell from a horse when I was ten and a rock gashed my leg."

They went back into the kitchen and devoured the sliced apples marinated in sugar and cinnamon, the air of lust still with them. "No need to be so proud, Mr. Cantrell." Jessica licked her upper lip. Beyond his half smile, she detected a touch of sadness in his eyes. It always concerned her, that look of his, as if haunted by memories. She couldn't bring herself to ask him about his past. Perhaps she didn't want to know.

Chapter Twenty

$\mathcal{S}$tanding at the kitchen window, Jessica watched the rain drip from the eaves as she warmed her hands around a cup of tea. She surveyed the field, the green, glistening wetland. With one hand, she pulled her shawl tighter around her shoulders. Soon she would go into her art room to finish the painting for her latest commission. The window in that room overlooked the barn and the narrow trail that led to Sally and Ben's home. The winding path had a lovely feel, and she took pleasure in its simple connection between their homesteads. The trees and bushes on each side of the path's entrance looked as if they had been planted with care. She loved nature's garden. The season would change and bring forth the wildflowers and new grasses and their heavenly scents. For now, the world was quiet, cool, and damp with the heady aromas of fir, pine, and deadened leaves.

This morning, her parents' visit loomed. With another sip of tea, she hoped her nausea would ease. *Caleb is right. They do deserve my love and respect.* A feeling of nostalgia softened her anxiety. *I suppose I can get through this, even if it's practically making me sick.*

Caleb came in from saddling up his horse and gave Jessica a kiss before going to work. Their days started early, and by the time he was ready to head to his workbench at the Higgins Silver Shop, the morning chores were done. In the two months since their wedding, they had purchased a batch of young chickens, a goat, and a cow. The goat kept the field mowed, the chicks would be laying soon, and the cow was giving milk. It was Jessica's job to get fresh water and food to the chickens, counting them each morning to be sure none were taken by a coyote or an eagle. The wire around the wooden coop was not always reliable—they'd gone from fourteen chicks to ten. She also milked the cow, Suzy, after a lesson from Sally.

Most days, as she gently worked the teats in the early hours, Jessica mused at how her life had changed. Today, while Caleb fed the horse and checked the livestock supplies, she milked Suzy, and recalled the social balls she once attended, the grand parties she was always invited to, and the theatre and ballet she and Frederick had attended regularly. As her mind wandered, she lost track of what she was doing and got a squirt of milk in her face. Letting out a startled laugh, she stopped her daydreaming.

Their large garden lay dormant, but for the tender starts of kale and cabbage. The only thing showing growth today were the puddles in between the rows. Caleb had taught her what he learned from his time with the Klamath Indians in Oregon and from Ben and Sally. Jessica took in all the knowledge and tried her best to perform her duties, though if it were not for her art, she would feel unsatisfied. It was one thing to make a meal, clean a house, and do farm chores while she waited for a painting to dry or inspiration to come, but it was quite another to have it as the sole purpose in life.

She knew her heart would not be content with only well-done chores. She observed Caleb doing the same in his world. He loved his land and his work at Higgins, yet he was intent on making his own art with silver and stones, eager to finish his shop. Sharing a passion for art with him gave her such pleasure, yet it seemed to be one of their only shared passions other than sex and the land. His talk of travel to the Klamath Reservation made her uneasy, as did the long walks he took in the surrounding woods. On several occasions, before he left for work, she would spy him standing very still in the middle of the field, as if he were contemplating the depths of his soul, a place in him she might never be invited to. There was so much to learn about this man she loved, and she had to remind herself that even though they courted for many months, they had only been married for just over two.

"No eggs yet," Jessica said. "I've made some warm oats, and there are nuts from the market. Suzy let me milk her without complaint. Not a moo from her." She decided not to tell him about the milk sprayed in her face. It was hard enough to earn his respect as an equal partner on their land.

Caleb gave a short laugh. "Good ol' Sally." She felt him examining her. "You look a little pale this morning. Are you getting enough food?" He gulped his breakfast and drank down the milk. "I'll bring home salted pork and beans for a stew." After wiping his mouth, he took a licorice bark stick from his shirt pocket and worked it around his teeth. He then grabbed the small tin she had filled with his lunch and kissed her cheek. The mere mention of salted pork made her stomach flop. She tried to breathe steadily. It didn't help.

"Jess, you need to eat. I have to go. Promise me you'll have more than a cup of tea."

"Yes, of course." She sighed. "I'm anxious about my parents' visit. They'll be here soon."

"It'll be fine, sweetheart." He kissed her.

His lips tasted bittersweet from the licorice bark lingering on his mouth. Then he was out of the house. "Stay, Boones," she called to the pup chasing after him.

She watched him ride down the road and onto the bridge, when suddenly, her stomach lurched. Barely making it to the kitchen, she threw off her shawl and vomited into the tub in the sink. With stomach spasms, she steadied herself against the counter and wiped her mouth. Another wave of warning, and again her body heaved up what remained in her stomach. With labored breath, a thought came to her in a rush. This wasn't her trepidation over her parents' visit.

"Oh, my Lord!" On trembling legs, she went into the parlor and sat on the red, paisley chair, the warm stove crackling in front of her. She counted on her fingers. A smile crept over her face, and she closed her eyes and placed a hand on her lower belly. Boones scampered over. She held him close to her cheek while he wiggled in her arms. "A baby, Boones. We're having a baby!" Tears rimmed her eyes as he licked her face. Setting him down, she paced the floor. *Caleb.* He had agreed to children, but not yet. How could she have let this happen? Then her mind turned to Jacob. This would put him even farther away. She sat and wiped her face with the towel tied to her apron. As hard as she tried, she couldn't lessen her love for him. He was like an old, beloved shawl around her heart—one she couldn't throw away, even though another of greater comfort had taken its place. She stored it safely to try on now and then when the memory of it became too great to ignore. Love and loss filled her now, and she touched the pleated material of her skirt below her waist. She said a prayer.

Chapter Twenty-one

"*P*oor Thomas!" June exclaimed. "How could Bethany even consider leaving him to come out here?"

"Sounds as if he's on the mend," Burt said. "Didn't she say Thomas was adamant that she visit us and Jessica? Let's not make more of this than it is, though my sister traveling alone is quite the news."

Jessica took the telegram from her aunt with a shaking hand and read it through watering eyes. She wept over the thin, yellow paper. Her father had suffered a heart attack. Her aunt guided her to a chair.

"Now, now. This is all there is to it. Just a bit of an interference in his life, as Uncle Burt has said. I'm glad you were here when we got the news. We can plan your mother's visit together. I'm afraid Christmas will be more subdued."

Jessica blew her nose into her handkerchief. "I came here with joyous news, but now I feel just awful to be so happy." Her aunt and uncle stared at her in anticipation. "We're having a baby."

"Oh! This is the best news!" her aunt cried to her uncle. "Did you hear that? A baby!"

"Yes, June. I'm right here. Congratulations, my dear. How is Caleb taking it?"

"How do you think he is?" Aunt June answered for her. "Overjoyed! Am I right?"

Her uncle smiled knowingly. Jessica tilted her head. "I know he wasn't expecting this so soon. I told him after the doctor confirmed it, and he's been very quiet." She put a hand to her head, her emotions confused by the dichotomy of life events clashing into one another.

"Of course he will," June said. "Oh, dear, are you all right? Should I get my smelling salts?"

Waving away her suggestion, Jessica steadied herself. "I'll be fine," she said, though inside, she battled with her emotions as she tried to keep her sensibility.

June clapped her hands. "Now let's see what needs to be done before Bethany arrives." She was off to the kitchen.

Her uncle Burt gave her a hug. "I'm sorry about your father, dear. And Caleb *will* come around, don't worry."

Jessica started for home with the weight of the world on her shoulders. Her father had suffered a heart attack. She couldn't believe it. Her mother was traveling out here alone. That was even more unbelievable!

Caleb brought the carriage around to the front of Burt and June's home. Jessica spied her mother on the front porch. Her heart lurched. As soon as Caleb helped her down, Jessica ran into her arms. It had been so long since she felt the warmth of maternal love. She didn't want to let go. To her surprise, her mother brought her closer. Joy rose in her. All was forgiven.

Bethany gently pulled away. Jessica waited for her appraisal. "Let me look at you. When did you grow into a woman?"

She met the question with a smile. Then it was her turn to appraise her mother. Bethany's height hid her thick waistline and ample bosom, yet she looked more matronly than Jessica remembered. "Mother, it's so good to see you. You're looking well. How is Father?"

"Your father is doing just fine. On the mend. Winnie has him well in hand. He sends his love and wishes he were here."

The thought of her strong-minded, active father lying in bed saddened her. Biting back her emotions, she turned to Caleb. "Mother, this is my husband, Caleb. Caleb, I'd like to introduce you to my mother, Bethany Messing."

Her mother's demeanor changed from warm and caring to cool and distant. Perhaps all was not forgiven.

"It's a pleasure to meet you, Mrs. Messing." Caleb's cordial response did not thaw the ice forming around her mother's gaze.

Bethany took a step back and looked him up and down. Jessica grew nervous and ushered them into the house. "Mother, I'm sure you've missed Aunt June's cooking. I can see she's prepared a banquet for us." Looking back at Caleb, Jessica found nothing in his expression that would cause dismay. In fact, he smiled at her with a wink. She felt her tension ease.

"Yes, and it's all too much," her mother exclaimed. "My goodness, she and Hannah wouldn't let me lift a finger, either. June, you'd think we were feeding a regiment."

"Our Hannah was very good in helping me." June smiled at Hannah, who stood apart.

"Yes, I suppose it's good to keep busy," Bethany said. After Hannah left the room, she commented, "She's thinner than the young girl I remember. The hardship of losing her husband, I suppose. I can't imagine. ..." Bethany took in a sharp breath and waved away any act of sympathy from her daughter.

The smell of the food added to Jessica's queasy stomach. She picked at her plate while her family feasted. Broiled salmon surrounded by steamed vegetables. Hot rolls and farm-fresh butter, mashed potatoes and gravy, and a dessert table laden with small pies and a two-layer chocolate cake.

"Thomas will have to eat sensible foods," June commented, lifting a rounded spoon of potatoes to place on Bethany's plate.

"He's as stubborn as a mule," Bethany retorted, receiving the food. "What's the latest news from your brother, Jessica? Does he ever write?"

"No, I haven't heard from either one of them." Feeling she had responded too quickly, she added, "I'm sure they will write soon." Then she noticed her aunt tilting her head toward her mother with expectant eyes. June was ready to burst with the news of the baby. "Mother, Caleb and I have good news." Jessica paused at Bethany's dour expression.

"Well, what is it, Jessica?" her mother demanded.

"Caleb and I are in a family way," she answered with dampened enthusiasm.

Bethany placed her fork to the side of her plate. She looked across the table at Caleb with one raised eyebrow, as if she were expecting an explanation from him for his actions.

"We are very happy, Jess and I," he said. "We hope you can be happy for us, Mrs. Messing. Perhaps you may offer us your advice on raising children. Your own daughter has turned out well." The room held its breath as Bethany surveyed her new son-in-law.

"Thank you for the compliment." Her response was curt, and Jessica swallowed the lump rising in her throat.

"Mother?"

"Children are always a blessing." Her mother arranged her silverware, then took a sip of wine. "I suppose this seals your fate, my daughter." Before Jessica could respond, Bethany continued. "Your father will be very pleased. I'm sure we'll be able to make things more comfortable for you here, though I'd hoped you'd come home with me. But I see now that would be unthinkable. I had plans for you, Jessica."

Recovering from her mother's comments, Jessica found her tongue. With a raised chin she answered, "Yes, my fate is sealed. And I couldn't be happier."

Her mother went on as if her daughter hadn't spoken. "Now that a baby is on the way, we must find you a suitable home in town with plenty of advantages for the child, including a good education and, hopefully, culture. June, we'll go shopping in the city. I want to see San Francisco for myself. I've heard so much about it. Jessica, according to your aunt, you'll need just about everything." She placed a fork pierced with salmon in her mouth.

"We have a home, thank you," Caleb said, his hand on Jessica's back.

As if sensing a brewing storm, Burt rose with his glass in hand. "To the coming of new life and new ideas."

June looked up at the large man. "New ideas? Whatever does that have to do with preparing for a baby, for goodness sake?"

Bethany was not amused. "My brother is trying his diplomatic best to let me know that I need to mind my own affairs."

This was what Jessica had dreaded. Taking a bite of potatoes, she tried to gain the strength of mind she had developed in her years away from her parents, but she couldn't think of anything to add in her defense. The subject was put aside as her mother and aunt talked between themselves, catching up with each other's lives. She knew her mother would take up her case more fervently once she had visited their home. Caleb had already expressed trepidations about being a father, and now this. She felt her belly tighten, and she had to breathe in deep and slow to keep it from getting worse. Caleb's warm hand moved over her back and she relaxed, if only for now. Her mother's visit to their homestead was yet to come.

Chapter Twenty-two

_T_heir simple home on Rail River Acres looked glorious in the clear, crisp light of the winter sun. Its brilliance shone through the kitchen and pierced the parlor. The new garden was beginning to burst with cool-weather crops, while the turned-up, raised beds waited for the early spring. A pot of daisies on the porch still held a few blossoms. Although the acreage was rough, it was a lovely homestead and admired by those who came to visit. She and Caleb were very proud. Today, however, Jessica almost felt sorry for the place, knowing that her mother would soon be there to judge it as inadequate.

When she stepped onto the porch, Jessica saw Caleb sitting on the bench, smoking a cigarette, coffee in hand. He kept silent about his mother-in-law's disapproving comments, which she had peppered into the conversation throughout the evening. She wondered if he would hold his tongue today.

"You've been awfully quiet, Caleb."

"I'll be saying 'no thank you' to your parents' offer for help, and that will be the end of it. You can take my lead or argue with your mother. It doesn't matter to me." His bluntness put her on guard. "If she wants to purchase a small gift for our baby, that will be fine … but that will be all. I can support my wife and family without anyone's help."

Jessica wanted to weep with joy—he said "our baby." At the same time, she found his naïveté about her mother to be amusing. "And I wish you a great deal of luck in convincing her of that."

"I'm serious, Jessica." He stubbed out his cigarette into the small, silver tray next to him and tossed his remaining coffee over the railing. Stepping off the porch, he leaned against the house with one boot-clad foot on the bottom stair. "I'll bet she has Burt looking for houses as we speak."

His tall frame against the house made her lust for his touch. "Will you come up here and kiss me?"

"You come here."

The look in his sensitive, blue eyes invited her to step onto the stair, and he brought her against him. Their passionate kisses aroused her, and if it weren't for her family's imminent arrival, she felt he would have taken her into the bedroom. Her condition hadn't diminished his desire for her. She wondered if it was right, but it hardly kept her awake at night.

The sound of the carriage on the bridge made them reluctantly pull apart, but before Jessica was completely off the step, he pulled her back, touching her chin. "Tonight." She smiled, butterflies dancing in her chest.

Burt's covered carriage always looked out of place on their land. Bethany alit from the carriage with his help as if she were going to a formal affair. Unfortunately, Boones didn't understand and leapt on her before he could be stopped. She gasped in surprise as Caleb found the scruff of the puppy's neck and pulled him away. Bethany wiped off her dress and seemed to tolerate the sudden attack, to Jessica's relief.

They began their tour, and her mother seemed interested in the land and its buildings. When they came to the outhouse, Jessica held her breath. This would be the end of all the pleasantries. "And what little building is this?" her mother asked.

"The privy, Mother."

Bethany turned to the house. "The back porch is very nice." The tour continued. Her mother even went down to the river with them in her fine clothes without one word of complaint. Jessica was so pleased, she felt as light as a feather. Later, she served tea and coffee, along with a crumb cake she made with her own hands. Although a little dry, everyone seemed to like it. Caleb gave her a wink, and she knew he was pleased. The conversation was easy, and Jessica felt her morning nausea lift.

At the end of the visit, her mother gave her a hug and before entering the carriage said, "This will make a lovely place for a holiday or a day in the country, my dear, and you both have done wonders with the land. I can see the river would be nice for a picnic with the children, and they could learn their equestrian skills in that field." She glanced at Caleb. "But you surely can't have a baby here." Before he could protest, she continued. "I've asked your uncle Burt to scout out houses in town for us. We can look at them tomorrow. I'm sure we can find something more suitable. This ... cabin can be let out, and there you'd have an income. See how it will all work so fine?"

June was already in the carriage and didn't hear Bethany's speech. Burt was about to help his sister in when it began. Jessica's eyes widened as she looked at her uncle, and her high spirits crashed back to Earth.

"Now, Bethany, I said we would feel out the situation, but I gave no guarantees. Can't you see the work Caleb has done here? This is their home."

"Caleb, don't you want the best for your family?" Her mother wasn't letting up.

Caleb stepped toward his mother-in-law and Jessica froze. Clouds moved over the sun and her world went gray. "I thank you, Mrs. Messing, and Mr. Messing for the generous offer, but we will not be moving. You're welcome on our land any time, and I hope you can both visit when the baby is born, but this is where we will be." He stood as proud as any man could, and she loved him all the more for it. "I've earned this land, and the right to live on it, and your daughter has chosen to share this life with me. There will be no further discussion on the subject of moving."

Her mother cocked an eyebrow at him so high, Jessica could feel the strain. "Is that so? Putting my daughter in danger each and every day out here in the wilderness? It doesn't appear as if you've taken her or your unborn child into account, but merely your own selfishness. How can I leave with a peaceful heart knowing this is what I can expect my grandchild to grow up in, let alone the physical work my daughter must do to make this a proper home? No indoor plumbing?" She turned to Jessica. "How can I report this situation to your father without him relapsing?" Smoothing the bodice of her waistcoat, she continued. "I see your expression, Mr. Cantrell. Yes, my daughter comes from good society. Plowing and milking and feeding chickens are not part of her upbringing. Jessica, how could you stoop to such a laborious life?"

"Beth, please," Burt implored his sister. "It's not that different out here. As you said, the town is close. Children grow up healthy on these lands. The work is satisfying, and Oakland and San Francisco are near enough for all the city they could want."

"What's going on out there?" June piped up from her seat in the carriage.

Burt took his sister's arm. "They clearly don't need help from you and Thomas."

Jessica's mother looked at Caleb and said in a tight, cold voice, "Excuse me." She entered the carriage. Burt shrugged his shoulders at the couple and patted Jessica on the arm.

"It'll be fine. This is all new to her," he said in a whisper.

Her family was not completely out of sight when Caleb let loose of his anger. "Damn her!" He retreated to the barn, Boones not far behind.

Jessica huffed and looked at the polished carriage making its way over the bridge and away from their home. She wrapped her arms around herself. What would her father say about all this? Perhaps it was a good thing he wasn't here, after all. With a look at the barn, she knew to leave Caleb to himself.

Entering the house, she went to her art room, her refuge. The smell of her paints, the squares of color in her open case, brushes waiting to be picked up ... all of it brought a peace to her and today was no different. Touching her belly, she felt a joy, one her mother couldn't take away. Beneath the joy, she felt guilt. Jacob's letter called to her. She had lied again to hide their forbidden love. How could she let the family know Will and Jacob were safe without exposing the letter? It almost met its fate in the hot stove, but she couldn't burn it or the other tokens that stayed in the box. Just as she couldn't let him go.

Resolved to keep it hidden, she peered out the window and caught sight of the sun's rays escaping from the clouds. Beams of soft, blue gray lit the land. Her and Caleb's land. *My life is my own, my heart is my own.*

Chapter Twenty-three

*E*nduring the rest of Bethany's visit was easy for Caleb for he made himself scarce. Along with his job, there was always something to do around the land and in his workshop. Then there was the saloon. A drink with Levi was a good escape. Tonight, he chose just that.

A sharp December wind picked at his coat as he walked the wooden boards to Clermont Saloon. He was early, and he sat down to wait for Levi. Motioning for a drink, Caleb noticed a thin, road-weary man dressed in a grubby suit. His hair was a tangled mess and stuck out from under his worn hat, and his boots were muddy. Not an unusual site in most other town saloons, but here in Clermont City, he stuck out like a sore thumb. The barmaid delivered Caleb's drink, and right behind her was the bedraggled stranger.

Tipping his hat back, he said, "I was wonderin' when I'd find you."

Caleb's throat tightened and his heart raced. He took a swig of beer and wiped his mouth.

"Who the hell are you?"

The man stuck out his hand. "Rex Conrad, at your service."

Without meeting the stranger's hand, Caleb sat back in his chair. He searched his face for recognition. "I don't know you. I'm afraid you have the wrong man."

With a laugh, the man withdrew his hand. "You're the one. Harper Davis gave a good description, and Soaring Feather gave me the name of this town. Not many men lookin' like you in a place like this. Maybe you should've cut that hair and darkened it so as not to attract any trouble."

"And what trouble would I be attracting, Mr. Conrad?"

"Ho! You can call me Rex and I'll call you Caleb, or is it just Cantrell?"

Feeling he had stepped into a trap, Caleb rose and pardoned himself. As he went to the door, Rex pulled his arm. "Let's not call attention to ourselves. We can have a nice chat right here. Ya haven't finished your drink." The barmaid came back to the table. Rex called to her, "Get me the same as my friend."

Sitting across from the stranger, Caleb's mind went in different directions. A scout from Colorado? A past trade coming to haunt him? This man couldn't be a marshal.

After taking a long drink of beer, Rex leaned forward. His eyes were a cloudy, brownish green. His breath was putrid, and his body odor was rank. Caleb brought his glass to his nose.

"I'm the scout they sent to find ya. Colorado Springs ring a bell?"

With a steady hand, Caleb set down his beer. The hope of putting his past behind him was suddenly shattered. A streak of pain went up his wounded shoulder. "Soaring Feather?"

"Now don't ya worry 'bout the ol' Indian." Rex ran his finger around the rim of his glass. "I let him off with only a warnin'. Abettin' an outlaw is a crime, but he told me where ya were, so I was mighty charitable."

"If I hear otherwise, you'll be *mighty* sorry."

"Ho! You're in no position to threaten me." He rubbed his chin whiskers and smiled, revealing brownish teeth. "Now let's get down to business. I've come all this way through the hellish land of this country lookin' for you and the others. Before ya think I'm goin' all the way back there with you and them in tow, let me tell ya, I'd rather jump in the ocean and swim to China."

Sensing the man's desire to be free of his career as a scout, Caleb grew confident.

Leaning back in his chair, Rex dipped his head. "Tell me, those three dead men in that cabin, whatcha got to do with it? And I know when a man is lyin'."

Caleb wasn't sure Rex was all that intuitive. He could outwit him. "I've been to Colorado Springs in passing, but what's this about dead men in a cabin?"

Cocking his eye, Rex sized up Caleb. "So … as innocent as ya are pretty."

Ignoring the barb, Caleb took a sip of beer.

"Three men dead in a cabin 'round the same region you and the Keaton group camped. One and one makes two. Don't suppose ya knew they worked for the law."

A chuckle escaped Caleb, and he wiped the moisture sitting on his upper lip. Adjusting his body, he looked at Rex. "Get to your point."

In a lowered voice, Rex told Caleb what he wanted—rifles, a handgun, ammo, and cash.

It was another trade, simple and direct, but Caleb had no store of rifles or ammo and most of his cash had gone into his land and. … His mind went to Jessica. He had to find a way to get rid of this man. Just then, Levi came into the saloon and headed right to Caleb's table. With a quick nod, Caleb signaled for Levi not to approach him. Levi turned to the bar and sat on a stool. His back to Caleb and the stranger, he hunched over and ordered a drink.

"I have no weapons. What I have is a life far from the dirty dealings in trade. I can come up with some money, but that's it. How much do you need to leave this town and keep your mouth shut?"

"Ho! We are testy now." Rex slurped the saliva leaking from his mouth. "I'd say two thousand oughta do me just fine."

"Talk sense. Where do you think I can get that much money?"

"Your wife. From what I know, she has some rich parents back East. Did I see them at your house the other day? The mother, dressed very well, and the carriage … my, that should be worth somethin'."

Caleb lurched at Rex and grabbed him by his collar, raising the man off his seat. Sensing Levi was off his stool, and others were watching, he released him with a jerk and sat down. Under his breath he said, "I'll give you two hundred and let you leave this town alive."

Rex adjusted his collar and whispered, "I heard the Keaton group were a ruthless bunch. You kill me and you hang."

"And who the hell would know? Who's coming to look for a scout who's on his last leg? They sent you on a fool's errand, and you went for it. How much are they paying you? Not enough by the looks of it."

"Marshal said I'd get a bonus if I return one of ya alive. But if ya offer me more, I'd be happy to go up to Canada and wash my hands of this filthy business."

"I'll meet you here tonight with the cash—two hundred, that's all."

Rex stuck out his hand and Caleb shook it, then wiped the moisture on his trousers.

After Rex left, Levi came over to Caleb. "What was that about?"

"Let's talk outside."

Walking to their horses, Caleb filled Levi in. "Damn that Harper. How did he know about the Klamath Reservation?"

Levi adjusted his hat. "Close quarters with a bunch of bored men gets them talking."

Caleb gave a side glance to Levi. "And I suppose you—"

"Not me, Keaton. I heard him speak of your Indian connections with the Klamath a few times, like he could use you to make some deals with them."

"Why didn't you tell me? I would've set him straight. I told him about the Klamath people in private. They had nothing to do with my business dealings."

"Yeah, we knew he was a hungry bastard. Sorry, Caleb. Sure glad no harm came to them. Now, how we gonna get rid of this piece of scum?"

Caleb untied his horse. "I have some cash put away. It should be enough to get him on his way. I don't trust him, though."

"Want me and Cork to take care of this?"

"After I give him the money tonight, I'd be grateful if you escorted him out of town. I'll warn him if he trespasses on my land again, it'll be the last steps he takes."

"What business do you have in town at this time of night?" Jessica folded her apron and placed it on the sideboard in the kitchen. "You hardly touched your supper."

Wiping his mouth, Caleb sat back in his chair. "Can't I have a drink with old friends?"

"Again? I'd like to meet these old friends sometime. They don't seem real to me."

"I told you, sweetheart, they're not your kind of company." He stood and went to the vestibule to get his overcoat. The night was damp and cold, and he was ready to have this deal done. "I won't be long. Make sure this door is locked."

Giving his wife a kiss, he was gone to make one last trade—this one for his life.

In back of the tavern, a sliver of moon prevented total blackness. Caleb handed the two hundred dollars to Rex, who counted it not once but twice. It wasn't in small bills, and Caleb realized the man wasn't schooled in numbers. "It's all there."

Rex looked up after shoving the bills inside his coat pocket. "I see it is. Don't take me for a fool, Cantrell."

Coming out of the shadows, Levi stood beside Caleb, a pistol in his hand.

"Ho now, I want none of this," Rex proclaimed.

"My friend is here to see you out of town," Caleb said. "You keep to your side of the bargain, and no harm will come to you."

Cork came out of the shadows next. "I've come along for the ride."

Raising both hands in the air, Rex gave a snarky laugh. "So the gang's all here. I surrender."

Caleb assured Rex of his intentions to deal with him if he ever caught him on his land.

"My business is done here," Rex shot back. He came close to Caleb. "You'll always be an outlaw, pretty boy. You'll never escape what you've done whether I'm dead or alive."

Stepping away from the thin, pathetic man, Caleb walked into the night, leaving Levi and Cork to do their job.

Chapter Twenty-four

The time had come to say good-bye to his mother-in-law. Three weeks of her visit had been enough to put his wife in a state of nervous tension. There was little Caleb could do, and he let the drama play out. The subject of houses was not over. Bethany said, "I still believe it would be best to have a home in town, and you must find a studio to do your work in, Jessica. The fumes would be too much for the baby." It didn't help that Bethany read an article in the local paper about a group of Indians breaking from the Klamath Reservation and heading south. "How can I leave with any satisfaction knowing this? Do you want both your parents suffering from heart problems?" Caleb would not reassure her. He paid the price with her squinting eyes each time he talked, no matter how pleasant his statements were. Indeed, this day couldn't have come soon enough.

At Burt and June's home, Jessica held on to her mother, embracing her as affectionately as she had in saying hello. Taking it as a good sign his wife had survived the visit, Caleb turned to Bethany and bid her safe travels. With June weeping alongside them and Burt misting up, his mother-in-law's farewell to him was predictably frosty. "I will be in touch with my daughter." Putting his true feelings aside, Caleb smiled.

Lost in his thoughts, Caleb steered the open carriage home. Jessica's talking brought his attention to her. "I think we came out of the whole thing unscathed, don't you? Other than a few gifts for the baby, I'd say Mother was respectful of what you told her. I'm surprised. She's never been one to back down."

Pulling on the reins, Caleb slowed the horses. He turned to her, his anger simmering. "Don't ever refer to her as if she's *our* mother. She's gone, it's over, so let's just get on with our lives." He commanded the horses to a brisker pace. When they arrived home, he helped Jessica down and said, "I'll be in my workshop. Will you be all right by yourself for a while? The fire needs only a little encouragement."

"Yes, but don't be long."

After entering his nearly completed shop, Caleb kicked the door closed. With a curse, he went for a canister on one of the new wooden shelves. He opened the rusting lid of the tin and removed the small, wooden pipe inside. Shaking the can, he looked to see how much remained of the dried cannabis Soaring Feather had given to him on his last visit to the reservation. Sometimes life couldn't be soothed with a couple of shots of liquor.

He filled the inside of the blackened pipe, lit it, and inhaled deeply. Sitting back in the shop's only wooden chair, his sleep and wakefulness intermingled. The many dreams he had of his mother swirled in his head. He saw her in the garden, picking stems of pink cosmos, then whistling cheerfully as she found the perfect vase to place them in, leaving one flower out just for him.

"My father called her a fine lady, and that she was," he said to Boones, who lay at his feet. "She'd always laugh at my silly jokes. Wonder what she'd think of me now? What would my father think of me and my simple home? He never designed barns." Caleb cursed, and Boones regarded him with sorrowful eyes. As he leaned forward, the remains of smoke left his lungs. "Do you think for one minute they'd come out here to buy me a house? No, goddammit!"

He sat back and gave a sharp laugh. "Maybe they would. I guess I'll never know. Shit, I should have stayed on the trails. I knew what to expect out there. A wife? A family? What the hell was I thinking?" Soaring Feather's niece came to his mind. *Meadow, sweet Meadow.* The memory of her body, her comfort, her simple way of living taunted him now. "No!" Then his thoughts swirled to Jacob and Jessica entwined in each other's bodies. He kicked the floor hard. "What the hell was I thinking?"

Looking down at Boones, he thought he heard the dog speak. "What?" he asked the puppy.

"You are one lucky son of a bitch."

Forcing his body from the chair, he opened the newly hinged pine door and let in the cold air of winter. He inhaled deeply, needing the scent and briskness to wake him before he was consumed by his demons.

Sitting outside on the cold ground, his back against the shop, feeling the earth under him, his mind went to the scrubby scout. What would his mother think of the man he had been, a man he no longer was but couldn't escape from? He sat very still, bringing her voice to mind. It was clear and musical. "You were my proudest moment in life." The words vibrated through his head, then swirled into the misty air. A chill ran through him, and he swiped the tears off his face. Placing his head upon his raised knees, he tried to recapture her voice but it had passed. The smell of winter wafted by him, carrying the aromas of the forest, clean and heavy. He took it into his being and felt himself settle, his fragmented thoughts becoming whole again.

After what seemed like hours, he rose to take in another deep breath. The crisp air awakened his lungs. Boones brushed up against him, and he lifted the pup into his arms. He squirmed and licked Caleb's face. "All right, little guy." Setting Boones down, he ran his fingers through his hair, deciding never again to smoke from the pipe of Soaring Feather's plant leaves. Lately, it had only brought back sorrowful memories. As he sat on the porch before entering the house, he wondered what made Soaring Feather give information to the scout. Was it tricked out of him or was there violence? The latter brought hot anger to his chest. Levi said they had taken care of Rex, and somewhere in Caleb, he hoped it was for good. God help him.

Stepping into the kitchen, he found Jessica folding a letter and tucking it into an envelope as the growing pup ran in, sliding on the polished, wood floor. They shared a chuckle at Boones' silly entrance, then she returned to her correspondence.

"Who are you writing to?"

"A thank-you letter to my parents for their offer of help. Don't worry, I also reminded them of our plans and ability to make our own decisions."

"You're damn right. I'm going to bed."

"So early? Well, I'll finish my tea." She took up the cup and saucer as if talking to a stranger, the rim of her china cup meeting her lips.

"Jess." His anger turned to amusement as she sat as stiffly as one would at a high-brow social event. He couldn't help but smile.

"Boones told me I was one lucky son of a bitch to have snagged such a fine society lady as yourself."

"Boones is right, but I think we need to teach him better language." A soft laugh escaped from her. "I'm more than that, Caleb, and you know it." He extended his hand to her. She placed her tea on the table and received his invitation.

A breeze stirred the curtains. Jessica felt the chill of December, but the sweet air held the future and it delighted her. Caleb brought the quilt up, then drew her chin in his direction. His mouth touched hers, a kiss so sweet, yet filled with strength and wanting. She whimpered and he pressed his lips harder, opening her mouth with his tongue. Her lust for him rose, and she let the natural rhythm of their lovemaking take her away from all her thoughts and cares. She was lost in him and he in her. So intimate was their coming together, it made her feel she had never welcomed anyone else into her body. When they came apart, his eyes were moist and she brushed a tear from her cheek. She wondered how he could sweep her away to soaring heights, then set her gently back to Earth with a few words, a grin. Her eyes fluttered, her body tingled. She molded herself into him and slept.

Part Two

Chapter Twenty-five

Rail River Acres–May 11, 1889

*T*he spring wildflowers made for a beautiful show by the river's edge, and Jessica wanted to capture the scene before they were gone. She finished all her morning chores and gave a thorough cleaning of the house, as she did every Saturday. Her baking skills had greatly improved, and she had a pie filled with meat and potatoes resting on the counter, along with Caleb's favorite—strawberries and cream.

With days getting warmer, she could indulge in a few hours of painting by the cool river. Carefully, she wrapped two slices of raisin bread she'd made the night before in a small, cotton towel and placed it in the pocket of her smock. The rectangular, wooden box Caleb had made for her was brimming with art supplies—a white, cotton cloth, small jars, brushes, pencils, and colored tiles of paint. After a quick assessment, she neatly arranged her supplies, closed the lid, and secured the latch. She then grabbed her pad of heavyweight paper and made her way outside.

Stepping into the warm sunshine filled her heart with gladness as she entered Caleb's workshop. In the acrid-smelling, dimly lit building, she found him trying to coax a long strip of silver metal around a fat, wooden dowel. He was bent over this latest project in a battle of wills, a cigarette hanging out of his mouth, strands of his blond hair escaping its leather tie and laying across his face, his brows tightly knitted.

"Caleb, I'm going down to the river to paint."

Without looking up he answered, "I'll be done soon, Jess. Wait for me to finish this, and I'll go with you. I don't want you down there by yourself."

Her hopes sank. She was familiar with the scene—his head down, a cigarette stuck to his mouth, the creases between his eyes in concentrated effort. This project could go on forever and she'd miss her beautifully planned afternoon.

"It'll be fine. I'll take Boones with me, and you can join us later."

She envisioned herself coming back and him still bent over his project. No matter. She was determined to paint her picture. It wasn't for any gallery or commission. It was for her home, to hang in her own parlor. "Caleb, did you hear me?"

"Yep," he answered without looking up.

"Please, sweetie, the light is just right. I have to catch it. I'll be gone for only an hour or so."

Caleb raised his head and brushed the hair from his eyes. Removing the butt from his mouth, he laid down the half-twisted piece of metal. "You look pretty today." A smile touched her face, and she adjusted the wooden box under her arm. She felt pretty. The blue day dress she wore was overlaid with the pink-flowered smock her aunt helped her sew just for these painting sessions.

Full of the creative spirit, she was well prepared and anxious to get going. The walk through the field would take a good ten minutes, then another five or so once over the knoll and down to the banks of the river. Her husband was delaying the precious time she had to paint. Then he smiled and held her gaze. "I'm glad to see you've become yourself again."

"I'm well, Caleb. You don't have to worry."

"I do worry." He was standing now, and she felt the strength of him in front of her, the strength she so needed when their life took a sad turn last winter. "I'm just happy to see you get back to yourself and your painting," he said.

The last thing she wanted to be reminded of were the days following her miscarriage. It had blunted her spirited nature for too long. "All right," he conceded, "I should be along shortly. I'll need a break from this damn thing anyway."

"Oh, thank you!" Without giving him a chance to change his mind, she raised on her toes, gave him a peck on the cheek, then cheerfully left to return to the sweet smell of spring.

Walking through the low-growing, grassy field, she held a twinge of guilt for being happy after such a grievous event. After miscarrying Jacob's child, she felt abandoned and alone in her grief and fought hard for her contentment. Today, she wasn't alone. Caleb mourned with her, in his own way. Her wounded heart had begun to heal, leaving another tender scar. She had reluctantly forgiven the powers of nature for its cruel and mysterious ways. Her forgiveness had been tested when her parents wrote, blaming Caleb for working her to the point of exhaustion, resulting in a miscarriage on that damp and dreary January day. By Caleb's hand, the letter was quickly turned into ashes and they never spoke of the accusations. Jessica had June to console her, but she didn't know who would console her husband, if he even needed it.

"Let him care for you and the land, my dear," June advised. "It's a man's way of showing his love and concern. And don't expect him to feel this as deeply as you do. Most men don't become attached to their children until the child recognizes them. It's just the way of it."

With her new knowledge of the workings of men, Jessica let Caleb take on the chores of the house and land until she felt well enough to continue to do her part. Although her husband expressed nothing of his feelings, she had peered into his eyes. Perhaps the loss affected him more profoundly than her aunt had described.

"We'll try again, sweetheart," he had whispered as they lay close only a few months ago. In the shadows of a half-moon, he had stroked her head and held her to his body. It calmed her unsettled spirit and lifted her hopes. He had finally given recognition to their tragedy, and it played an integral part in making her feel safe to plan their family.

Today, with the spring in its fullness, she was ready to let go of her grief and meet life head on. As she walked over the knoll, the river came into sight. The smell of clean water and warm grass was intoxicating. Soon, she was able to find the perfect place to view her subject from. The dense woodland was to her right, and on her left, the meadow peeked out among the mighty pines. The clear, blue-green waters of the Rail River winded along the field and cut a path under the bridge and off into the trees and fields, making its way to other tributaries and ultimately to the Pacific Ocean. Feeling as if she were like this river, she contemplated the smallness of herself as part of a greater whole.

Arriving at its banks, she set up her work. A carpet of buttercups in front of the tall grasses across the water was more vivid now, and she checked her paints to make sure she'd included the right colors. The variety of greens in the landscape, the blue of the sky, the wildflowers in the distance—she wanted to capture all of it.

Boones explored the area, sniffing and snorting at all the de-lightful odors as Jessica hummed a little tune. She assembled her palette and filled a small jar with river water. Finally, she hiked up her skirt and crossed her legs beneath her. She placed her sketch pad on her lap, pencil at the ready. Looking up at the clear, blue sky, she took in a deep breath of the delicious air. The walk had made her warm, and she was glad for the river. "Aaahh," she sighed. Boones turned his attentions to his mistress and leapt happily to her. "Careful, Boones, watch it. Go away, go away!" she gestured to him, affectionately. He went off sniffing again, his tail wagging behind him.

Falling easily into her creative rhythm, she was lost in the colors and sounds around her. The petals of the wildflowers seemed to turn in her direction, allowing themselves to be mimicked on the paper. The grasses sang a shushing song as the warm breezes made them dance. The water dominated the air with its full and steady current, gliding past her as the wild birds sang from so many perches and the ducks quacked and chortled.

As she was about to start the pencil drawing, she sensed she was being watched. Turning to look up at the knoll, she smiled, expecting Caleb to be standing there. When he wasn't, she dismissed the feeling as simply herself becoming one with her surroundings while the birds and wildlife busily went about their lives. Returning to her picture, she sketched the basic scene, but she couldn't shake the feeling that someone was near. When Boones barked wildly in the direction of the dense wilderness, she sprang to her feet, her heart pounding. She tried to look everywhere at once, searching for signs of danger. Nothing had changed. The birds continued to sing, and the breeze of the wind blew lightly through the trees and grasses. Caleb said he'd be along shortly. Placing her fists on her hips, she decided she might be overreacting. Boones was always barking at the birds and squirrels. She turned to the knoll and wished Caleb would instantly appear. Boones was still barking, and his fur was ruffled on his back.

"Hush, Boones!" Her heart beat faster. "My goodness! What is it?" Remembering Caleb's warning about the bears and cougars, she decided to collect her things and return to the house. As she bent down to retrieve her paints, Boones hunched down and bared his teeth, growling at something behind her.

Chapter Twenty-six

A heavy weight encircled her waist, knocking the wind out of her. A muscular, dark arm pulled her off her feet. A stirrup grazed her legs as her body was lifted away from the ground. Pounding her fists against the hard muscle, she struggled to get loose. The steely grip made it impossible, and suddenly, she was flung atop a huge, black horse. As she tried to turn to see her assailant, her body was thrust against his. Surely, Boones' barking would alert Caleb. With a sharp pull on the reins, the horse was turned toward the wooded land and dread consumed her.

"No!" she cried. "Boones, get Caleb! Help!" The river was on her left, the knoll on her right, the forest ahead. Then, all at once, they took flight. The dog's barking receded into the distance. Trees surrounded her and the sunlight diminished. She was being pulled into a nightmare.

The horseman turned the large beast one way and then another through the dense forest that Jessica no longer recognized. Her rib cage burned with pain as he held on to her body, encasing her arms. Her legs dangled helplessly. At each turn, long, straight, black lengths of hair whipped around her. The pressure of his arm cut off her breathing, making it impossible to yell for help. His chest slammed against her again and again as he hurled them through the many trees and low-hanging branches. It was like a brick wall, practically knocking her off the horse. She tried to grab the base of the horse's mane. It, too, lashed at her face, but she was able to grasp a handful of the coarse, black hair. The world swirled around her, greens and browns, light then shade. A thin branch wiped her forehead. The blood ran down her face like a warm finger.

Her captor continued to maneuver through the underbrush of the towering firs and cedars. A loosening of his grip, and she finally caught her breath. She screamed for help, her body shaking from the inside out. His arm tightened again, silencing her. Feeling as if her head would explode, she tried to fall from the horse. Once on the ground, she could run home. It was no use. His strength overpowered her. Deeper and deeper into the thick forest they rode, the horseman relentless. He took his arm from around her and concentrated both hands on the reins. This was her chance. She prepared herself for the rough landing. The ground blurred beneath her, and as the horse lurched to clear a fallen branch, she found herself holding on for dear life. Fear was in control. It felt like an eternity as she rode imprisoned by this stranger. When would he stop? Knowing horses, she hoped he'd bring the beast to a state of lameness, then she could leap off and. ...

The light changed as they emerged from the darkness of the forest into a vast, open landscape with a great leap over a giant tree trunk. She screamed in fright. Squinting from the sharp sunlight, she adjusted her eyes. A vast, grassy land with giant hills dotting the landscape lay before the Diablo Range. Jessica had heard of its breathtaking beauty, but for her it was indeed like facing the devil. Its craggy hills would swallow them up, and Caleb would never find her. A million places to hide was all she could think.

The animal snorted hard as the stranger commanded it to continue its furious pace. How could they cross the open landscape without being noticed? She searched desperately for a homestead, a wooden marker, fencing, even a cow—anything to indicate people were nearby. Then the base of the first mountain range was before them. Entering a canyon, the warmth of the sun vanished behind the high ridges. They road on. Finally, the ground below her moved more slowly until it came to a stop, even if her body did not, and it took a moment for her to feel she had also become still.

Jessica sat motionless as the horse's labored breaths made her legs rise and fall, her own breathing just as labored. Her abductor dismounted, and for a wild moment she thought to command the beast and flee. Moving her leg to the other side, she was about to take the reins when the stranger's hands were around her waist, pulling her to the ground. Her feet hit the solid earth, and she lurched forward before catching her balance. Standing before her was a Native man. Tall and muscular, his face was placid, and his long, black hair hung over a leather vest that rose and lowered with his breathing.

"Your name?"

Jessica was surprised that he spoke English. Her throat was dry and tight, and she could only produce an unintelligible sound. Clearing it, she tried again. "My name is Jessica Cantrell."

"Cantrell, yes."

He seemed to affirm something in her last name. "What do you want?"

Without a word, he turned to his horse and searched in one of the packs.

Escape! Hiking her dress in her fists, she sprinted to the opening of the valley. The floor beneath her was treacherous with low-growing shrubs littered among the rocky terrain. Looking back, she saw him watching from his horse. *Maybe he'll let me go!* Running with all her strength, she headed for the open land. Her heart felt as if it would burst out of her chest, her legs becoming weaker. Suddenly, her foot caught the edge of a bush, and she tumbled onto the rocky floor of the canyon.

Then the sound of horse hooves. Wiping her mouth, her hand came back with fresh blood. She got to her feet and continued, her head down, her body contesting her every move. "No!" she cried as the horse bore down. She fell again, twisting her ankle. The stabbing pain went up her leg, and she collapsed onto the hard, dry earth. Determined, she dragged herself forward. The pain was too great, and her foot felt as if it would explode from her shoe. She stopped to untie the leather laces and yanked off the low-cut boot with a scream of pain. She crawled on the ground, shoe in hand, determined to get away. Looking over her shoulder, she saw him coming closer. The land was bleak, and she would not get far. Sitting like doomed prey, she watched him approach.

He dismounted and she felt him study her. She dared not look directly at him. Under her brows, she saw him remove a long, leather pouch from his saddle. He hunched down close to her and brought the opening of the pouch to her mouth. The oddly shaped animal skin smelled like horse dung, and she turned away in disgust. He drank from it himself, and she could see the clear water run down his chin. He poured the water in a cupped hand and brought it to her mouth for her to drink. Recoiling from his touch, the liquid touched her bodice, pink with her blood. Grimacing from pain, she tried to stand. It was no use, and she crumbled back down.

She crawled backward from him, her hands scraping across sharp stones. The sound of her rapid breathing was loud in her ears. He pulled her toward him. His hand reached for the injured foot, and she jerked away only to be met with a shooting pain up her leg. He went back to his pack and brought a strip of what looked like soft animal hide. Again, he was hunched down in front of her. Unsheathing the knife that hung from his belt, he sliced the length of it in two. She dampened a cry and let him wrap her foot and ankle. She would need his help to get back home again. The pressure of the tightened leather eased her pain, but only by a little. The throbbing continued. "What do you want? Why did you take me?" She was near hysterics.

He sat back on his haunches. "You are Caleb Cantrell's wife?"

"Yes. How do you know my husband?"

He only nodded, and she wished she hadn't given him any information. "This is kidnapping. You could go to jail—or worse. Take me home and I'll tell no one."

Standing now, he towered over her. "If they do not pay, I take you for my wife."

Jessica couldn't believe what she was hearing, and if it were not for the gravity of her situation, she would have laughed in his face. "I'm already someone's wife. Are you taking me for ransom? It's against the law." A feeling of hope washed over her. He would realize his mistake and return her to the river.

He grinned. "Your laws are not our laws."

"Oh, but they are." She searched his face for understanding. "It is the law of the country. Now, please take me back!"

"Where are your people from?"

She stared at him, wide-eyed. "You just took me from my people." Jessica detected a slight recognition in his expression, but he gave no response. "It doesn't matter, just take me back." Tears filled her eyes and spilled onto her cheeks. He reached up to touch her and she jerked away. "Return me to my home." She shook with fright.

"Come."

"No, I'm not going with you." He pointed to the horse and again she refused. Before she could reason with him, he lifted her up and she was atop the horse, her cries lost in the open air. Her strained voice became a whisper, and she realized her calls had no place to go but onto the harsh land among the prairie dogs and coyotes. He mounted behind her. They rode again, but at a gentler pace. To her relief, he mostly followed the edge of the range. Each time he rode higher in elevation, the ridges became slippery with dirt and pebbles and the horse was unsteady. The sheer cliffs terrified her, and she choked back a scream. Then, to her relief, the ground would level again. Where would she end up?

Her thoughts reeled, colliding into her fear as she tried to reason. By now, Caleb must have known she was gone. Surely, he would be here soon to rescue her. Did this horse leave a trail? His hooves will give Caleb the clues. She prayed she was right. Then an arm reached around her waist, and she was pressed up against this man, this strange Indian man. The sun descended, raising her dread. The darkness of night was still to come.

Chapter Twenty-seven

The cold, cavernous, moonless night brought Jessica's reality crashing in. Where was she? How would she find her way back? They were in a small clearing in a wooded area, but that's all she could figure. The scent of pine filled her nose. Tomorrow she would take note of the rising sun and what direction they took. Earlier today, her life was full of promise and love, and now she was in a world of complete unknown.

Shivering, she found little comfort in the woven blanket he had given her. She squinted to see his form come in and out of the blackness as he gathered wood. Stooping in front of a small stack of broken branches, she saw him work the flints. Sparks flew once, twice, three times. Finally, a low flame came from the tip of a stick and a small fire formed. He coaxed it, and she could feel its warmth. The urge to lean into it was stopped by her inability to move, her fear so completely engulfed her. Then his arm was on her, and he dragged her closer to the fire. Her hands shook as she reached for the heat. He sat down with a grunt.

The pit of her stomach ached with emptiness. Remembering the raisin bread in her smock, she reached in and drew out the towel. Unwrapping it, she found the slice in several pieces. Taking one, she ate it with satisfaction. His hand pulled the bread from her mouth, bringing it to his nose. She lunged forward, not letting go of it. Making a face, he pushed it away and she devoured the piece, saving the rest for later. He offered her dried meat and what looked like dried fruit. The leathery meat had a bland, gamey taste, but she knew she would need her strength if she were to escape. The dried fruit was tastier and she ate her share. From the back of her mind came all the horror stories she had heard about Indian kidnappings. Shaking the thoughts from her head, she tried to settle her nerves. This was her, not them, and it would be … *must be* … different. She would stay awake and look for any opportunity to run away. "What is your name?" she asked.

He crouched by the fire and Jessica studied his features. His dark, bronze face was round with a straight, flat nose, and his black eyes sat atop high cheekbones. "Blue Heron," he answered. A sound, like music, came from his full lips, exposing his white teeth. *How could he sing at a time like this?* She would get up and run, disappear into the night. Moving to stand, she slumped back down. Her ankle pained too much. A wave of heat came her way, and she thought of Caleb's warm body. She wiped her eyes with two quick swipes.

Then he spoke. His voice was clear and quiet. "I will not hurt you. If you try to leave, I will come get you." Tossing another stick onto the fire, he looked up and she caught his eyes piercing into her, full of confidence. "We will not be with my people for many days."

Many days? The children's story of *Hansel and Gretel* came to her mind—bread crumbs were all she had. With a jerky breath, she wrapped the blanket tightly around herself. "You must return me. What money are you talking about? What do you know about my husband? Tell me."

A shrug of his shoulder was all she got. He took the blanket from her, and a cold chill ran up her spin. Laying the blanket on the ground, he gestured for her to lie with him. She hugged her knees to her chest and leaned in closer to the fire, turning her back to him. When she dared look over her shoulder, she saw him waiting with a stony stare. "No, I'll sleep here. I'll be fine here."

She held her legs closer to her chest, her head bent to her knees, trying to make herself small.

"The fire will go out and you will be cold. That is not good. Our bodies together will keep us warm." The strength in his voice frightened her, but she couldn't let him have his way.

"No, I will not!" Rocking back and forth, she stared into the flames. All of sudden, she was being raised up, his arms forcing their way under hers. She cried out in pain. "Let me go! I will not lay with you!" She fought him off and stumbled into the blackness, brushing up against rough tree bark and low-hanging limbs. Branches lashed at her neck and face. Fighting to keep her attention on escaping, she ignored the pain. Her efforts came to nothing. In no time, he was upon her, forcing her to return to the fire.

Placing her on the blanket, he pushed her down. Then he was laying next to her, covering them both. She sat up, and he pushed her back down again. "Stay!" he demanded. Helpless, she consented for the sake of life itself, and soon she lay with her back to him. He smelled of dirty, sour sweat, and she could hardly keep from choking on her own bile. He held on to her strongly. Would she wake tomorrow from this horrible dream? What unthinkable things would he do to her? She tried to stay alert, but eventually her body gave in to a fitful sleep.

Waking with a start, her eyes darted around wildly. Her heart sank, as dawn brought no relief from her nightmare. Standing against her body's will, she gained her balance, then looked around. The sun was still low in the sky, but its radiance felt warm on her face. A few trees crowded together where they camped on a slight hill, a valley below and the Diablo Range still looming. By her best calculation, the north of California was in front of her, home was to the west. She looked at the sun's position and decided she was right. Blue Heron was at the fire.

As she smoothed her crumbled dress and adjusted her smock, she came across the lump of bread in the pocket. Unwrapping the towel that held the last piece and mostly crumbs, she choked back tears. The towel from her kitchen, her sweet kitchen. Would she ever see it hanging on the peg alongside the pantry? She ate the last of the bread and shook it out, then placed it back in her pocket.

The horse grazed on the rocky terrain. The packs on either side looked full, and she hoped they held more food. Her mouth was dry, and she looked for the water pouch. A rifle held in a leather casement was at the side of the saddle, and beside it, a quiver full of arrows. The bow hung below the horse's belly on the other side. Her thoughts went to Caleb showing her his bow and arrows and trying to teach her how to use it. She wasn't very successful. Learning to shoot a rifle had been more useful to her, even though she had been intimidated by it. She knew she'd need to learn the skill if she were to live away from town. Why hadn't she taken a gun with her to the river? How could she get to Blue Heron's rifle? "May I have water?" she called out to him.

His back was to her and he didn't answer. She hobbled toward him. He turned around and she stood still. "May I have water?" In his hand was a small, skinned rodent on a stick, which he was roasting over the small fire.

"Oh!" She hopped several steps back, turning her face away.

When she dared look back, she witnessed him ripping the flesh off his prey with his teeth. She felt sick. Through a mouthful of the greasy meat, he said, "You are a stupid woman. I have food to bring to my people. They wait for me. You must learn quickly. You cannot be a burden."

"Leave me here. I will find my way home."

Blue Heron laughed a loud, penetrating laugh. "You will die, and I get no money."

Jessica placed her hands on her hips and looked around the unfamiliar landscape. Another step had her wincing in pain, a reminder of her plight.

Wiping his mouth with his sleeve, Blue Heron got up and went to his pack. Coming back, he held a small pouch in one hand and the water skin in another. He sat down and untied the string of the small pouch with his teeth. "Sit." He patted the ground next to him.

With slumped shoulders, she huffed and sat down. Taking her hand, he turned it palm side up. With care, he emptied grayish powder onto her cupped hand. "Be still," he said as he dripped water on the powder.

Jessica tried to remain steady as he rubbed the water and powder together into a loose paste. His large thumb felt odd in her palm as he swirled the mixture. She rubbed her chin nervously.

"It is ground from willow bark and will ease your pain. Put it into your mouth, then water and swallow."

She took some with her finger and smelled it. There was no scent. She touched the tip of her tongue to the paste. It was bitter. She remembered Caleb mentioning this medicine to her. She licked her hand and her face puckered uncontrollably, then she quickly drank from the skin. Gagging, she thought he was trying to poison her. Pain or not, she bolted up from the ground but was yanked back. Holding her arm, Blue Heron brought the water to her lips, encouraging her to consume all of the medicine. She took a second drink and swished the stale-tasting water around her mouth until the bitterness was gone. It soon reminded her of the small tablets her mother would make her chew whenever she got sick with a cold or fever, but they had been followed by a spoonful of jam.

After a while her ankle hurt less, and she was on the horse again, wedged against Blue Heron's back and the edge of the saddle. Her legs splayed over the horse's broad back, her dress and petticoat raised up around her thighs. She was thankful she had worn her pantaloons.

Jessica tried to remember her train trip out West, what seemed like a lifetime ago. There were hills and valleys, mountains, and large expanses of green. Where were the people? She didn't recognize anything. The heat was already bearing down. Blue Heron was right. Without food or water, she would perish out here, yet she was only one day and night away from home. What optimism she held was upended as they entered a trail carved into the rugged hills. He rode with renewed purpose.

Chapter Twenty-eight

C aleb placed the fat, coiled piece of silver on the workbench. With a good base and polishing, he would have a place for the stove tools. It would give a nice touch to the 'parlor,' as his wife liked to call it. Maybe he could eventually commission sales of his design. He fished into his shirt pocket for a cigarette and lit it when he heard Boones frantically barking in the distance. Something was wrong. He went for his horse and rifle and rode to the river. Boones' relentless barking was getting closer by the second.

Reaching the top of the knoll, his first sight was the frantic dog walking in circles, sniffing the ground. Caleb looked for his wife, her shiny, dark hair, her pink smock—anything to make the sick feeling in the pit of his stomach go away.

At the river's edge, he called Boones to him. The dog's fur was littered with leaves and debris from the forest. "Settle down, Boy, settle down." Looking around, he found her art supplies strewn about, a jar tipped on its side, and paint brushes spilled on the grass. "Jessica!" He ran along the riverbank, then returned to where she had been. On further inspection, he saw that the grass around his feet was smashed, and divots from a horse's quick exit trailed into the thick, dark woods. "Christ!"

The trail left trampled vegetation and broken branches, taking him deeper into the forest. Determined, he rode on, calling her name. The open prairie came into view, and looking beyond that, he saw a valley marked by the Diablo's rockiness. He knew there were farmlands up north, but also wooded areas. His mind was a jumble of possibilities. With his adrenaline surging, he searched the landscape. The afternoon sun was beating down, and he saw no one in the blaring light. "Jessica!" he called to the north. Then he called her name to the east. Waiting for a sound, he only heard the wind hissing through the low brush.

Weighing his odds, he decided to ride to the valley. The wind picked up and whistled around the hills and slopes of the land. Caleb stopped. He was on a wild chase. By his calculations, her captor or captors would be a good twenty or more miles ahead of him, yet he called her name again. A gust of air blew it away. Reluctantly, he turned back. This would take more than a day's ride. He'd need help and a plan.

On his way back, he cursed himself for not going down to the river with her. His mind searched for answers. Who was behind this? Rex Conrad was his first thought. "Damn it!" He commanded his horse to ride faster.

The sun played with shadows in the forest. As he weaved through the trees and brush, a shiny object caught his eye. Slowing, he directed his horse to a branch where he carefully removed a short string that held two small, metallic beads and a few strands of black hair. He tucked it into his coat pocket. It was another clue, but one he dreaded.

Caleb rode straight to Levi's parents' farm on the outskirts of town and found his friend in the barn.

Levi came from around a stack of hay. "Caleb, what brings you here?"

Caleb got off his horse and hurried to Levi. "Jessica's been taken."

"Good God. Who you figure?" Levi looked around, then walked farther into the barn. Caleb followed.

"What happened the night you led Rex out of town?"

Levi removed his worn cowboy hat and scratched his head. "He was mighty arrogant and barked he'd get his money one way or another. Thought it was an idol threat."

Reaching into his coat, Caleb brought out the string with the beads. "He could have hired them to help."

Levi gave a low whistle. "That sounds about right, but damn it, if that's so, then we could be looking at a fight. I reckon those runaways could be pretty desperate."

"I need to find her, Levi. I need your help."

In the early dawn, Caleb headed to the end of town where Levi would be waiting. After informing Ben and Sally yesterday, then Burt and June, he felt profoundly responsible for his wife's safe return. His neighbors' expressions of concern barely hid their horror of something happening to one of their own. "We home-steaders stick together," Ben had once told him. They assured Caleb they'd watch after his livestock. As for Burt and June, Caleb had been relieved June hadn't been awakened. When Burt came out of his shock, he vowed to inform the sheriff, start a reward, and have posters made up. Caleb thought about the thread this would pull that would start unravelling the truth. What would these good people do if they knew why she was taken? What will Jessica think of him once she finds out? He would have to deal with that trouble later. Caleb could only shake Burt's hand and promise him he would do all he could to return with Jessica.

Once he met up with Levi, Caleb took on the search with a vengeance. He was going back on the trails and away from the life he worked so hard to achieve. The person or persons who stole his wife had also stolen his peace. He had no ransom money, only a gun full of bullets and the determination to get himself and his wife back home safely.

Chapter Twenty-nine

North Sacramento River

*A*s their ammunition ran low, the cousins' gunrunning days fell behind them. They supplemented their income by selling housewares and home adornments to the farm wives. It was the alibi they gave to their family to cover their illicit dealings. Now it had come true, and Jacob felt he was scraping the bottom of the barrel. He couldn't bring himself to write to Jessica until he could claim success. With the real chance of her finding someone else, he let his pride lead his decisions. He looked at the map but his mind was elsewhere.

Sitting by the fire, Jacob thought of her smooth skin and soft lips, and of quiet moments wrapped in each other's arms in a place outside of society's reach.

"What about all this stuff we packed on that tired ol' horse?" Will asked.

Without looking up, Jacob replied, "We'll sell it. We have to get rid of the rest of the guns … and ammo, too." He went back to poring over the map. "Before pulling you out of that saloon last night, I caught wind of runaway Indians along the northwest side of the river. It might be a waste of time, but it's on the way. No more trading, though. Cash only." He smirked at his cousin.

Will shrugged. "I was on a winning streak."

"No, you weren't." He was worn thin from this vagabond life and his cousin's appetite for gambling and prostitutes. A deep desire for a more respectful living had taken hold of him. He got up and went to an old fallen tree. After swiping at the surface of wet leaves, he sat and lit a hand-rolled cigarette. He peered up into the changing sky. The clouds were rolling in, leaving only a patch of blue above their camp. Then his mind wandered. He pulled on his cigarette. "I want our import business to sell fancy things, like items from the Orient and Europe"—he exhaled the smoke from his lungs—"not that junk." He raised his chin to the packhorse laden with blankets, pots and pans, and scrub boards, along with an array of useless trinkets. The horse shifted his weight.

Will inhaled the last drag of his cigarette, then snuffed out the butt under his crusty boot. He pointed his dented tin cup toward the animal. "If we can sell this shit, we can sell anything." Then he drained the last dregs.

"I think you'll have to call it by another name. 'Shit' just doesn't sound sellable, unless you're a farmer."

Will laughed and raised his cup in the air. "To china and porcelain and silk and all the beautiful things we can get our hands on!"

Heartened to see his cousin come around, Jacob rubbed his whiskered chin and murmured, "Women."

"What about them?"

"Women will love what we have. We'll get the finest goods … those little treasures they can't get enough of. Buy cheap, sell big."

"Aunt June and Sophie and Laura could help, too," Will added. "What about Jessica? She has refined tastes. Last time I saw her, she was up to her elbows in it."

It didn't take much for Jacob to remember the September when the family gathered in Clermont City to surprise him and Will. Their journey from Colorado was long and tedious as they ran from the law while selling the guns and ammunition they had acquired from a deal gone wrong. Their foreman, Caleb Cantrell, haunted Jacob's dreams. He had killed a man to save his life and, to this day, Jacob wasn't sure the sin of murder was worthy of the man, a man he would most likely never see again.

Visiting his mother's brother in Clermont City was just what they had needed. The shock they got was almost more than Jacob could bear. His mother and father had moved to Clermont City from Hartford, Connecticut, and Jessica and Frederick lived in San Francisco—all without his knowledge. Reuniting with Jessica all the way out west was like a dream to him. It lifted him up from his troubled life. Making love to her in his parents' home the night before her husband was to join the family was worth giving his soul to the devil. He drank her in like a refreshing stream after a long walk through the desert. Now she was divorced and a free woman, and their lovemaking in her tiny art studio nearly a year ago brought a rush of blood to his chest. It was a memory he cherished each day. It got him through the hardships of a life that no longer served him.

Jacob heard Will talking about doing their research on foreign trade. He coughed. He couldn't let himself linger in his escape from reality. "Let's get on our way." He stood and kicked dirt on the campfire until the fire was smothered.

Will gathered the blankets and adjusted the load on each horse. "Hey, Jake, I wonder if Burt can lend us the money to start our business. Why not go straight to him and ask?"

Jacob gave Will a doubtful look. "Yeah, I think my father would be overjoyed with me right now." His glibness was not lost on Will. "Why, he would positively jump at the chance to back our risky, if not impossible, enterprise."

Will laughed. "And *my* father would be delighted. Good God! The looks on their faces if they could see us now."

"We'll be rich someday," Jacob said and went to his horse. He mounted Otis and waited for Will to do the same with Drake.

The morning sky was darkening as they rode with renewed purpose, lumbering along with the packhorse in tow, heading down the west side of the Sacramento River.

Chapter Thirty

May 20, 1889

*J*essica heard a distant yelp, and Blue Heron answered as if to echo it. A fresh wave of nerves rose up in her chest and her ears rang. He turned to her. "We are close now."

How could she alert someone—anyone—that she was being held against her will? She hadn't seen a soul in days. She tried to hold on to the thought that Caleb was not far behind, yet her hopes were fading. Ten days, she counted ... a ten-day journey back home. Every step she took, every clip clop of the horse, took her farther away. Each day blended into the next but for the rising and setting of the sun.

At nightfall, she was afraid of what Blue Heron would do to her, yet every night, he slept soundly. Or so it seemed. Stealing his horse, once he began to snore, proved harder than she thought. One night, she crept toward the towering beast. Out of nowhere, Blue Heron appeared, sending her heart leaping into her throat. "I was relieving myself," was her excuse.

"Then do it away from my horse," was his reply. She winced with acute humility and decided she would have to escape on foot.

The next day, they came to a ridge. A valley lay before her in swirls of greens, browns, and golds. In the distance, a stream of smoke rose above a rocky hill. Blue Heron stopped his horse and slid down behind Jessica, then helped her to the ground.

"We will rest here," he said.

It was an odd place to stop, Jessica thought. Nothing but a rocky cliff. "Why here? Why not go to your people now?" She pointed to the stream of smoke.

"How do you know that fire comes from my people?"

"I just assumed. Am I right?"

He huffed and curled his lip. "We stay here for now."

The day was sweltering, and her clothes felt more like heavy wool than cotton. With modesty a distant concern, she sat down and removed the strip of leather from her ankle and took off her shoes, then her stockings, sticking each black hose into the pocket of her smock, which she also relieved herself of. After rewrapping her ankle, she loosely tied her shoe around the swollen foot. Rising, she placed her smock around her waist. The kitchen towel would become her shield from the midday sun, and she wrapped it around her head. All the while, Blue Heron looked out onto the valley. There had been only sporadic conversation between them in the days they had been together. Jessica grew curious.

"How old are you, Blue Heron? How do you know English?"

Turning from his outlook, he answered, "I am twenty-four years. My father's brother married a white woman and she taught me. She's dead now. The white man stays on our land and brings with him teachers. What age are you?"

"I'll be twenty-four in July." She took another stab at reasoning with him. "Why can't you understand? I cannot marry another man when I am already married. I love my husband. You are in danger by kidnapping me. You place your people in harm's way."

"I will make *you* understand." He stood closer to her, and she smelled the now familiar heavy musk of his body. "Your husband is an outlaw. He will bring in good money. We trade you for his freedom and money—a good price for me and my people and a good price for the scout. If he does not pay, he will no longer be your husband … I will." She spoke, but he cut her off. "You will know our way, and you will be happy with me and my people."

She shook her head. "This is preposterous! My husband is a silversmith, a farmer, and a good man."

Blue Heron shrugged. "I do not know him." His answer rang true to her ears, and her fear of Caleb being a part of this man's plan eased but wasn't totally washed away.

"How did you let a scout talk you into kidnapping me? He might be an outlaw himself." By his expression, Jessica thought she struck a chord. "Yes, this might be all for nothing and he will cheat you." She backed away as he rushed to her.

"Quiet! You know nothing!"

Cowering from his rage, she limped back to the ridge and evened her breath. The horse whinnied, and she stroked its dark, shiny coat. "Nice fella," she said as her hand petted his neck. If only she could steal away on him.

Nothing changed for what seemed like hours. She sat on the ground against the trunk of a squatty tree bent in one direction from years of wind. She dozed until Blue Heron nudged her shoulder. "We go."

Wiping her sleepy eyes, a thought sparked. She suppressed a yawn. "Caleb Cantrell knows the Klamath tribe and has friends within the reservation there." She waited.

Blue Heron's expression became serious. He lifted his chin up, his eyes looking down at her. "They have given in to the ways of the white man. We"—he pointed to the line of smoke in the distance—"were not so willing to farm the land for your government or cut the trees for your houses and forts. Much money comes from it, but it does not buy our freedom. We are free now. We do not live on the reservation you speak of."

His words gave new insight to her circumstances. He and the others who waited were a group of renegades, and the scout, for reasons still unknown to her, had hired Blue Heron to take her. What had Caleb done to have this thing happen? What secrets did he keep? Her loneliness and despair grew.

"Can we not be friends? My husband and I will do what we can to help your people." She gave him a slight smile.

Blue Heron's eyes widened and he laughed out loud. "You are not as I hoped." He tapped a finger to his temple at her lack of intelligence. "I will ask the spirits to help you learn."

The ride down the ridge and into the valley was treacherous, and Jessica held on tight while Blue Heron led his horse on foot. The horse stumbled and nearly toppled onto the jagged rocks and gravel. The motion made her head swim. Coaxing the horse along the switchback trail, Blue Heron turned for a moment and looked out onto the land. Suddenly, the large beast reared up, throwing Jessica all the way back and onto the ground. The towel flying off her head, she landed with a thud. The wind was knocked out of her. The sound of a rattlesnake shot panic through her, and she rose and ran down the side of the rugged hill. A sharp shriek and whish of air came from behind her. Stopping, she turned to see Blue Heron standing with a large, decapitated snake held high in the air like a trophy. She slumped to the ground, heaving sobs of despair.

Once they got to level ground, he helped her remount. The coiled, dead rattler had been wrapped in her kitchen towel and tied to one of his packs. She remarked, "Must we take it with us?"

"Good food," he replied, as he again revealed his disappointment in her with a shake of his head.

As they made their way across the open plain toward the smoke, she wondered with renewed fear what the next chapter in her nightmare would bring.

Chapter Thirty-one

$\mathscr{T}$he expressions on the faces of the Indian men surrounding Jessica were serious, almost foreboding. Piercing, black eyes looked at her from under thatched, grass rimmed caps. Other faces were framed in bandannas with feathers sticking out of each side. Long, braided hair accented with ribbon and beads fell on their bare chests. Deerskin pants decorated with more beads and shells covered their legs. The women looked shy and curious in their cotton shirts, dyed blue or light yellow, tucked into colorful skirts that reminded Jessica of her husband's woven rugs and blankets, but with frayed edges. Intricate beadwork, shells, and feathers adorned their clothing, and felted wool caps. It was a small group, no more than twenty people by her calculation. She was no longer in the world she knew.

When the group parted, she got a good look at the huts—domed structures of roughly thatched layers of sticks, woven grass, and tree bark, with animal hides laying upon the thatch. A small firepit held long sticks leaning over the flame holding what looked like skinned rabbits. Jessica wondered how no one bothered to follow the smoke and capture them. Her hopes rose. Perhaps it wouldn't be long until they were discovered.

Blue Heron rode to one of the larger huts, which looked much like the others. He told her he shared this dwelling with his younger brother and his brother's wife, and now she would live with them. He added that this was home until the elders decided it was time to move on. Its crudeness added to her misery.

Once on the ground, she nervously pulled on her dress and petticoat. Bringing her pantaloons down, she wished her legs weren't bare. Even though her stockings now had holes and tears, she would replace them as soon as she could. Three men came toward her and she stepped aside. They took the laden horse away.

The sun was setting, and the wind had picked up. A chill seized her, and she jerked with a shiver. Jessica felt a blanket being draped over her. With trembling hands, she caught the heavy, woven material and brought it around her shoulders. A woman with dull, strawberry-blonde hair appeared in front of her. Her complexion was rough and deeply tanned. She was not one of them. "I'm Cara," the woman offered.

Clearing her throat, she replied, "I'm Jessica. I was taken, and I would like to return to my husband. Can you help me?" Blue Heron spoke sharply to Cara, and the woman receded behind the others.

She spied an older Indian man emerging from another hut. He walked over to Blue Heron and spoke to him in their native tongue. The conversation was heated, and the elder glared several times at her as he talked. She nervously awaited her fate. A hand grabbed her arm, and she looked down to see an old woman pulling at her. "Go with her," Blue Heron instructed. The woman's face was heavily creased, her gray braids lay under a headband of dyed-blue material. For all her frail appearance, she had a mighty grip.

The old woman opened the deer flap of the hut next to the one Blue Heron said was his. They both ducked in. Jessica suddenly felt cold and she shook. Sitting on animal pelts were Cara and a younger version of the old woman. The blanket slipped from Jessica as she went to Cara and fell to her knees. "I need your help. Tell Blue Heron he's wrong about the money, and I must be returned to my husband and family. It will go very badly for them if my people find me here."

Jessica turned around to the old woman, hoping she was sympathetic to her plight, but to her disappointment, she laughed a toothless cackle. The woman next to Cara looked at her with wide eyes. Finally, the older woman spoke in slow, broken English, and loudly, as if Jessica was hard of hearing. "My child, you need rest."

"Take a seat." Cara's voice was deep and hoarse. "I can only help you here. I can't help you escape. Sorry, young lady. What's this about money?"

Jessica closed her eyes for a moment, rubbing the back of her neck, then her shoulder. The pain from her fall took her attention. "Never mind." She slowly looked around. The makeshift home was larger than she expected. Worn animal skins covered the ground. Several furs and blankets in one area looked to be for sleeping. Small, wooden stumps, smoothed from wear, held copper mugs and wooden plates. A few pipes hung on leather straps from the structure's frame. To the side of the entrance, arrows stuck out of fur and leather quivers, their bows leaning against them, along with several rifles and boxes she recognized as containers for bullets. It smelled like a barn on one of the farms back in Connecticut, but smoky, with the aroma of incense. The only comfort she could manage came from the sound of the river not far from camp. It might be the Rail River.

"I am From-Wings," the older woman said. "This is my daughter, Lea. She is John-Tooth's wife. John-Tooth is Blue Heron's brother. They share Blue Heron's home. Jessica acknowledged the woman's daughter, who looked old enough to be her own mother. Lea gave a shy, toothy smile, then bowed her head.

Cara turned to From-Wings. "I'll look after her. Let us be alone now."

The old woman shook her head and reprimanded Cara in her native tongue. Cara argued back, and Jessica was intrigued by her speaking their language. From-Wings and Lea left abruptly, the heavy, hide door flapping shut behind them.

Jessica spoke as quickly and precisely as she could. "Where am I and how can I escape? The mountains are to the east or maybe northeast? We crossed plains, but then there was–"

"Shush!" Cara snapped at her. "You speak too fast. You make my head hurt."

Jessica caught herself, shocked by the woman she thought certain to be her ally.

"I told you, I can't help you. Do you know what would happen to you if you tried to leave?" Cara sat up straighter. "You'd be eaten by wolves or bears. Or worse, Mallow would kill you. Don't give him any reason to do so. Do you really want to die this young?" It seemed as though her eyes would burst into blue flames.

Jessica sat back on her heels. "Where is the scout Blue Heron talked about? Who is Mallow?"

"You must be talking about that lousy excuse for a man, Rex Conrad. He came into camp talking about money and a cut for everyone. He stayed awhile, spouting his tongue about how he could make us rich. He spent most of his time around the elder, Sam Farrow, and Blue Heron. He disappeared a few days ago. Now as for Mallow, he's a mean one. Doesn't like this business of money for flesh. He might think you to be a spy. I wouldn't put it past him."

She got the feeling that Cara could be helpful, but not as she first thought. "I'll be careful."

"I'll point Mallow out to you. Meantime, lie back and wait. If the elder and Blue Heron get what they want from Rex, you go free. If not, you marry Blue Heron." She raised her hand to stop Jessica from protesting. "Yes, you have a husband, but that will not stop them from doing what they want."

By now, Jessica was worn out, and the pelts looked soft. She slowly laid her tired, sore body down on one, and Cara covered her with a blanket. With half-closed lids, she listened to Cara speak. "You will help them continue their lives, away from white folks, to bear Blue Heron's children. You must do your share. Then help pack up when it's time to move on and carry as much as you can," she explained, making a circle with her arms to show a large load. "And as far as knowing where you are, well, I certainly don't have a map. Hells bells, I don't know where we are. We've traveled far from where I once lived … or maybe only in circles. I've lost track." She went silent for a moment, as if a memory had taken hold of her. She brushed away a strand of hair that hung from her loose bun. "This is it, missy. Learn to love this life. It's yours now." Cara ran the palm of her hand over her faded, woven skirt. Her legs were covered with long, black stockings dotted with darning. "At least Blue Heron is one of the most handsome and bravest of them all." Her cheeks blushed a deep red. "The elders have great respect for him, and one day he will be the leader of this new tribe."

Jessica listened with disbelief. This woman spoke as if she sat in a house of great repute. She reminded Jessica of a silly schoolgirl with a crush on the handsome eldest son. She had seen her fair share of such girls back East in Hartford society, yet this environment sharply contradicted Cara's words and tone. Her next thought was this couldn't possibly become her life, even if this woman had clearly resigned herself to it. "How long have you been here?" Jessica spoke softer now, her mind slowing as sleep took her. "Where are you from?"

The sadness on Cara's face told Jessica she had asked too many questions. "My husband, Harold, was killed when the tractor he was on turned over. I guess I went a little crazy. We were newly married. I wandered from our farm and they took me. I've been with Jo Horn for over a year now, or maybe closer to two. This is our hut. Don't know what became of the farm, don't care. My family probably has taken it over. Fruit trees and nuts, that's what we made our living off of in the valley near Medford."

"I'm sorry," Jessica said. "Why do you remain here? Don't you want to go home?"

Cara got up, stooping over so as not to hit the rounded walls. She went for a large pelt, then placed it over Jessica's road-weary body. "I reckon this life suits me just fine for now. Jo Horn is as good a husband as ever there was one. A good warrior, too. I have nothing to lose here. It's them that take their lives into their hands." Sitting, Cara bowed her head and twirled a strand of her reddish-blonde hair around one thin finger. "I'd hate to see anything happen to any of them, though. They've become my kin." Their eyes met. "I suppose I'm a traitor, but I'm here as long as Jo and the rest of them will have me or they get arrested by the government. I suppose if it comes to the worst of it, I'll pretend I was a victim all along." She was quiet for a moment, then got up and opened the flap. "You better get some rest. I'll see what I can find out." She gave a half smile and left, the makeshift door slapping shut.

Jessica lie under the warm blanket and pelt, plotting her escape. The bears and wolves didn't concern her. Will and Jacob had taught her how to climb trees. It was being captured again that frightened her the most. This Mallow man Cara spoke of sounded dangerous. As she made her plans, her eyelids became heavy and she could no longer fight sleep. She felt oddly peaceful.

By the end of the next day, Jessica still didn't know her fate. She spent her time in From-Wings' hut. It felt good to not be moving. The old woman joined her. She brought out a jar from a woven basket, then examined Jessica. A sudden, sharp pain ran through her back when From-Wings touched her left side. Unscrewing the rusted lid of the jar, she said, "Blue Heron say you fall off horse. I will help the pain."

Jessica recognized the smell as lavender and chamomile, with a hint of peppermint. She unbuttoned her dress and gave herself over to From-Wings' touch. The smooth, round hands of the Indian woman moved over her body with intention, and she felt her muscles become like jelly. The tension dripped off her like the warm salve running down her back. From-Wings gave a soft whistle when she came to the torn flesh on her legs. She took another jar from her basket and applied a paste that stung at first, then the flesh became numb. *Stinging nettles.* Caleb had showed her how to soak the stems and leaves to create a liquid for the garden. The smell had been awful, and she had quickly abandoned the project. Now she could see its benefits, and she would add it to her remedies when she returned home.

After redressing her ankle with a fresh piece of soft leather, From-Wings gave a chuckle.

"You will be good for Blue Heron. It is fine."

It was no comfort to Jessica. The tension returned to her shoulders and back, even as From-Wings continued to work the muscles loose.

The flap opened and Blue Heron ducked in. From-Wings hurried out.

Jessica sat up. "What has happened? Has the scout returned with the money?"

He sat down crossed-legged in front of her. "We are to marry. Money is not coming. The scout is dead."

"The scout lied to you. My husband is not an outlaw." Tears filled her eyes. "We cannot marry!"

He leaned forward and looked her in the eye. "Your husband caught by your lawmen ... or dead. Scout tells so to Mallow. That is why there has been no money, Mallow says."

A surge of acid rose in her throat and she gagged and coughed. "No!"

Blue Heron shrugged. "Mallow says scout was a spy, and now he is dead."

The thought of Caleb no longer on Earth drained the blood from her head, and she felt as if she might faint. She clenched the blanket. With her breathing becoming shallow, she pleaded with Blue Heron. "Please, tell me exactly what you heard. Is my husband alive or not?"

"I told you. You will get ready." He left without another word.

She lay back, trembling. Mallow had killed a man he thought was a spy, and now he may think she was one, too. The flap lifted and Jessica cowered. It was Cara, and she came forward, sobbing.

"Missy, don't cry. What did Blue Heron tell you?"

Taking a ragged breath, she enlightened Cara.

"Well, doesn't sound for sure, so wipe your tears. That Rex Conrad met his fate. Let's say your good husband wasn't part of it."

"Yes, you may be right." She wasn't convinced by her own words, and her chest was heavy with worry. Then she realized she would have to marry Blue Heron. "I can't marry him, I can't."

Chapter Thirty-two

Lea entered with a basket of feathers and beads, along with some leaves and flowers. Having no choice, Jessica let them place the adornments on her. She felt the weight of the beaded and shell necklaces. The animal hide cape draped over her head fell around her shoulders. It was laden with beaded work and stitched decorations. Lea plaited her long hair and put flowers and feathers in the braid that ran down her back. Jessica's own comb that held up her hair was placed on the top of the braid. Resigned to the fact that she would have to go through with their ritual, she played along, her sights set on escape. When they walked her out for all to see, she thought for sure there would be great laughter and she would be made to feel foolish. To her surprise, most of the small group did not laugh, but a few snickered.

Blue Heron came to her and took her hand, nodding his head in satisfaction.

The ceremony was held around a large, round firepit. Its flame was low and spread out. Men with sweeping gestures danced around it as if trying to change the flow of air. A flower dropped from her hair and she didn't retrieve it. Another shell necklace was hung around her neck. Behind her, a hand grabbed the comb from her head, strands of hair pulled with it. She reached back to stop the thief, but it was too late—the young woman was putting it in her own hair and looking at Blue Heron with an alluring eye and saucy grin. Jessica furrowed her brow. What kind of society was this? Though she vowed to stay alert, she found herself lured by the quiet chanting and rhythmic dances that went on throughout the night.

During the celebration, Cara came up to Jessica and sat down beside her, crossing her legs. "This is nothing. When I married my Jo, there was lots more dancing and it was much louder. He says we are more vulnerable in these parts, and we have to keep quiet and not be seen." Jessica followed Cara's loving gaze to a squat, older man sitting cross-legged on the other side of the ring of people, his mouth shiny with grease as he ate with gusto. Jessica barely felt present. Then a tug to her sleeve brought her attention back to Cara. "And you see him there?" She pointed to a muscular man standing beside Blue Heron. "He is Mallow." Jessica studied his face. He was shorter than Blue Heron and strongly built. His expression was serious, even angry. He gave her a ruthless look and jerked his chin up at her. With her fright newly ignited, she would take Cara's warnings to heart.

The meat was freshly killed venison and rabbit. Jessica was ravenous and ate her share, including dried fruits and cooked root vegetables. She recognized the black licorice they passed around. It tasted sweet and reminded her of her childhood. She licked her lips to get every bit of it. The fermented juice she drank made her light-headed, but she didn't mind. The fire's flames mimicked the dancers, and she stared into it, slightly rocking, falling into a trance.

Blue Heron was standing above her with his hand held out. Jessica took a gulp of her juice and stumbled as she stood. Blue Heron steadied her. The muffled chants stopped, and everyone lined up on either side of them. She floated along the haze of laughing faces. She saw Cara among them and reached out to her, but she could not touch her.

The tribe quietly encouraged the couple as they entered Blue Heron's dwelling. The low hum of chanting and giggles swam in her head. Jessica immediately went for a large fur pelt to wrap herself in and fall away to sleep. She closed her eyes, but it wasn't long before Blue Heron joined her. She struggled as he made his advances. He took both her arms and pinned them down above her head. His face was close as his body hovered over her. She turned away. He set her arms free, and she immediately crossed them in front of her. They fumbled in the dark. Only the light of the moon piercing the hut kept it from total blackness. Shadows danced around her. *More dancers.*

Blue Heron brought her arms from her body. Her own strength was no match for his. She reluctantly gave in, knowing he would eventually win. He lifted her dress and petticoat. Huffing impatiently, he drew down her pantaloons. She tightly closed her eyes. It was soon over. He laid back, his breathing deep, and then he was snoring.

Jessica wept, overwhelmed by anger and shame. She quickly adjusted her clothes and brought the blanket to her chin.

Wide awake, Jessica crept from the hut and into the night. She was rattled but determined. Barely able to see in front of her, she hunched over and slinked away like a cat making its escape. She was making progress, when suddenly, a hit to her back brought the ground smacking into her. A forceful blow of a boot struck her side. She yelled out in pain, struggling to see who was assaulting her. She was dragged by the collar, nearly choking. The flap was flung. She was on the floor by Blue Heron's feet. In the low light, she saw the side of Mallow's face recede from the hut, the heavy skin thumping shut. As she bent over, retching, Blue Heron jerked awake.

"What is this?" he asked.

She could barely speak. Finally, she wiped her mouth with her hand. "The food. I think the food made me sick. I will clean it up."

She looked for her smock. He turned over and fell back to sleep before she could ask him for willow bark.

The next day, Lea tended to her bruised side. "Mallow is furious," Lea said in warning. "Blue Heron is his friend, but you are not. Try to stay away from him."

"Why would he care if I left?" Lea carefully rubbed the scented jelly onto her bruises. With every touch, she winced from the pain.

"His heart tells him you will bring men to take us back to the reservation."

"No, I won't. Tell him I will not do that. I don't care if you all want to hop a boat to China! I just want to go home!"

Lea's laugh was rich and Jessica smiled. Lea's hands worked in the same skilled way her mother's had. Jessica closed her eyes and let her mind rest, along with her body.

After that night, Jessica kept an eye out for Mallow who, in turn, pretended to ignore her. But she wasn't fooled. She knew he was watching. One day turned into the next. Days passed as she worked alongside the other women. They helped to keep the small camp fed and warm. They picked berries, dug up edible roots, collected water fowl eggs, prepared the cambium under the bark of the yellow pine, and gathered firewood. The men hunted for meat and fish. Living completely off the land had been an unfathomable idea to her, but these people were doing it and Caleb wanted to do the same. She took note. When she returned home, she would have a new perspective on her husband's ideas. The thought struck a chord of deep longing, and she was more determined to find her way back to him. She prayed he was alive.

Jessica also helped care for the two small children in the camp. It was as Cara had told her. She worked hard each day and was exhausted each night. Some nights were more difficult to find rest. Living in the hut with John-Tooth and Lea was challenging.

With four, the space turned cramped and provided no privacy. Jessica would be awakened by John-Tooth and Lea making love. She would draw the pelt up to her ear and continue to design her plans. More upsetting was when Blue Heron reached for her. She would refuse until John-Tooth and his wife left the hut. It caused such disagreement that, at times, she would give in to Blue Heron, biting her lip so as not to make a sound.

Mallow's watchfulness did not deter her. She would adjust her plan as she gained more knowledge of her surroundings and the tribe's routine, and most importantly, Mallow's routine. As a scout for the group, he would be gone for long hours, yet she never knew when or for how long. Cara had informed her that a few of the young warriors, including Mallow, would travel onto the reservation where supporters of the renegades would risk supplying them with food and more ammunition, blankets, candy, alcohol, tobacco, and other necessities and comforts. She also learned the group would be moving soon, but where to, no one would tell her. Still, she couldn't help to be encouraged by the change. Perhaps someone would discover them.

Her efforts to keep from becoming pregnant kept her vigilant with the remedies Cara had suggested, along with the knowledge of the rhythms of her body. It went far beyond the speech she remembered Jacob giving her after their first time together. Through this, she found a sense of empowerment throughout her captivity.

While the opportunity for any plan of action had not presented itself so far, she did what was expected of her and tried to blend in with the others. She observed the way the group respectfully and lovingly interacted with each other, as they worked together for the same purpose. Their ingenuity had impressed her, until she found her dress and petticoat had been cut up into pieces and spread among the women of the camp for use in various chores. They took her clothes as they hung out to dry. Her smock was turned into a garment for one of the children. It was too late to claim any of it, and she had to prepare herself to travel with what they had given her to wear—a heavy fabric patchwork skirt, the deer hide shawl from her wedding, and soft, worn cotton shirts, big enough to cover a man. Her camisole, pantaloons, stockings, and leather, lace-up shoes were still hers. She washed her undergarments once a week and hung them to dry, keeping an eye out for anyone who waited to claim them. She also kept her footwear close. One morning, she woke to find a few of the women taking turns trying them on. She stormed over to them in her stocking feet and snatched each shoe from their hands, walking away from the mocking sounds behind her.

The day had been long and she welcomed sleep. The weather was changing, and the coolness of the earth penetrated the hut. She brought the blanket around her and adjusted the fur to cover her body. She lay beside Blue Heron, lost in her thoughts of getting home, her back to him as usual. As she dozed off, she heard him speak. She tensed. The tone of his voice was low above her head. "We will be moving on soon," he informed her.

"Yes, I heard."

He huffed softly. "You work hard. It's good."

"I don't belong here."

"Is it why you do not have a child in you?"

Jessica turned to face him. "Yes, that is why. The spirits see I am not one of you and won't let a child come into this world in such a way. You must let me go and find a woman more suited to you." She looked down, as if to mourn the unfortunate circumstance.

He raised her chin up. "I will speak to the spirits."

She sighed and turned back on her side.

With her own world beyond her reach, she harkened back to the memory of her and Jacob, their love, so very sweet and tender, before the rules of society squashed their hearts' longing for each other. Her thoughts immediately turned to Caleb, his strong, trusting arms holding her. Had her world vanished, never to be seen, touched, or smelled ever again? It could not be so. She would never give up.

Chapter Thirty-three

*T*he California sun bore down on Caleb. He and Levi had been riding for over a week, heading east then north, taking the most likely trails that would end their search. The Sacramento Valley was hot and nearly deserted but for a few people on horseback or walking with packed donkeys. When he could stop someone, Caleb pulled out his wedding photo and pointed to Jessica. Each person he encountered merely shook their heads and walked on. In every town, he did the same and received the same reaction. Riding beyond civilization was even more disappointing. The valleys were desolate, the farmlands open, the rugged hills hiding their secrets. None of it gave comfort to the twisting guilt and grief he now wore like a heavy coat.

Today had been long and fruitless. The sky was a splash of rust among a light-gray background. It was time to make camp for the night. They had gone as far north as Red Bluff. Finding a spot by the Sacramento River, they stopped and refreshed their horses, then sat down to build a fire. Taking food and drink, they discussed tomorrow's agenda.

Chewing on a piece of the leathery jerky he himself had cured, Levi removed his hat and scratched his scalp. "If I might offer some advice?"

Caleb knew what his old friend was about to suggest, but he didn't want to hear it. "I have to find her."

"Yep." Levi clapped his hat on the grass, dust flying like a cloud of gnats, then placed it back on his head as he continued to speak. "Fact is, we're not going to find her traveling like this. Where do we go next? North? East? I reckon we just close our eyes and point in a direction."

Caleb stared at Levi. "I can't go home without her." A moment passed. Looking out at the water passing over the glistening rocks, he rubbed his chin whiskers. "Damn it, she's out there somewhere, and I haven't a clue where."

"Maybe Rex, or whoever took her, will be in touch with you—for money, that is."

Huffing, Caleb released the tension in his shoulders. "Waiting is not my strong suit."

"Mine, neither. But if they want to make a deal, you're gonna have to be waiting—at home."

"It's a ten-day ride to the Klamath Reservation. I have to speak to Soaring Feather. Rex talked to him and he must know something."

Levi bowed his head, then looked up. "You've been my friend and my boss. I can't say I ever doubted ya, but here's the plain truth. We can't go up north. I know you see them as kin and need your Indian chief's advice. You're mighty keen on this, I can tell, but"—Levi gripped Caleb's arm and their eyes leveled—"we gotta head back and play this right. Get the ransom note and pay up. It'll be done before ya know it. We already have Cork on the lookout. Then we'll deal with the bastards once she's back."

Caleb rose and walked away. Finding a spot to reflect, he sat in the shade of a cottonwood tree overlooking the river. The color of the sky reflected a muted tone of red in the river. Caleb took a heavy breath. It was as if his heart bled into the water. Frustration seethed in him and his anger surfaced. "Damn!" he shouted, pounding his fist on the ground. Never had he been so trapped. Lighting a cigarette, he inhaled deeply, then released the smoke, watching it drift away. He knew Levi talked straight with him, but he couldn't surrender.

They would search for another week, leading them to the base of the Siskiyou Mountains.

As Caleb sat on his horse contemplating the journey to the reservation, he thought carefully about what Levi said. His own instincts had been dulled with the fear of never seeing Jessica again. Levi was right. The best thing to do was to wait on his homestead. He reached into his pocket and took out a cigarette. The wind blew steadily, and it took both hands for him to get it lit. His horse swayed at the loosened rein. Inhaling, he said a prayer to the spirits and blew out the smoke. It was time to go home.

Rail River–July 1889

The evening light threw long, dappled shadows across the grassy field. Caleb walked down to the place where his wife had been taken from him so abruptly and where he had set out to look for her. Coming back to wait took every ounce of his strength, and after a few weeks, he was more disheartened than ever. At least on the trails, he could do something. Cork had no word for him when he and Levi returned. Ben and Sally had nothing to offer, and Burt and June were in a state of heavy grief. He had no one to turn to. The sheriff had called on him, and he could offer him only what he wanted the law to know—someone took his wife for no good reason.

"I had my men post her likeness and the reward in as many of the surrounding towns as they could get to … all the way up to Yuba and down as far as San Jose," said Sheriff Randall. Then he said something that chilled Caleb. "Heard there was a scout in town looking for you a while back. What do you know about this, Mr. Cantrell?"

Gathering his wits, Caleb shrugged. "I've no idea. Reward money brings out all kinds."

"But he was in town before your wife was taken. Maybe he has something to do with this."

Again, Caleb shrugged. "All I know is my wife is gone and I want her back."

The sheriff stepped off the porch and Caleb's stomach relaxed. "All right then, Mr. Cantrell, we will do our best." Before getting on his horse, the lawman turned to him. "I think it's wise if you stick around here. Going to look for your wife only complicates my job."

With a nod and a thank you, Caleb went inside. The sweat ran down his back, and he fixed himself a stiff drink.

Chapter Thirty-four

*C*aleb's days blended one into another as he kept himself busy with his land and found solace in his silversmithing. His employer, Mr. Higgins, let him work on several pieces in his own shop. Slowly, he came back to life, though to a life that held no joy.

Standing on his porch, he looked out onto his land. The sound of the river still haunted him. Jessica's favorite season—summer—had come and gone. He had celebrated her July birthday by getting drunk and passing out.

Today, with little resignation in his heart, he stood here, a victim of life's cruel twists. He breathed in the scented air, then closed his eyes. Upon exhaling, he opened them as if a curtain were rising to present another act in a play—she was sitting on the grass by the river, her back to him as she focused on her painting. "Jess," he said softly so as not to startle her. She turned and looked up at him gleefully.

"Caleb, come see what I've done so far. Let me know what you think."

A heated jolt filled with anguish shot through him. How violent was her kidnapper? "Damn it! Why didn't I follow her down there?" He had rarely let his regrets set up any permanent residence, but since that day, he found the practice to be a difficult task.

Why did you have to be such a selfish bastard? With no answer to be found, he stood for a moment longer. The forest beyond beckoned him to search for her again. He shook his head and walked into the house. He had to change his mood or fall back into the deep depression he had struggled to overcome.

Except for a drink with his friends, Levi and Cork, he stayed to himself. Burt invited him to the house several times, but he felt he could not share his grief with Jessica's family. The one time he had consented sunk him deeper into melancholy.

"We certainly cannot blame you, Caleb," Sophie began as the family gathered for the Sunday dinner, "but your property *is* out of town and quite wild."

"I don't know what I would have done if Carl had taken my Sophie out into the wilderness like that," Laura had exclaimed. She turned to her son-in-law, who looked up from his mashed potatoes at the mention of his name. June had wept most of the time, and Burt tried to console her. The boys clamored for more food and asked many times about dessert. Caleb left as soon as it was courteous to do so. Riding home that evening, he ached to have Jessica by his side to commiserate with.

A knock came to the door. Caleb peeked out the front window and saw Ben standing on his porch. The smiling neighbor waved. Caleb let him in.

"Can't stay," Ben said, "just here on a mission. Sally and I insist you come to dinner tonight."

⸙

Riding up to the large, white farmhouse, Caleb saw the cozy light inside reveal three figures moving about. He wondered who else had been invited. "Come in, Caleb. Glad you decided to join us," Ben said.

Caleb had been grateful for his friend's support in the months following Jessica's disappearance. Even through their own shock and sadness, Ben and Sally's optimistic spirits helped to raise him up, if only for short periods of time.

As Caleb removed his coat and hat, Sally came in from the kitchen to greet him. Behind her was a woman whom Caleb recognized as Martin Cabot's stunning wife, Jane. A catch in his chest made him clear his throat.

He had seen her on occasion in town with Martin. Her beauty never failed to capture his eye. She wasn't too tall, but she had a way of holding herself, giving a presence one could hardly ignore. Her features were unlike any other woman he had ever seen—ancient and exotic. She had a long, straight nose, high cheekbones, and almond-shaped, brown eyes. Her black hair accentuated her light, olive-colored complexion. She provoked his curiosity every time he saw her, and he wondered what a refined woman such as herself was doing on a farm.

Sally made the introductions. "Caleb, this is our friend, Jane Cabot. Jane, our neighbor and friend, Caleb Cantrell."

"Good evening, Mrs. Cabot." She had a basket of biscuits in one hand and raised her other hand regally. Caleb stopped himself from bending over and kissing it. He stood up straight, almost embarrassed at the thought.

"Oh, please, call me Jane, Mr. Cantrell." Her smile lit up her face. "We're all friends here."

"Then please, call me Caleb." He followed her lead, but wished for something more formal.

"I was so sorry to hear about your wife, Caleb. It must have been an awful shock to you and her family." She brought the basket to the table. "I met her once, in town. It was some time ago, and we only spoke briefly, but she was very sweet. I wish we could have been better acquainted." Her voice was soothing, and her eyes held only kindness.

Sally placed the plates on the table while Jane and Caleb conversed. Ben was uncorking a bottle of spirits. "Thank you," Caleb said. "I was sorry to hear of your husband's passing. I heard he worked that farm as well as any man could, considering he had little experience coming into it."

"Yes, he was … determined."

Rumor had it that Jane Cabot received a monthly stipend from her wealthy family in Ohio and Martin's death, and the selling of the farm had not caused her hardship. It was also rumored that she was relieved to be off the land and living in San Francisco.

"Come now, supper is ready," Sally announced.

The meal was hearty, as Caleb had hoped it would be. His cooking skills hadn't improved since Jessica's disappearance, and he was craving some good home cooking.

The small group fell into easy conversation. Jane's opinions were smart and thoughtful. Caleb's attentions fixed on her beautiful, light-brown eyes and how one of her eyebrows lifted almost innocently as she spoke. His eyes wandered to her tulip-shaped lips, then to her slender wrists peeking out from the long-sleeved blouse. Catching himself, he reached for the jug of wine, or perhaps he had had enough. The widow Cabot reminded him of wanting a woman's touch, Jessica's touch. Nevertheless, it felt good to converse and laugh again.

"Sally and Ben were so kind to me after Martin's death," Jane said. "I love San Francisco, but I need the country air and friendly faces of Clermont City every now and then."

"Jane is staying with us through her home's renovations," Sally explained.

Jane gave Sally a smile and turned to Caleb. "The whole thing is a big mess. I sometimes wish I had bought another home entirely."

"Jane has money to burn," Sally teased. "A house here, a house there."

"Now stop that, Sally. You have what money can't buy—a home with a husband in it!"

Her melodic laughter made Caleb light-headed. He smiled. "Though being solvent can have its advantages," he added.

"Sally says you built yourself a fine home. I'd love to come and see it while I'm here." Sally gave Jane a startled look.

"You and Sally are welcome to come over. I keep the door unlocked. I'm mostly at work or in my shop." He swallowed more wine to soothe his discomfort.

"Now, ladies, let's not intrude on a man without a woman around to keep things orderly," Ben said. The room went silent and Ben looked away, then to Caleb. "I'm sorry, I didn't … I didn't think before I spoke."

"No need, Ben. It's true. My home has been without a woman's touch. Fair warning."

"More wine," Jane commanded.

"I think I've had enough," Ben said sheepishly.

Sally and Jane cleared the table, and the evening wound down with coffee and cake. By the time Caleb left, he felt satiated physically if not emotionally. The deep desire in him for 'that woman's touch'—for his wife's touch—dulled the levity he had enjoyed earlier in the evening.

Jane floated into the kitchen with the last of the dirty dishes. "Oh, Sally, I think I may have fallen in love tonight." She dreamily placed the stack on the sideboard.

"Jane, how can you even consider it?" Sally washed the dishes with gusto. "My Lord, you had barely said two words to him, and suddenly, you were on a first-name basis. It isn't proper!"

"Sally, I know you're a God-fearing, church-going woman, but I won't have you making this out to be a sinful thing."

"That's not it at all." Sally kept at her chore. "Ben told me that he won't sign Jessica's death certificate so they can have a decent ceremony for her. He'll never love you as he loved her."

"Of course not. He'll love me as he loves me." Jane grabbed a cotton towel to wipe the squeaky-clean plates.

Sally stopped, turning to Jane in mid-scrub. "You're nearly six years older than him. What will people think?"

"Well, I don't care. Why should it matter? Love is love. I mean, is there some kind of law against it?"

Sally turned back to the bucket of suds in the sink. There was an awkward silence until she said softly, "I just don't think Caleb is ready."

Jane put down the towel and leaned against the counter. "I am sorry. I was just thinking of myself. How wrong of me to express my desires like that. But we are friends, and I thought you might be happy for me *and* for him. I know you miss her terribly. Please, forgive me?"

"Yes, of course." Sally's sweetness returned. "But what makes you so sure of all this? How do you know he's even interested in you ... in that way? He gave no indications of it that I could see."

Jane laughed into the back of her hand, then tilted her head. "Oh, my dear, you've been happily married for what now, eight years?" She picked up the towel and continued to wipe the dish.

Chapter Thirty-five

*T*he chilly October dawn forced Caleb from bed sooner than he would have liked. Tomorrow was the one-year anniversary of his wedding. *Where are you, Jess?*

He stoked the fire, then poured himself another cup of coffee. The pork, eggs, and beans he had for breakfast would have to last him until noon. He went into the kitchen and tore off a piece of bread from one of Sally's loaves and shoved it into his coat pocket. After lighting a cigarette, he headed to the barn, his thoughts taken again with Jane Cabot. He had seen her out in the Loggins' pasture on his way to work and there had been another supper invitation. He was glad she wouldn't be around for long. Leaning into his chores, he worked through his demons, taking care of the livestock and digging and hoeing the garden beds until sweat ran down his face. Boones gave a bark, and Caleb looked at his pocket watch. It was time for lunch. "All right, Boy, let's get us some grub."

He pumped water into the kitchen basin and washed his hands and face, his empty stomach beginning to hurt. He brewed more coffee and searched the pantry for lunch. Before he could satisfy his hunger, there came a knock on the front door. His heart leapt into his throat, then he settled himself. *Jessica wouldn't knock.* He shook the thought away. Boones barked and wagged his tail, crowding Caleb in the vestibule. "Settle down, Boy." He opened the door and to his surprise, Jane stood alone, a pie in her hands and a basket on her arm. He looked around for Sally.

"I hope you don't mind me bringing you some lunch. Sally was busy, so I thought I'd just walk myself over here." The sweetness in her laugh disarmed him. She extended the food and he took it, nearly dropping the pie.

"Come in, Mrs. Cabot. Jane." His nerves flared. "Thank you. I was just about to have something to eat. You must have ... I mean, you and Sally had this timed just right. Come in."

With a wide grin, Jane took back the basket, letting him free to handle the pie. "I think there's enough for two, if you don't mind me being so forward. The walk over here gave me an appetite."

Caleb's insides were quieted by her warm, inviting voice. "Not at all. I would love to share this with you."

She looked over his shoulder. "Is that the kitchen through there?" He stood back, then followed her in. Easily making herself at home, she placed the meal onto dishes and found cups for cider. Before he could intervene, the table was set. He'd be sentenced to hell for letting this woman into his wife's kitchen.

Their conversation flowed as they ate Sally's meat-filled pastries and apple pie, along with Ben's cider. Their small talk eventually moved to more personal topics, sharing the struggles of losing their spouses and of happier times in their lives. Caleb felt he could tell her almost anything and she wouldn't judge him. She knew nothing about his life, his world, and yet she showed great empathy and understanding.

A knock on the door and a bark from Boones interrupted the visit, and Caleb noticed that the light had changed. He looked at his pocket watch as he opened the door. Hours had gone by. Ben stood there, a look of concern on his face. "Have you got our guest with you?"

"My God, Ben, come in." Caleb stood back, passing a hand over his hair. "We lost track of the time. Jane was telling me all about her childhood in Ohio and I was. ..." He stopped talking as Ben gave him a quick nod and wink. "We were having a friendly lunch."

Jane emerged from the kitchen with the empty basket. "Ben. You've come to walk me home?"

"Why, yes. Sally and I were worried about you."

"Oh, I was in good hands." Her generous smile made Caleb uncomfortable.

"Thank Sally for the food. I'll return the pie plate as soon as I can," he said.

"No need for that." Jane waved a dismissive hand. "I'll come by and pick it up tomorrow. Will you be at church in the morning?"

Caleb looked at Ben, then back at Jane. "I don't attend church."

"Well," she said, as if startled by his admission. "I'll be by after church then."

"All right, Caleb," Ben piped up. "We'll be on our way. It looks like you've got some pie to finish off before tomorrow." He gave another wink. "We'll leave you to it."

After seeing them off, Caleb went back inside. He rubbed his neck as he peered from the parlor window to see Jane walking beside Ben, the basket swinging from her arm. He sat in his leather chair, stroking his goatee, imagining a place in his life for Jane Cabot. The profound loss of Jessica engulfed him with its now familiar ache. He closed his eyes, then opened them. *What am I doing?*

As he did every Sunday, Caleb walked to his field and found a space to sit and meditate. The open sky gave way to the opening of his mind, and he would often find his place of peace and wholeness. Today, however, there was none of that to be found. He had left the pie plate on the   porch for Jane to retrieve. His vulnerability agitated him. The spirits he talked to today sent him no relief. He tried to bring forth the answer to finding his wife, but none came. Given that he was too tied up in knots, his usual routine was fruitless and he rose with a huff.

Before heading home, he would visit the river. It had become a sacred place to him. The last of the wildflowers still bloomed along its banks. Picking a few, he placed them in the spot where Jessica was taken. He knelt down and asked the spirits for her safe return. He kissed the cold grass, then stood up. Hoping the pie plate was gone and Jane caught his message, he took long strides over the knoll. He could go back to his life of grieving for Jessica and working on his land.

When he came to the porch, Boones was inside and leapt to the front window, barking. He looked down at the bench. The plate was still there. He brought it in and placed it on the kitchen counter.

That afternoon, Jane was in his parlor. They had tea and conversed easily, taking up where they left off yesterday. "I'd love to hear about your beliefs," she said.

Looking at her sitting in Jessica's paisley chair gave him an odd feeling. *How long would he wait before he removed it from his home? Jane looked very much at ease in it.*

"Caleb?"

"Oh, I was just thinking how to describe them." He scratched his cheek. "I suppose you could say my beliefs come from my experiences, and some of those experiences include my relationships with Indians. Their beliefs and rituals seem more real to me than others." He cleared his throat. "To each his own."

"I don't know much about Indians. My father was so afraid of me coming out west because of them. I see now they were the least of my worries." She grinned.

"I take it you didn't care to be on a farm."

"Not that one, anyway. I love land and fresh air, but ... well, Martin wasn't the right man for me after all. I'm sorry he's gone, and yet, I would have divorced him sooner or later."

Caleb could only nod his head. She was outspoken, to be sure.

Arranging her skirt, Jane moved to the edge of the chair. "The heat feels nice. I should be going, though."

Rising, Caleb took the tea cup from her. "Thanks for the visit."

"It was my pleasure." She walked to the vestibule to retrieve her coat, Caleb behind her.

"Oh, the pie plate."

When she suddenly turned around, his hands were on her arms, preventing a collision. Why they traveled to her slim waist, he didn't know. Suddenly, she was against him and her lips were on his … the warmth of her body, the tenderness of her mouth. She gave no resistance, and he was weak with lust. He cupped her face and his tongue met hers. A hand to her bodice, and he was lost. She moaned, and he was jerked from the spell. He felt the racing of his heart, the heat in his loins. He took several steps back.

"I'm sorry, Jane. Forgive me." He ran his hands over his hair, coming to the tied tail. "I don't know what came over me."

"No need to ask for forgiveness. I'm sure you noticed I was enjoying your advances." She smiled, setting her chin at a most provocative angle.

"More like *your* advances." His smile felt fake. "I can't make love to you, Jane." There, he said it. He could be just as outspoken, yet it didn't seem to bother her in the least.

"Your heart is still attached to her. Of course it is. Maybe someday you will be free to love again, or she will return and you will be free in a different way. Grief is a terrible companion, Caleb. Will you let me be there for you?"

Tongue-tied, he couldn't meet her question. "I'll get the plate." He went into the kitchen and she was standing outside.

He handed her the pie plate, and she took it slowly from him. "Good day, Caleb."

"Good day, Jane."

The moistness of her sweet lips remained on his skin as he watched her cross the yard, pass the barn, and step onto the path that led to the Loggins' home. He turned to his land and the field. The smell of the river wafted over him, and taking out his handkerchief, he wiped his mouth.

Chapter Thirty-six

Sacramento River, California

*J*essica walked on the carpet of dropped pine needles, the scent reminding her of home, the sound of the river close by. Emerging from the woods with the bundle of sticks she'd collected for tonight's fire, she decided to rest on the banks of the river. It would be a welcome respite from her morning.

Her one-year wedding anniversary was in her thoughts today. It would have been one of these days early in October. She wondered what she and Caleb would be doing to celebrate. He had promised her a special dinner at a favorite restaurant in town. Her heart was heavy at the thought of touching his hand and looking into his eyes, while her mouth watered from the bite of steak she would partake of.

Adjusting the basket strapped securely to her body, she reached in and took out a piece of dried meat. Although it was meant to sustain her in her escape, her belly ached from hunger. She had found the long, woven basket, limp from use in the woods, and claimed it as her own, but with much tugging and demanding. The barely healed scratches on her arm were a reminder of her fight with a younger woman in camp. Once it was known to everyone that this basket was hers and only hers, she stole a bit of dried venison here and there to stash away. She only ate half of her share of food, hiding the rest in her clothes or tucked in her hand to later deposit into her basket. One day, she stole a small knife from one of the younger women while she was away from her hut. The tribe searched for it the next day but left Jessica's basket alone. She waited for a few days to pass before she took a piece of rawhide from another woman to make a strap with. This time, there was no fuss. Jessica figured the woman hadn't noticed it missing yet.

Moving toward the shore, she stopped in her tracks and scurried behind a tree. Peeking around its wide trunk, she spied Blue Heron emerging from the cold water. He flung back his wet, black hair, the spray of droplets sparkling in the sunlight. He then laid on the grass above the edge of the gently flowing river, his face serene, his body like a carving of a man, the light revealing every muscle and contour so perfectly chosen by nature. She barely breathed. She couldn't help admiring the artistic scene of the wilderness ... and the man.

Her mind went to her art. When would she be free to paint again? She quietly adjusted the bundle of twigs and leaned up against the tree while she etched the scene in her mind. She couldn't look away. Her desire to paint him and this scene was palpable. He rose and put on his deerskin pants and a leather-and-fur vest. She stepped away to resume her task.

Soon they would be packing up the camp. By listening discreetly, she learned what she needed to know—they were headed for the Rogue River in Oregon. They had allies there to help them in their pursuit to remain independent. If anything, Jessica could count on Cara to tell her about the goings-on of the tribe.

Her plan to escape was taking form. Her basket held a small blanket, a piece of flint, and a few sticks. She wasn't sure if she was collecting, or *stealing*, the right things. When asked about it, she would look naïvely at the inquirer and produce a rock or cone from the top, which she kept there for just that occasion.

Jessica had followed the sun's movements and kept track of the days by scratching a mark on a small piece of dried deer hide she had found laying outside a hut. She figured out the month, but she had lost track of the exact day. She chided herself for that. Could it be five months since her capture? She knew she would have to travel south, and her only compass was the sun.

Today, the bright orb brought warmth to her body. She bent down to pick up several more sticks, lingering in the quiet serenity of the forest. Over her shoulder, through the thick stand of trees, she caught a glimpse of Blue Heron walking to his hut. She dismissed her growing fondness for him as merely being part of her survival.

After a while, she noticed something quite odd—she was alone. Mallow was not in sight. She walked farther away from the camp, searching for any faces or movement. All was still, but for the spattering of voices in the distance and the rippling of water cresting the pebbled shore. She moved more quickly now. Then, in a sudden, unbridled surge of energy, she threw down the sticks and ran without looking back. She was escaping! She turned from the river and ran deeper into the surrounding brush to hide herself. The branches and prickly wild blackberry ripped her stockings and tore at her legs. A few of the taller vines whipped across her face. Ignoring the pain, her survival instincts took over.

She hunched behind a great northern pine. Her breathing was labored, and blood trickled down her face. She waited.

Shaking with fright, she slumped down on the moss-filled base of the tree. It was cool, and she resisted the urge to wipe her hand on it. They would see her blood. With the sun's position as her guide, she resumed her escape through the thick forest. Scurrying like a crab on a beach, she stealthily moved her body along the floor of the forest, traveling as fast as she could, her basket bobbing at her side. She refused to let herself be captured.

A woman laughed. Jessica froze. She listened through the sound of blood surging like the ocean loud in her head. The laugh got nearer. Calculating the risk, she slowly moved in the opposite direction. A twig snapped under her foot, and she dropped to the ground.

"Where are you?" It was Lea's voice.

Jessica did not answer. Lea asked again. She stilled herself, her breathing shallow. A rustle of underbrush and Lea was upon her.

"You hurt?" she asked.

Jessica slowly stood. "I tripped."

Lea laughed as she removed twigs and leaves from Jessica's plaited hair.

Smiling at the Indian woman, she told her she was gathering mushrooms and to go on back to the camp without her.

"No. You are bleeding. I cannot leave you. I get in big trouble."

With a deep sigh, Jessica followed Lea back to camp. To her surprise, she had gone in a circle and would have ended up back there herself. Her poor navigational skills deepened her fear of never finding her way home.

Chapter Thirty-seven

*S*unlight filtered through the forest as Will and Jacob rode the trail along the Sacramento River. The midmorning air smelled of the change in season—fresh and slightly cool. Sparkles of light could be seen in the distance as the sun played on the water. As they rode, Jacob caught a whiff of burnt wood. They followed the scent and soon came upon an Indian camp. Staying out of sight, they looked it over. The huts were roughly put together with branches, thatched grass, and animal hides. The fire was barely visible. Women sat around it with long sticks. The roasting of meat settled in Jacob's nose and churned the acid in his empty stomach.

Stilling his horse, he looked at Will. "What do you think?"

"The runaways, I reckon. Might as well let them be. Looks as if they don't have much."

They turned their horses away and headed in another direction. They didn't go far when out of the woods came a young Indian woman. She looked at them with a startled expression, her black eyes wide and her mouth open. Dropping the basket in her arms and spilling berries on the forest floor, she ran to the camp, her voice clear with warning.

Will and Jacob decided to follow her rather than have the Indians come after them.

Approaching with caution, but with an air of confidence, Will dismounted and led his horse, and the packhorse, into camp. Jacob followed on Otis.

"We come peacefully," Will announced to the gathering of women around a firepit. The young woman who had spied them peeked out from behind the skirt of an older woman.

A tall Indian came from behind one of the huts, a rifle at his side. He came forward. "What do you want?"

"I'm Will. This is my cousin Jacob. We're traders. You are?"

The Indian waved his hand to dismiss the question.

"We have things to sell that you might need. Cash only," Will informed him.

"Traders? We have no use for you." He gestured for them to be on their way.

"You might want to look at what we have. It may save you a trip up north."

The man stopped and turned to face Will. "Who tells you we go up north?"

Jacob held his breath. He knew Will had to tread lightly. "We've heard rumors, that's all."

The Indian yelped, and the piercing cry echoed throughout the forest.

Soon the cousins were surrounded. Some men drew their loaded bows, and several of the men had rifles. They motioned for Jacob to dismount, and he came to stand with his cousin. Without daring to make a move, the cousins watched helplessly as one of the Indians took the packhorse, leading it toward their own stand of horses.

"Give us your money," the Indian commanded.

Jacob let Will do the negotiating. "We need our money and you need our silence. You'll have to kill us to get both," he said. It was not what Jacob wanted to hear. He hoped Will knew what he was doing.

"We will kill you!" a squatty Indian shouted as he came forward to stand by the tall one.

"Let us keep our lives and we'll keep your secret. We have no business with the government."

Jacob raised his hand. "I have money in my pocket." The tall Indian nodded, and Jacob slowly and carefully reached into his pocket and brought out several worn bills. "Here, this is all we have. Take it and let us be on our way. We wish you no harm."

The squatty Indian went over to Jacob and snatched the money from him, then stepped back.

The women had retreated to the huts, and Jacob could hear their feminine voices in the silence of the standoff. Suddenly, a commotion from one of the huts nearly broke its structure. A woman burst from the flap, flinging herself onto the ground. Everyone turned to see her rise up and run to them, shouting, "Help me! Please, help me!"

The tall Indian stopped her, grabbing her arm as she wrestled to break free.

The woman's face struck a chord of familiarity with Jacob. Her hair hung in two braids down her chest, her skin browned by the sun, yet Jacob saw in her someone he knew. Weapons still pointed at them, Will and Jacob moved toward the woman but the men closed in. Peering between them, Jacob saw her being dragged back to the hut. Her pleading shouts grew stronger, moving him to take action.

He drew his gun and cocked it, pointing it at the tall Indian. Before he could make his threat, arrows flew and gunshots ricocheted. Within a fraction of a minute, Jacob was pinned to the ground, his gun hot in his hand. A mighty force from the squatty Indian made it impossible to move his arm and make use of his weapon. Will was taken against a tree and held by several men, while another pointed a gun at his face. Then a command from the tall Indian and the action stopped.

The cousins stood side by side, still in the site of an Indian with a rifle. The tension was thick. The tall Indian waved the others away.

The men in camp gathered and watched. Some retrieved arrows, and others assessed themselves for wounds. One man lie on his side, holding a bloody arm. A woman helped to stop the bleeding. As far as Jacob could see, the skirmish had resulted in no deaths, only a few injuries. He himself was bleeding from his shoulder, but it was only a flesh wound. Will was roughed up but nothing greater than that. Jacob straightened his coat and addressed the tall Indian. "Who is that woman? Why do you have her here?"

"Do not kill them!" The woman was back. She fell to the ground and pleaded at the feet of the tall Indian. The sight moved Jacob.

The woman rose, her eyes penetrating deep into Jacob's. A moment of recognition ignited a burning in his chest. "What is your name?" He knew what the answer was, yet he couldn't believe what he saw.

"I'm Jessica. It's me, Jacob. Will, it's me! You found me!" She reached out to him and he took her hand. Blue Heron stepped between them and yanked her back.

Will let out an audible breath. "Jessica, my God!"

Turning to Blue Heron, Jessica trembled and sought his eyes. "My kin, my family. They found me. Please let me go with them. We will go and tell no one about you. Please, Blue Heron, let us leave in peace."

With a grunt, Blue Heron took her arm. "Go to Lea."

Stepping back from her brother and cousin, she turned and reluctantly walked away from them. Her nightmare was over. Blue Heron would have to concede. Sitting in the hut, she cried tears of joy. Lea and Cara were there. "Those men look dreadful. They can't be your kin," Cara said. "I wouldn't go with them. Stay with us."

Jessica looked at her through watery eyes. "They're the best site I've ever seen."

The slow, deliberate negotiations went on for hours. Sitting around the small fire, a pipe was passed between Blue Heron, the squatty Indian, Mallow, Will, and Jacob. Some dried meat was offered. Will was agitated and Jacob became restless. He couldn't believe Jessica was so near and in such a bad situation. So many questions needed answers, yet Blue Heron offered very little. They would not leave without Jessica, and Blue Heron was reluctant to let her go. Finally, the Indian spoke the words that would seal their deal. "We take your horse with pack, you give us all your money and leave us to our life. If we know you have sent the government, we will find a way to repay your disrespect." He looked over at the hut where Jessica sat within.

Tired and hungry, Jacob nodded in agreement. Will did the same. "We must take Jessica with us," Jacob said.

For a moment, Jacob didn't know how he and Will would take her by force, but he was willing to do anything to get her out of there. Blue Heron sat, staring at the fire. It seemed like hours instead of minutes when he stood. The rest of them followed.

"Take her."

Jacob went to the hut and removed Jessica from it. She wrapped her arms around his neck and sobbed. "Take me home." His heart lurched, and his eyes stung with the salt of his tears. There was still so much to learn about what happened, but first they had to get far away from the Indian camp.

Part Three

Chapter Thirty-eight

*R*iding as far from the Indians as their horses were able to, they made camp at nightfall. Jacob made a note to himself to find a blacksmith to reshoe his horse. Both Otis and Drake had been driven hard, and it was time to find a town for their care before heading to their next destination. It was hardly in the forefront of his thoughts, but with their extra passenger, he knew they needed to make sure the horses were well cared for. This remarkable turn of events had him thinking in a different direction. He took it as a sign that his days of trading and trails had come to an end and being with Jessica was his future. The details would have to be worked out. He didn't care. He wanted her more than he ever had.

Tall cedars and pines surrounded their camp, and thick undergrowth covered the small clearing. Interspersed alder trees noted the change of season with their leaves a variety of yellow shades. A smear of reddish orange ran across the sky. Jessica looked upon the canvas of color and her heart swelled. But for the wind creating a swishing sound among the trees, a quiet fell upon the land as creatures bedded down in holes and burrows, trees and underbrush.

Jacob crouched and teased a gathering of sticks into a small fire while Will counted what was left of their money. Jessica sat off to the side in awe of her rescue. The event played over in her head. One wrong move and her cousin and brother might have been killed. Mallow had been ready to take their lives as soon as he heard white travelers were near the camp. She would have gone with anyone. Having it be Jacob and Will gave her the notion that Caleb and the family had been searching all this time, and they were the ones to find her. Could Caleb be far behind? The thought both thrilled and disturbed her—Jacob and Caleb face-to-face. Jessica looked up at her brother, who was speaking to Jacob. She heard him say, "Jake, we don't have a whole lot left." She turned her back and listened.

Will placed the money back into a pouch strapped to his stomach. He ran his hand over his light- brown mustache and beard. Crouching down beside his cousin, he said in a quiet voice, "I have a confession, but given our circumstances, it's good news."

Jacob didn't like the sound of that and swiveled to face his cousin.

"Don't give me that look, Jake. Listen, I have money … and rifles, too. I left them up in Medford. Sorry I didn't tell you about it. I guess I thought if I returned someday for Mi, we would have resources, her and I and the baby, if she had waited."

Jacob stood. "Is that so? Medford? Why did you hold out on me? After all we've been through together? For a woman? A woman who gave up on you?" Jacob's anger boiled over.

Will spoke over Jacob. "The Indians would have taken it. It's safe up north."

Turning his back on his cousin, Jacob squatted in front of the fire. "We have to ride up there and get it," he said bitterly. He let out a breath. "I suppose I should be grateful."

Will turned from the growing breeze to light a cigarette. He blew the smoke from his lungs. "Yeah, you're damn right you should."

Jessica turned to them. "Where do you need to go?"

"Nothing. Don't worry about it for now," Jacob answered. "Rest." He laid a thick blanket on the ground and brought another to cover her. She didn't argue, and soon he saw she was asleep. Her face dirty and smeared with blood, she was still so beautiful to him. His heart wrenched.

Jessica woke on a blanket, her body wrapped in another, a soft pack under her head. The ground beneath her was hard and damp and she was hungry. Sitting up with a jerk, she looked wildly around her. Where was Blue Heron? Where was the tribe? Then she remembered. Clutching her stomach, she cried out. Jacob and Will were by her side. She wept into Jacob's coat and held on to him, begging God to let this be real. Fully awake now, she composed herself, wiping the wet grit from her face. She offered Jacob a weak smile. "I'll be fine. Now that I'm with you and Will, I'll be fine."

"We'd planned to ride today. Are you up to that?" Jacob asked. "If not, I think we will manage another night here."

Panic rose in her. She needed to keep going. "It's a good day to ride. How far are we from Clermont City? How far from the Indian camp?"

Will scratched his head and looked at the ground. "Several days' ride, I'm afraid, and don't worry about the Indian camp." He peered at Jacob. "We should let her know, Jake."

"Let me know what?"

Will turned to his sister. "We have to go to Medford, a town in Oregon. It's practically on the border, give or take a few miles. We have resources up there we need to claim. The Indians took most of our things."

Jessica had another plan. They could take her to a train station. They could telegraph Caleb, and he would come get her. Before she could verbalize any of it, Jacob stood.

"Jess, it won't take too long, then we can ride to Clermont City, all three of us together. I can't—we can't—let you go off on your own. It's too dangerous and you're in no shape."

Jessica raised her body from the ground, suppressing a moan of pain. "I'm strong enough." She swayed and Jacob caught her.

"Then it's settled," Will said. "I'll send word to the family that you're safe with us, and we will return in a few weeks."

Conceding, she smiled at her brother as he wrapped an arm around her shoulders.

Where had her strength gone? So determined was she to escape, she would have crawled home through the forest among the wild animals. Now she felt weak and tired. Her mind could not spin any more plans. Settling back on the blanket, she watched her brother restore the fire. "I'll get us a rabbit later today," he said, "but first, coffee. I think we have a bag." Jessica looked over at Jacob pulling a small pouch out of his pack. He held it up in triumph. She gave a chuckle.

A lump formed in her throat and her eyes misted. When would she sit with her aunt and a good cup of tea again? She could almost taste her aunt's scones. Thoughts of home she dared not dwell on when she was captive came swarming into her mind. Wiping her eyes, she came back to the present. "Are you sure we are far enough away from Blue Heron and … Mallow? Maybe we should ride today."

"Nah, they won't bother us. They took what they wanted. I doubt we're heading in the same direction anyway," Will explained. This calmed her, but her body was ready to move within a second's notice.

After her share of coffee, hardtack, and a handful of berries, the men prompted her to tell her story. *Where to start?* How would she explain her new life to Jacob without hurting him? A cold wind passed through, and she gathered the blanket around her.

Without mentioning her new husband, she began when she was taken from the Rail River. After she finished, they remained silent. She could see they were trying to make sense of her story.

Jacob was the first to speak. "My God, Jess, I don't know what to say. I mean, are you well? Beside what we can see, are you well? Were you?"

Will looked at her with the same question written on his face.

"Yes, I think I'll recover. My body hurts all over, and I haven't slept well, but I wasn't taken advantage of in the way you might be thinking. I did what would be expected of a wife"—she lowered her head—"to survive." She hoped they caught her meaning without having to go into detail.

Will cleared his throat and Jacob looked away.

She continued. "Mallow had it in for me. As you saw, he was the hardest of them all."

Will slapped the ground. "Those sons of bitches! I have a mind to—"

"Settle down, Will. Nothing we can do," Jacob said.

Her brother flung questions and comments at her without waiting for answers.

Jacob stopped him. "Will, let her tell us in her own way."

Waiting for Will to calm down, Jessica recounted her experience.

"I still don't understand what their motive was. Do you, Jess?" Jacob stared at her, and she felt his look penetrate through her. She hesitated. What did she know? Her husband might be some bandit the law is after, and she was taken for ransom by the Indians a scout hired? This couldn't be the whole story, and she wouldn't let anyone think wrongly of Caleb.

"Never mind. We'll talk again later. You're safe now." He touched her hand and she grasped it.

Will hunched in front of the fire, mumbling and cursing.

"Where is this Rail River?" Jacob asked.

Her heart pumped in her chest, but not out of fear or the adrenaline that moved her forward as she tried to escape. It was her love for Caleb and the pain she was about to deliver to the other man who also had her love.

The fire was full now, and she told the rest of her story.

"I remarried. My husband has land a few miles from Clermont City, *our* land by the river. He named it Rail River Acres." She stopped to catch her breath. The look in Jacob's eyes, his jutted chin, his body slightly withdrawn, pricked her heart. She would give anything to keep him from hurting. In a low voice, she said, "You were gone. I didn't know where to find you."

Will cleared his throat and sat back from the fire and congratulated his sister on her marriage while Jacob sat quietly. Finally, he spoke.

"That's fine, Jess. Sounds like a good home. And you say your art was selling? That's good, too. You can get back to it soon. I'm sorry you were taken from all of it."

His tone opposed his words, and she was not at all convinced he was so easily resigned to her marriage. "Thank you."

"I'm sorry, too, Jess." Will patted her. "I'm happy we found you, Sis." He turned philosophical. "Some say there are no coincidences and that all things are preordained. I have to admit, this seems to fit that thought. Don't doubt for a moment if we had known, we would have been looking for you with everything it took."

Jacob shook his head. "Also, we were tracking renegades and needed money. We tracked this tribe and ... well, there you were. I'll have to agree with Will on this much—it seemed destiny pulled us in that direction."

Jessica's mouth fell open. "You didn't set out to find me?" Her thought that Caleb was close vanished. She had to get home. "Please, Will, send the telegram to the family soon."

Will nodded. "We'll find a town along the way, Jess. I promise."

"I suppose whatever it is that brought you to me, I am so grateful," she said. "I spent every waking moment planning an escape.

It seemed so out of reach. I tried twice but was caught both times. She rubbed her ribs, still slightly tender from Mallow's beating on that first night.

Will went to relieve himself in the woods, leaving her and Jacob alone.

Jacob scooted over and pulled her close to him. He whispered in her ear, "I don't want to let you go."

The years of love for him rose to the surface, and she buried her head in his chest, his smell as intoxicating as ever. She sat up, nervous now. The thought of him from a distance was one thing, but being so close confused her. Will returned and they sat apart again.

She passed the rest of the day quietly, resting on the blankets. The forest framed the blue sky. The smell of nature readying for winter gave her a sense of anticipation she could hardly contain. Her life would be returned to her. What of Jacob, her first and forever love? Her feelings for him must remain secret. She could not let their love re-emerge, no matter how much she wanted to touch him and talk with him intimately. Caleb waited. Jacob must have read her mind, for when she looked up at him, he frowned and shook his head.

Chapter Thirty-nine

$\mathcal{T}$he rising sun brought large beams of light through the forest and onto the open land. Jessica marveled at the sight. The trio were wrapped in wool blankets around a cold, charred campfire. She stirred at the intoxicating smell of a new day, cool, damp, and clean. Each whiff of pine needles, fir cones, and boughs of spruce filled her with joy. Jacob turned in his blanket and faced her. His smile was like honey on warm toast. She smiled back and he mouthed, "Good morning."

Will tossed his blanket aside. Stepping high in his bare feet and long johns, he hurried into the woods, cursing the cold morning. Jessica laughed. Her brother was still her brother. Part of him remained the same and she was glad.

Jacob stood up and put his pants over his long johns. "I'll make some coffee as soon as the fire gets going."

Jessica didn't turn away. During her time with the Klamath, she had grown accustomed to seeing scantly clothed men and women, to the extent that she wondered why her people wore so many clothes and not just for warmth—all the petticoats and undergarments, gloves in the summer, hats, too. She stretched her limbs, the aches and pains so familiar to her now. After relieving herself in the woods, she was ready to help. She gathered sticks and thick branches.

"Don't go off like that!" Jacob scolded her.

"I had to—"

"Let me know next time."

"I think I can manage that without informing you first."

Jacob scratched his head. "I know, sorry."

Will was still away from the camp. Jacob moved closer to her and then gently pulled her forward as he lowered his head to kiss her lips. She didn't stop him, in spite of her vow. She touched his handsome face, tan and beautifully etched, his knowing, dark-brown eyes with the bit of yellow flecks. Their love opened in her like a treasure chest full of riches. Regaining her sense of obligation to her life and her husband, she stood back, touching her mouth. "I'm sorry, that was—" Before she could get out the last word, his mouth was on hers again. So complete was his kiss, it made her feel faint.

He came away. "It's always been wrong. It always will be." His voice was hoarse and full of emotion. They could hear Will return to camp.

The coffee was strong, and the oak and fruit cakes were dry. Jessica dunked hers into her cup and slurped up the drippings. She realized her unladylike behavior and could only laugh at herself. The men chuckled. "Get me back to civilization!" She laughed.

Jacob saw in Jessica's face the toll that life in the wilderness had taken on her. He loved her even more. Her thin, unkempt appearance made her more real to him than when she had adorned herself with expensive clothing and fancy hats. She was more mature and down-to-earth. He never imagined she wouldn't wait for him. His words from his last letter—"Be free"—rang in his ears. He would have done whatever it took to have her at his side, but now she was another man's wife and again his desires had no home.

"We'll try to get you back as soon as we can."

Jessica smiled at Jacob, then turned to Will. "Isn't Medford where you convalesced?" Before he could answer, she continued. "I was happy to hear about Mi. Is that her name? Then I was so sad to hear she abandoned you."

Will cocked an eye at his cousin. "And how do you know all this, Sis?"

Jacob cleared his throat. "One of us had to write to her. The world could have swallowed us up with no one the wiser."

Jessica looked at her brother. "I was grateful to receive any news of you."

"I hope you kept it away from our parents."

Jacob noticed that Jessica's face saddened as she wrapped her hands around the tin cup of coffee, and took a sip.

"Father had a heart attack at the end of last year. It was before I was taken. He was recovering, last I heard."

"I knew he would work himself into the grave." Will became agitated. "Does he think he is above death?" He shook his head. "I'm glad he's still with us, though Lord knows when I will choose to see either one of them again."

"Will, I hope someday you and Father will declare a truce. Life is too precious. Mother came out to visit us. It was good to see her, though she looked tired."

"Our mother traveled across country? Alone?" Will laughed so hard he nearly fell over.

"The women in this family are braver than you think, Brother."

"And what did she think of your new husband?"

"Not much. You know how she can be. Mother and Father wanted to buy us a home in town, and with the baby coming. ..." Jessica bit her lip and averted her eyes.

"Where is the baby now?" Will asked as he reached over and touched her hand.

"I didn't ... I mean ... I wasn't able to carry it to birth." She lowered her head and took in a long breath.

"Ah, Jess." Will leaned in and hugged her.

Jacob said nothing but thought plenty. She carried his own

child and lost it, and now she'd lost another man's child. Was it fate that made them suffer? Were their sins written in stone?

He ran his hand over his whiskers. "Jess, to be honest, we don't know how long it will be before we can get you home to your ... husband. And, Jess, I hate to say this, but don't be surprised if he's gone on with his life. I know men, and it doesn't take them long to replace a wife." He wasn't sure why he wanted to add vinegar to her wounds, yet the words flowed easily. He pulled on his cigarette and stared into the fire, his words lingering in the air.

"Geez, Jake, for Christ's sake." Will turned to his sister. "He's become quite the cynic."

Jacob expected backlash from Jessica. Indeed, her chin was raised, her words tumbling out as if stored up for too long.

"I may not know men as well as you do, but I do know that Caleb Cantrell is not just any man. I'm sure he's searched everywhere for me and hasn't given any thought of replacing me. We had a good life together." She glared at both men in turn. "Did you hear me?"

Jacob heard nothing after "Caleb Cantrell." A cold chill ran up his spine at the mere mention of his name. "Who?"

"My husband, Caleb. He would never abandon me like that."

Slowly removing the cigarette out of his mouth, Jacob enunciated every syllable and asked, "You're married to Caleb Cantrell? Jesus."

Will turned to his sister. "So this husband of yours ... he isn't a tall, blond fella with a shit look on his face, is he?"

"He's tall and blond, but he has a beautiful face with the bluest eyes I've ever seen!" Her breathing was audible as she searched both men's faces.

"I'll be a goddamned son of a bitch." Will sat back and crossed his legs and arms. "Pardon my language, Sis."

A rush of regret flooded Jacob's heart, burning his chest. "How the hell did you get involved with a man like him?"

"Stop it, both of you! This isn't funny!"

Will rested his arms on his crossed legs. "Fact is, we've met your husband. This is a shock to us, too."

She pulled back. "He never mentioned it to me."

Will looked at his cousin, indicating he would let him explain.

Jacob snuffed out his cigarette. He spoke plainly. "It was on the trails a while back. We shared a camp with him and a few of his friends, then parted ways. My guess is, we didn't leave much of an impression on him."

"He did say he traveled around a lot. What was he doing when you met him?"

"He ... he was trading, as we were. I think that's why our paths crossed." Will coughed.

Jessica smirked. "I see." She huffed. "You traveled with him, didn't you? You don't have to hide his past from me. I know he led a somewhat lively life before we met. Was he a gunrunner, too?"

"Jess, if he didn't tell you about his life, then I don't think it's right for us to say," Jacob said.

"Oh, nonsense! I don't care. He's a devoted husband now. He works hard on our land to make a good home for us, and I work alongside him. He's also a fine silversmith, and one day, he'll have his own business, if he hasn't already."

"Good for you, Jess."

"Don't patronize me, Jacob."

"I wasn't. I really mean it. I just find it hard to believe we're talking about the same man, that's all."

"Well, I guess a leopard can change his spots," Will joked. "As long as you're happy, Jess, then you've got my blessing ... and Jake's, too, right Jake?"

"Yep." Jacob pushed out the word. Had she forgotten their lovemaking? Had the years erased her devotion to him? "I guess I've been fooling myself," he said under his breath.

"All right, let's get going. We have a six-day ride ahead of us." Will stood and began to break camp. Jacob stared at the ground.

"Will, I want to talk with Jess a moment. Jess, will you take a walk with me?"

Jessica walked ahead of Jacob as they entered the dark forest, the sun slicing through in soft shafts of yellows, giving them the light they needed. She sat on the thick trunk of a fallen fir tree. Her skirt and pantaloons barely buffered her from its rugged, damp bark. Jacob stood in front of her.

"I still can't believe this. Here you are. Here we are, together. How has fate arranged such a thing, yet you are married. Quite cruel, as I always expected fate to be."

She reached out her hand, and he took it and sat down beside her. "I thought you didn't care to be with me. You abandoned me. I had to live my life."

His eyes held sorrow. "I know. I thought you'd be better off without me, without this complication we so naïvely wove for ourselves." He looked away, and she wondered what he could say that would stop her yearning for him. She thought of her husband, and it restored her resolve to go home.

"My life is with Caleb now, and I must get back to him."

He squeezed her hand. "I love you, Jess."

"I love you, too, Jacob." The words were smooth on her lips.

They sat in silence. Finally, with their fingers still entwined, they walked back to camp without a word. She would follow him to Medford with the hope that it would lead her back home one day. A faint feeling of wanting to be with him crept up inside her. She felt as if she were in another kind of abduction—one of the heart.

196

Chapter Forty

Rail River Acres–October 1889

*K*eeping to his life, Caleb avoided the widow Cabot as much as he could. The invitations from Sally kept coming, and he was keen to find an excuse to decline. Today, he found it hard to be alone. The stove was ablaze, a good book waited, and his duties around the house were finished —for now. He could relax in peaceful solitude, yet the company of soft voices and gay laughter tempted him to invite the Loggins and Jane over for dinner. He got up to look at what he had in the pantry. A rough stew was all he could manage still.

In the distance, he heard the sound of carriage wheels making their way over the planks of the bridge. He went to the porch and waited. Soon Burt's carriage appeared from around the bend.

Stepping off the porch, he felt heartened by the company but his anxiety grew. When the carriage finally came to rest, Burt leapt from his perch and rushed over to him. Caleb was alert, his heart beating faster. Looking at Jessica's uncle, he saw a flush of rosy exuberance in the man's face.

"Burt, what is it? Come in and sit."

Burt took Caleb by the shoulders. Taking in great gulps of air, he said, "Jessica is safe. The boys have her. Will and Jacob found her."

Stunned into silence, Caleb stared at him. He stepped away and ran his hands through his hair. Turning to Burt, he asked, "Are you sure? Where did you get this information?"

Burt was already reaching into his pocket, revealing the telegram from Will.

It gave little information. They would be home in three or four weeks. Nowhere was the how, when, and where Caleb ached to know. His mind racing in too many directions. "Why on earth doesn't he give their location? Damn it! I need to get to her."

"Caleb, this is extraordinary news. What does it matter the circumstances? We'll have our Jessica back in only weeks and my son and nephew will be with her."

Coming out of his thoughts, it hit him—Jessica was safe. She was coming home. He took Burt's shoulders. "My wife is alive."

The men hugged, patting each other's back. They came away with watery eyes. Caleb laughed and brushed away the tears. "My God, I can't believe it!" He laughed again. Questions invaded his mind, pushing aside his joy and relief. He looked at the ground, shaking his head.

"We'll find out soon enough, Caleb. I have to get back to June. As you can imagine, she's
in quite a state."

"Say no more, Burt. June expresses what we're all feeling."

"Aye, and much more," he said with a chuckle.

That night, Caleb could not find sleep. His mind was a flurry of questions. His body was ready to act. After examining the telegram, he came to the conclusion it was sent from a town up north. With a fresh horse and supplies, he could be there in less than a week. Even after agreeing with himself of the impracticality, Caleb still fought the urge to get riding. Again, he would have to wait ... nearly a month. Why would they not bring her back sooner? What was Jacob up to? He was with Jessica, and Caleb's jealousy was at a fever pitch.

He got up and paced the floor. The room was cold, the stove barely lit, and he hadn't eaten. How was he going to wait for her return without going mad?

Chapter Forty-one

Late October 1889

*J*acob, Will, and Jessica traveled north along the Sacramento River into Southern Oregon. Jacob felt the warmth of Jessica's body at his back as they rode together, her arms around his waist when the trails got rough, her breath on his neck as she spoke to him. On day four, they camped along the Pit River before they began their easterly route to Medford.

The evening was dry and cold. Jessica huddled near the fire. The blanket over her body kept the heat in. She was reluctant to take it away, yet she needed to examine her body. The scars from her attempts to run away were fading. She turned from the men and rolled down her torn stockings. The memories of her time with Blue Heron and the camp were still too fresh. The bruises and scratches remained, and new ones from traveling dotted her inner thighs. She rubbed her legs and thought of Lea's salve. Her scalp itched, and she knew she smelled pungent. The small town where they stopped to send the telegram held little in the way of accommodations, and they camped outside of it. The bruises would fade, the scratches would heal, but she wondered how she would resume her life after this. What would be expected of her? She was changed and didn't know who she was anymore. Would she fit back into her life as wife, niece, daughter … artist? She covered her legs, lowered her head, and heaved a sigh.

"Get that blanket on you," she heard Will say. She brought the scratchy, wool blanket around her and turned her attention to Jacob. He'd skinned and gutted a rattlesnake and was now wrapping it around a stick.

"Why are we camping like this? Do you know any towns where we could find decent lodging?" Will and Jacob defended themselves by saying they did not have the luxury of spending their money on hotels. Although she knew it may be partially true, she suspected they liked being free in the wild. She did not. "Will we find a train station in Medford?"

Jacob turned from his crouched position. He was trying to keep the snake meat from falling off the stick. "Yes, but how will the horses get to Clermont City?"

Her anxiousness to get home was blunted by her circumstances. She would have to be patient. She needed clothes, money, and perhaps a chaperone if she were to leave without them.

"I thought that it was all settled." Jacob turned his attentions back to their supper.

"Yes, it is." The roasting meat made her mouth water. She thought of the meals she cooked for her and Caleb, and their life together. How was he getting along? Was he resigned to her being lost? Her stomach rumbled and she was back to the present. The food she would never have eaten before smelled delicious to her now and she couldn't wait to taste it. Survival had become the most important thing in her life.

Finally, they entered the town of Medford, Oregon, a town with many memories for Jacob. The town he came into with his wounded, unconscious cousin draped over Drake while he maneuvered Otis. The desperation he felt with Doc Middleman being his last hope.

They had closed a deal with a group of men when, out of nowhere, came riders with bows and arrows, guns and tomahawks—Indians of the Northwest region of Oregon. He still recalled the urgency to ride as fast as he could to get clear of the small war that had broken out around them. The words *not fast enough* still echoed in him, for a bullet had shot through Will's arm and another had grazed his left side.

This town held no future for Jacob, yet here he was, back at Doc Middleman's. Will had begged him to stop here before they went to the bank to get their money and a few stored guns. The place where the doctor stitched up Will, the doctor with the sour-faced wife and pretty, Chinese assistant, Mi Lee, Will's love and the mother of his child. Guilt rose in him as he recalled Will's anger for having to leave Mi behind while they made their money. He knew his cousin still blamed him for not taking her along, but Jacob had made it clear that traveling with a pregnant Chinese woman did not fit into their plans. There was no room for remorse today—it had been for the best. How was Jacob to know Mi wouldn't wait for Will? *It seems to be a way with women,* he thought sourly. He looked down the middle of the town. Rows of buildings lined the packed-dirt streets. Nothing was different, except now Jessica was with him. How extraordinary was this twist of fate. He set his sights on the hotel across from Doc Middleman's and was anxious to get off his horse and into a real bed.

Jessica remained behind Jacob. She stroked Otis's backside and promised he would be taken care of soon. Will approached the Middlemans' home. Sitting on the edge of town, it was a large, white-washed building, two stories high, with little adornment. The porch creaked when he stepped onto it.

Moving restlessly in the saddle, Jessica felt a brisk wind blow through her torn stocking. She felt dirty and ragged and brought her cold legs in closer to the horse's warm belly. Her brother's eagerness pricked her heart. She hoped this would go well for him, though her intuition told her it wouldn't.

A young girl answered the door. She looked to be no more than fifteen, a tall girl with a pretty face and neat attire. "Yes, may I help you?" She surveyed Will, and then beyond to the other travelers. The door closed slightly.

Will removed his cowboy hat. "I'd like to see Doc Middleman."

"He's not here!" a strong voice behind the girl called out.

It was Mrs. Middleman. Soon she was in front of them, and the girl was forced to stand aside. "Get back to your work, Sassy," the robust matriarch instructed.

"So you've come back. And who is that?" Mrs. Middleman looked at Jessica.

Jessica became extremely self-conscious in her hodgepodge of skirt and hide, her roughly plaited hair hanging down one side.

"My sister, Jessica. Do you have any news of Mi and my child? Has he been adopted yet? Please, tell me what you know."

"Yes, she's in Portland with her new husband." Mrs. Middleman tilted her head, her hands folded in front of her full skirt. "That's all I know."

"Are you sure? I know Mi was close to you. Please, tell me about my child."

She raised a brow and cleared her throat. "Very well. The baby boy died right after she moved. Caught some nasty bug. She's got her husband to take care of her. Your part in her life is over. Be on your way now."

Will staggered backward off the porch. "A son."

Jessica scrambled to get down, but Jacob stopped her. "Let him be, Jess."

"Sorry to be the one to tell you," Mrs. Middleman said with little compassion. "Losing it was all for the best, in my opinion. Heard his complexion was too white for her husband's liking. Now if you'll excuse me, I have things to attend to. Doc Middleman is in his office and doesn't care to be disturbed. Good luck to you." With that, she closed the door.

"Will, let's get to the bank and then find a place to stay." Jacob tried to keep his tone even, but he found himself struggling not to break down the door and corner the bitch.

Will kicked the ground and looked up at his cousin. "This is all your goddamn fault!"

"We couldn't take her with us." Jacob's voice was strong and tight.

Once again, Jessica tried to get down, but he wouldn't let her. The look on her brother's face frightened her. "Will, let's go. We'll rest and talk." Will returned to his horse and led it across the street to the hotel—the same hotel where he fell in love with Mi. Jacob followed without a word.

The rooms were decent enough for the weary travelers. Jessica closed the door and surveyed the sparse but neat area. A single bed with a thin mattress, one pillow, linens, a wool blanket, and a quilt. The dresser had a mirror above it, and a plain, blue rug covered most of the worn, wooden floor. The cotton curtains framed a small window that looked out onto the street.

Jessica lit the kerosene lamp on the dresser. The face looking back at her from the mirror gave her a start. "Oh, God!" She turned away and began to undress. The skirt was smeared with her own blood, along with patches of grass and dirt stains, and the blouse was no better. Her ripped stockings were weathered beyond recognition, the rips creating large holes. Only her camisole and pantaloons were still somewhat intact.

She looked around for a clean cloth. To her relief, there was a pitcher of water sitting in a basin near the window. She washed herself as best she could and undid her hair, running her fingers through the tangles. Her body was sore, and she ached to be home. She entered the bed, and the springs creaked and squeaked. The feather pillow was luxury in itself, and the blanket and quilt would keep the chill away. She gathered them up to her chin.

Alone and safe, her thoughts swirled around her head. Jacob was with her, his presence unearthing the love for him she had kept so well buried. Her thoughts went to Caleb and desperation undid her. For the first time in a long while, she let her tears flow and cried without restraint into the soft pillow.

In the next room, Will and Jacob laid their packs on the floor, and Will threw his body on the bed, his weight causing the mattress to sink into the springs.

Will sat up, his voice tight with emotion. "You were right about Mi. Shit, I knew it all along. I would have moved a mountain for my son. His skin too light? Devil! He brought his legs to the side of the bed. "I want to ride up to Portland and kill her husband."

"No, you don't. You want to hurt Mi and you can't, even if she was standing in front of you. That's the shitty part of all of this."

Will laid back down and shoved the pillow under his head. "I had a son."

Jacob felt the heaviness of Will's statement. "I'm sorry, truly I am. I wish … I wish things had turned out differently."

"Yeah." Will smirked. "When are we getting back to June's cooking and a fine bed under us?"

Jacob rolled his eyes at his cousin. "All I know is I'm dog tired. He sat on the edge of his bed. "I think I should check on Jess before I pass out."

"All right, Jake, but I hope you've made up your mind to get her home."

Jacob went to the door and looked back at Will. "I've made up my mind."

Chapter Forty-two

*S*tartled by the knock on the door, Jessica sat up and pulled the bedding up to her. "It's Jacob," she heard from outside her room. She went to the end of the bed and put her skirt on, tucking her blouse into it. "I'll be right there."

She slowly opened the door a crack. "I'm fine. Go back to your room."

He held the door open and gave it a slight push. "Jess, I need you." She relented. Stepping into the room, he took her in his arms, shutting the door behind him with his foot. His smell filled her head, and she caught her breath as if she were drowning. He moaned and held her tighter. She was pressed up against him and felt his manhood rise, his hands caressing her eager body.

"Jacob," she whispered. "No."

He came away from her. The look on his face revealed his anguish.

"Please don't make me choose, Jacob. Please go back to your room."

"Don't make me go. We've waited too long to be together … or at least I have." He stepped away and ran his fingers through his loose mane.

The sting of his words stabbed her heart. She bowed her head. "I waited as long as I could." Only her eyes rose to meet his. He took her chin and raised her head. The kiss they shared sent her tumbling into the warm waters of their love.

Slowly, he brought her clothes to the floor and removed his own. Standing naked, flesh and heart eager to be satisfied, Jacob laid her on the bed.

After many hours of sharing their bodies with each other, Jacob reluctantly returned to his and Will's room. The love he held for Jessica had drawn the devil out of him, and he cursed the fact that remained—she was married to a man whose life he'd saved. He collapsed into bed, letting the touch of her skin lull him to sleep.

The morning light woke him. He rubbed his eyes and peered out the fogged-up window. Wiping the condensation away, he looked out onto the road. Drake and Otis were still there. He stretched and yawned. Will was standing in front of his bed, dressed in new clothes and clean shaven. He held a cup of coffee in his hand. Gesturing to the dresser, he said, "I brought you up a cup. It's lukewarm by now."

Jacob took a deep inhale and exhaled with a moan. "Thanks." He shivered in his gray long johns as he left the warmth of his bed to retrieve the coffee. He searched his jacket for a cigarette and match. Returning to bed, he sat up with his back against the wooden headboard. Aware of Will's stare, he took a sip from his cup. After swallowing with a wince, he laid into his cigarette with a long drag. "I see you got the money," he said, blowing out the smoke in a long stream. "You look almost human. I'll need some for myself. It's time I got a shave."

"Didn't hear you come in last night."

"You snore like a den of bears. When do you ever hear anything when you sleep?"

"We're leaving tomorrow. She's going back to Caleb where she belongs." He raised his hand. "Don't say a word."

Jacob took another drag and turned back to the window.

When Will and Jacob arrived in Jessica's room at the Medford Hotel, they found her in a highly agitated state.

"I can't go out like this! It was bad enough standing there in front of the hotel manager yesterday dressed like an Indian ... but not out in society! And just look at my hair!" Jacob became self-conscious as she sized him and Will up and down. "Well, I see you two wasted no time in spending money on yourselves."

Jacob felt his clean chin and grinned. He thought of her mouth enjoying its smoothness. Then it occurred to him that she had been traveling in the same worn and stained garments they had found her in. "We'll get you some proper clothes, Jess."

Jessica's eyes lit up. "Now just get me something simple. I don't need anything too fancy, but with a little style ... something I could ride in as well ... or maybe a house dress will have to do. The shopkeeper will know the proper petticoat, and I'll need a coat, too, and new boots and—"

"Hold on." Jacob raised his hand. "We're not going into a lady's shop."

Will stood by Jacob, agreeing with him wholeheartedly.

"Well, what am I going to do?" Her panicked voice raised the hair on the back of Jacob's neck.

Both men pursed their lips and lifted their shoulders.

She had been given no choice. Standing in front of the first dress shop she came upon, she peered into the window. The inside of Lorretta's Women's Wear looked expensive. She walked in with her head held high. The stares and whispers she had received as she made her way along the boardwalk were nothing compared to the looks of the ladies in the store. Then, from the back, she heard a woman boom, "My Lord! Where did you come from?" The patrons immediately turned to the neatly dressed and coiffed boutique owner, then back at Jessica.

She held her pride. "I need a dress, and one I can ride in, please. Also, a pair of boots and a warm coat."

"You most certainly do!" The boutique owner came around a display case and then wound her way past a finely outfitted mannequin before coming to stand in front of Jessica. "I'm Loretta. How much do you have to spend, miss?"

Jessica's chin went back into her neck. No one had ever asked her such a question. How rude. "It's Mrs.," she said. Then Jessica whispered, "I have six dollars." She felt the embarrassment rise to her cheek, hot and uncomfortable.

"Mrs., huh? Well, you had me fooled. You look like some urchin living on the streets."

The snickers and giggles vibrated around the shop.

Jessica smoothed her patchwork skirt. "I need clothes. I want my husband to see me in something nice when he does see me again."

Loretta surveyed her with a skillful eye. "I think I have a few things that may work for you. Anything would look better on that pretty figure of yours than that. I'll be with you shortly. Stand over there, and please refrain from touching the garments."

Jessica was cast to a corner near the back of the store. She waited anxiously. Once the last customer left, Loretta placed the CLOSED sign in the window. She came to Jessica and stuck out her hand, palm up. After placing the six dollars in it, she was lead to the back. "I think I can do something with that rat's nest of yours. First of all, you need a bath. You can use the tub outside. Don't worry, it's private. I'll run some hot water for it."

Tears filled Jessica's eyes. "Thank you. The hotel only had a privy and wash basin."

"Yeah, they've been meaning to upgrade that place for years. Drape your clothes over the fence, and I'll burn them for you."

Jessica couldn't think of a better way of disposing of them.

Leaving Loretta's with a spring in her step, she reentered the world with a renewed heart. The walk back to the hotel was much different than earlier. Women smiled at her and men tipped their hats. When Jacob and Will sited her, their broad smiles gave credence to the fact that she was moving closer to the person she once knew. "You look beautiful, Jess," she heard her brother say, but it was Jacob's loving expression that held her interest. He nodded in agreement.

After a hearty breakfast, it was time for her to return to Clermont City. It would take them some twenty days by Will's account. She mounted Jacob's horse with the confidence of a seasoned rider. They rode out of Medford, slowly and deliberately, each in their own world. Jessica was full of anticipation, even as her heart was being torn in two directions. Jacob's back rose and fell deeply, and she knew he was taking in the lavender and chamomile smell of her hair and body. His own scent of cedar soap made her smile. She leaned into his back and he drew her hand around his waist.

Chapter Forty-three

November 1889

*C*aleb opened the door to Jessica's uncle. "Burt, come on in. What brings you up here?" He held his breath. It had been three weeks since Will's telegram.

Sally and Jane sat in the parlor. Burt tipped his head in acknowledgement of them, and Caleb could see he was flustered.

"Burt, you know Mrs. Loggin, and this is her friend, Mrs. Cabot. They came over with a cake. Would you like a slice and some coffee?"

With a wave of his hand, he politely declined. "Caleb, I've got some news," he said soberly, then glanced over at the women. "Can we talk … alone?"

Hearing this, Sally and Jane rose as one and said their good-byes. Leaving, Sally gave Caleb a squeeze to his shoulder. "If you need Ben or me. …"

"Thank you, Sally. It was nice to see you both." Before Caleb shut the door, Jane gave him a smile. It was generous and caring, her eyes full of compassion. He turned away, hoping he didn't need it. Returning to the parlor, he blurted, "Tell me she's coming home. I can't stand to hear anything else."

"Yes, yes. I'm not here about that. All is still well as far as I know." Burt sat down and leaned into the room, his hands clasped together. "This does concern her, though. Thomas died yesterday. The telegram came this morning."

Caleb puffed a sigh of relief, then took in the news. "Oh, Burt, I'm so sorry to hear that." He sat in the other chair, feeling the warmth left by Jane. A silence engulfed the room. The wood burning in the stove cracked like a whip and both men came alert.

"I thought you should tell her," Burt said. "Bethany will no doubt want her home for the funeral."

"I don't know what my wife has been through. She might not be well enough to go to Connecticut." Caleb stood and paced. "I'm sorry, Burt. I haven't gotten my wife back, and now you're telling me she has to leave."

"It's all too much, I know." Burt rose from his seat. "I'll let you decide what's best."

"Is there anything I can do for you and June?"

"Nah. June is driving me crazy with all her plans to have Bethany come live with us. I don't think my sister is going anywhere. Not for now. This has been a blow to her. First, no word from her son, then Jessica's disappearance, now this." Burt reflected. "Thomas shouldn't have had to run the law firm by himself. My silent partnership seems selfish to me now."

Caleb listened, sad for his older friend. "Burt, he made his own fate. You can't be blamed for anything. Besides, if you hadn't come out here, I never would have met Jessica. We owe you our happiness with many more years to come."

"Yes, I suppose you could look at it that way, too. Who knows, I'd probably be in the grave with him if I hadn't left. When I think of my son and nephew following their own lives, I have to be grateful in a way. No one needs to work themselves to death."

Caleb couldn't help think that Will and Jacob had simply found another path to the same end.

Before leaving, Burt opened the subject of the reward money. "As you know, the detective Thomas had hired turned up little information. We had several fellas coming around to offer their help—and some claimed they saw her—but none had anything concrete."

Caleb knew his wife's family had gathered their resources for a reward, and five thousand would attract attention. It would also attract every thief trying to get rich quick. His own money would be put to better use, although he hadn't heard from Rex, and with Jessica safe, the point was moot. He simply acknowledged the information.

Burt lowered his head, then looked into Caleb's eyes. "What I kept from you is that Frederick Moore added five thousand to the pot. He came to Dunbar's about a month ago, claiming how overwrought he was over her disappearance. We needed as much reward money as we could get our hands on, Caleb. He made sure we had it in an account to earn interest. I know how this sounds, but trying times—"

"I understand, but Frederick? What the hell has he to do with this? I thought he left her high and dry? Earn interest? For whom?" His anger seethed, thinking of Jessica married to such a scoundrel, and a man handpicked by her own father.

"I think it's his guilty conscience," Burt replied.

"I hardly believe that, Burt." Caleb paused. "There's no point in it now."

Burt stroked his silver-streaked beard. "I think the boys should get the reward. After all, they found her."

"It's not my decision to make, but I'd advise you to give Frederick's part back to him."

Burt nodded. "It may be the best course of action, but as far as I'm concerned, he owes this family something. The boys could finally settle down, and you and Jessica could benefit by it as well."

"I know you mean well, Burt, but I would prefer you leaving Jess and me out of this."

Burt nodded. "It will all work itself out, I'm sure."

Watching Burt's carriage saunter down the road, Caleb was restless. Again, he would have to muster up his patience, which grew thinner each day. He was saddened for Jessica, and he knew the death of Thomas would be hard for her to take. First, she had to be in his arms, then he'd decide what to do next. He made up his mind on one thing—she would not be traveling to Connecticut. Another stab of jealousy hit him. Jessica and Jacob together. *Come back to me, Jess.*

Chapter Forty-four

The trio were two full days into their journey away from Medford and heading toward Clermont City. After coming together in Medford with Jacob, Jessica held herself in check. It would be too easy to fall back into their love affair. Will rode just a horse's length in front. She touched Jacob's back this morning, their third day, then placed her head on the soft leather of his new coat. The smile on his face when he glanced back at her warmed her heart, then it thumped hard as her mind went to Caleb. She straightened up and looked out at the scenery.

The mountains stood in the distance, the open land around them filled with light then shadows as the puffy, white clouds swept across the sky. There were wild, picturesque hills nearby with snaggy-toothed rocks protruding along the green slopes. Farms dotted the landscape. Jessica yearned to have her paints and paper to capture what she saw. Humming, she let it pass by her, setting it to memory.

The early November air was fresh, and she felt cozy in her new wool coat, leather boots, and the knitted scarf and hat Loretta had thrown in for good measure. Jacob's warm body added to her comfort. She let herself be with him without judgement. It was temporary, and for now, she would indulge in their togetherness. He was a part of her, and she would not let guilt take that away.

They stopped for a quick lunch of dried meat, cheese, and apples. They spoke little, then they were back on the trail.

Jessica grew weary of riding, yet she reminded herself that she was safe and Jacob was the one at the reins. The air grew colder as they entered a canyon, the jagged walls of rock towering up alongside them. She looked up at the rocky edges and noted their color and form. The muted reds and greens, dark yellows, and earthy browns swelled her artist's heart. She wondered if Caleb had left her room undisturbed. Jacob's words rang in her head. Surely, Caleb hasn't found another wife. She sighed and shifted her weight. The saddle felt as if she were sitting on the rocks she surveyed.

Cutting through the serenity, a sharp ping ricocheted from the rock face. Another, then another, and her brother looked back at Jacob with urgency written on his face. The dirt in front of him danced as the bullets landed only feet from his horse. Drake reared up, and Will struggled to get control. Jacob took his gun out of its holster. "What's going on?" Jessica asked, alarm bells ringing in her head.

Jacob shouted to Will, who had turned Drake to face his cousin. "Who?" he asked.

"Don't know," Will responded. He pointed to the trail leading out of the canyon just as another bullet hit the ground.

In one unified motion, the horses were in full gallop. Jessica held on tight, overcome by the fear she thought she had left behind. Out of nowhere came a rider from the left of them, his face masked by a ragged, faded kerchief, his gun pointed at Will. Jessica heard him cursing at her brother and the two exchanged gunfire.

"Jacob!" she shouted. Jacob fired a shot, then another, but they went wild. He turned his horse toward a nearby hill, and they rode higher up the small mountain. Will was no longer in sight, and only the crack of the gunshot could be heard. They reached the highest point and Jacob stopped his horse. He dismounted, then helped Jessica. He pulled her down to crouch beside him near a large rock. She followed, then tried to peek over the edge.

"Stay down," he whispered. She dropped to her belly. Jacob crawled over to the rock's ledge. "Good, he's still riding south," she heard Jacob say.

"He's safe?" Her breathing was irregular and she felt dizzy.

"For now." Jacob returned to her. "A man may be dead down there, so don't look down."

Jessica raised her hand to her mouth. She made the sign of the cross, and before her hand could finish, Jacob grabbed it and was leading her back to Otis. "We have to get out of here."

He looked around. "Down that way. Can you make it?"

She looked at where he pointed. It was rough, and her new boots were causing sores on her heels, but she was sure she could climb down into the valley on the west side of the hill. She nodded.

"Stay close. We'll have to get Otis down."

It took longer than expected. The land was gravely dangerous with slippery grasses between sharp rocks. Otis was difficult to encourage, but the two of them managed to coax him all the way down, his breath visible in the air with every snort and whinny. Once on the valley floor, Jacob gave his horse a quick drink and then they were off. The wind had picked up, blowing dirt into them. Jessica closed her eyes and buried her face into Jacob's back. Her thoughts went to the times she and Jacob raced in the field near their homes in Hartford. The time her horse went lame, and she had to ride to the stalls with him to get the stableman. How he commanded his horse to gallop, and how she had held on for dear life as they laughed freely. The wave of sweet nostalgia gave way to fear. Jacob moved Otis forward. "Yah!" he shouted, and she held on tighter.

"Will is headed south to a place we said we'd meet if we were ever separated in these parts," Jacob called back to her.

His voice was caught by the chilly wind as they cut through the landscape. "When will we be there?" she asked.

"A few days, maybe more," he said. "We're still heading south, Jess."

◦◦◦

The cave-like alcove in the hill gave Jessica and Jacob a place to bed down. Jacob lit a small fire, and they huddled together in front of the blaze.

"It's getting cold. We'll have each other for warmth, though," he said. His arm was wrapped around her, and she placed her head against his chest.

"Jacob, tell me what happened today. A man might be dead and Will is gone. I'm afraid for him."

Jacob kissed the top of her head. "I can't tell you not to be afraid, Jess, but Will got away. This isn't the first time he—we—got chased by someone whom Will had cheated at cards. This guy must have found out we were up in Medford again."

She lifted her head and turned to face him. "This is about gambling? Cheating at cards?"

"Or a woman," Jacob said matter-of-factly.

She was sitting upright now. "Not the first time? Good God, Jacob!"

Jacob reached around her and poked a stick at the fire. "Jess, calm down. I told you my life wasn't legit. Did you think I was kidding?"

"How can you go on like this?" she asked.

"Come here. You feel so good. It's the most comfort I've had in years."

Jessica remained seated upright, staring at him with tightened lips.

"All right, Jess, I'm sorry. We've both been through a lot. Get back here. I'm sorry."

There was nothing she could say. He drew her to him and wrapped his coat around them. His chest was warm and his heart beat strong.

"Are you taking me home, or do I have to find a stagecoach station? I'll get there one way or the other."

"I know you will. I was hoping you'd want to be with me."

"I will not stay with you. This life, this awful life you lead, is not for a woman—not for this woman anyway. I have a husband and a proper home." His chest heaved, and the breath he let out touched her face. The urge to be with him rose, yet she did not let it sway her.

"I wish to God your home was with me," Jacob said, "but I have no one to blame. I chose my life. I told you someday I'd be legit and have my own business. You didn't wait. You didn't have faith in me."

An awkward silence followed. "I tried," she whispered.

He grunted and cleared his throat. "Did you? How long before you married him? A month? Two?"

"I don't want to talk about this, not now. We're here together. For some reason, we're together."

He touched her cheek. "Are you warm enough?"

"Yes," she replied. "Tired mostly."

"Very tired? We might not have a chance to be alone like this again. Our timing is unpredictable."

Jessica chuckled. "To say the least."

He reached down and brought her lips to his. She kissed him, and the fury of passion ignited in her with a flush of heat. She pulled away, and he brought her back to him. This time, her head was buried in his chest. It wouldn't be right, yet there they were, away from everything that held them apart over the years. He removed her coat, then his own, and covered them with the blankets. Otis whinnied in the background, and a few crows gave their last end-of-day caws. The sun set early this time of year. They had a long night to share and no one to tell them it was wrong.

Chapter Forty-five

*J*acob took them along the Rogue River to the hiding place he hoped Will had escaped to.

The river's edge was cold and uninviting. The wind nipped at Jessica's ears and nose. She bravely rode behind him, hiding her face in his back. "How far, Jacob?"

"Not long now, Jess," he answered.

He told her he would have to take all the back trails he knew still remained—Indian trails, some overgrown, some still intact, others barely recognizable. Towns were being built up at an accelerated rate. "Damn civilization!" Jessica heard him curse on the most challenging paths.

They kept each other warm each night under the stars and in between the trees. A few kisses and sleep would take them. Last night, the kisses turned more passionate, reaching a dangerous boiling point. Jessica had to force herself to pull away. "I can't, Jacob." She had taken her blanket and slept on the other side of the fire. He didn't say a word, but she knew he was disappointed. He kept her at arm's length all day.

Finally, after nearly exhausting themselves and Otis, they came to a dense, wooded area. They walked into a small clearing by a huge boulder. Jessica smelled smoke. She looked at Jacob with wide eyes. "Could it be?"

Jacob let out two short yelps, then a longer one. They waited. Two long yelps and a short one came back. Jacob grabbed Otis's reins and practically ran with his horse. Jessica followed, hiking up her skirts and coat to step high over undergrowth.

Will stood by his campfire with a cigarette in one hand and a cup in the other, grinning from ear to ear. "Hey, it worked!" he said to Jacob.

Jacob went up to his cousin, took the butt from his hand, and pulled a long drag on it.

Letting out the smoke, he nodded. "Yep." His own grin matched his cousin's.

Jessica leapt for Will. "Thank God you're well!" She hugged him, then scolded him.

"I want to strangle you, Will Messing, for giving me such a scare! Gambling? I swear, I don't know how you've survived this far. Either of you!"

Will shrugged. "It's good to see that you both made it out." He turned to Jacob. "We have to talk."

Jessica waved her hand at them. "Go. Just make sure I get home soon."

Will and Jacob walked deeper into the woods out of earshot. "Jesus, that was Thompson I shot. Thankfully, he didn't die. I saw him get back on his horse and ride after me for a while, then turn around. Damn!"

Jacob walked back and forth. "He won't travel out of Oregon. You best never come back this way, cousin. Shit, I thought he was dead. Glad he isn't."

"We'll get to Clermont City. It's safe there," Will said.

"Yeah, there aren't any dirty saloons," Jacob lashed out.

"I need to get a different way of life, Jake. I've decided I don't want to die young."

"Glad to hear it," Jacob said.

"For now, let's get Jessica home. She's been through enough, Jake."

Arriving in Brandon, California on a warmish day at the end of November gave Jessica an uneasy feeling. Clermont City was only a day's ride. Her apprehension didn't make sense to her. This was her goal, after all. She felt alone and couldn't wait to be in her husband's arms. The past many weeks traveling with Jacob was not her life, nor would it ever be. She didn't wait for him. She married Caleb, and that was the way it was. She eased her shoulders, trying to calm her anxiety. Her and Jacob's love sat heavy in her heart, and she felt a pang of nostalgia for everything they were and everything they had become to each other.

The small, dusty town showed no signs of real comfort. Jacob stopped the horse in front of a line of storefronts that included a saloon. He and Jessica joined Will, who was already heading for a drink.

"Can we eat first?" Jessica asked wearily. She put her hand on her stomach and felt her ribs protruding under her bodice.

A passerby said, "They serve food and drink in there," and continued on his way.

They entered the dimly lit saloon and sat down at one of the small, worn, wooden tables. The smell of baking bread, mingled with the lingering odors of stale coffee, cigarette smoke, and booze, gave Jessica pause. She felt nauseous.

"What is it, Jess?" Will asked. "Are you feeling all right?"

"I'll be fine." She ordered a cup of tea and placed her hand to her mouth.

The men ate gladly of the offerings of biscuits and gravy and a slab of pork belly. They settled in with a shot of whiskey in their coffees and talked about their next route.

Jessica sipped her tea and nibbled on a dry biscuit. Her mind was cluttered with so many thoughts, her emotions were turned upside down. While Will and Jacob discussed business, she went outside for air.

Jacob and Will came out of the saloon, their bellies full and their spirits intact. Jacob was about to call out to Jessica when a man bumped into him. A short man, his head down, wild hair sprouting from his head offered, "'Scuse me."

"Hey, Levi," Will said casually.

Levi Landsburg looked up at the two men, squinting his eyes, then he opened them wide. "I'll be a son of a bitch!" he exclaimed.

"It's been a long time," Jacob announced with a grin.

Levi scratched his unkempt hair. "Well, I'll say it has!"

They shook hands and gave each other a pat on the back, then Will embraced the small man, almost picking him off the ground.

Levi caught his breath, and his face lit up to see his two friends. "What are you boys doing these days?" Before they could answer, he added in a lower voice, "Glad to see you made it out of Colorado."

Jacob found himself checking for eavesdroppers. Levi chuckled, then he looked at them with a serious face and said, "I was sorry to hear about your kin. Bad news, that was. Me and Caleb searched for weeks, and here you two found her. I'll be damned. Where is she? Resting, I reckon."

"Resting," Jacob answered.

Levi looked around them, then he laughed. "You know, they could have knocked me over with a tadpole when I found out he had married your kin. Sure is a small world." His toothy smile showed his amusement. He came in close. "A scout came looking for all of us. Caleb paid him off, and me and Cork led him out of town." He gave a wink. "Cork had some fierce words for him, and we thought he was out of our hair. Caleb thinks he had something to do with his wife's kidnapping. Can't say when Caleb will stop tearing himself up with guilt."

The cousins looked at each other, then back at Levi.

"You fellas heard anything? Does Rex Conrad ring any bells?

The sheriff came snooping around Caleb's place, too, but nothing came of it."

Will made sure his sister was out of earshot. Thankfully, he spied her several shops down the boardwalk.

Jacob stepped forward, running his hand over his chin. "Damn it. Never heard the name. We found her in a renegade Indian camp. No sign of any white men. We share the guilt, all of us, if that's the case." He swallowed the acid rising in his throat.

"Let's hope it blows over now that you got her with ya," Levi said. "Caleb is waiting hard on her return. Had to stop him more than once from going back out to find her. Well, we'll have to catch up on ol' times … yous, me, Cork, and Caleb." He laughed and scratched his disheveled hair.

The last person Jacob wanted to spend time with was Caleb, but he couldn't deny Levi the thought. "Good seeing you, Levi. We'll catch up for sure. Now we've got to get to our lodgings."

"Hell of a thing running into you boys!" He patted each on the shoulder and left them.

They stood in silence as they watched Levi enter the saloon, taking in the sight of their former campmate.

"Shit." Will looked over at Jessica. "What the hell are we supposed to do with that piece of information? Jess was taken because of us? We've got to find out what happened to this Rex Conrad. Caleb must know something."

Jacob shook his head. "Maybe Clermont City isn't as safe as we thought."

Chapter Forty-six

*W*ill opened the door to his and Jacob's second-floor room, then he turned to Jessica.

"Yours is the next door down, Jess," he said, handing her the key. "Are you sick?"

"She just needs some sleep," Jacob answered. "I'm going to stay with her for a while." He took the key from Will.

"Fine, do what you please," Will said. "I'm done in for the day."

Jessica remained in her own thoughts as Jacob glanced around the room. There was one narrow bed and a small table with a kerosene lamp next to it. A chest of drawers near the window offered some resemblance to a bedroom, but the plain, little room was a dim reminder of the comforts of a real home. The view from the dirty window looked down onto the main road. Jacob went over to it and checked on the horses.

"I'm afraid," she said. He turned around and saw a weary young woman standing so alone. "Things might well be very different when I return." Drawing himself from the window, he took her in his arms, his chest stabbed by sadness.

Jessica held on to him. Here and there her thoughts landed, her head hurt, her back ached, and her stomach refused to settle. Suddenly, her insides lurched, and she had to find the washroom. She pushed herself away and ran out into the hallway, desperately searching for the door that would end her suffering. She entered and turned the lock just as she heaved into the basin.

"Jessica," she heard Jacob say outside. He knocked again and again.

"I'm fine, Jacob, go back to the room."

"Open the door, Jess."

She splashed water on her face and cleaned up, then looked at her reflection in the small, scratched mirror above the sink. The person looking back was thin and tired, her skin was darkened by the sun, and her brown eyes were not as bright. Her straggly hair was mound atop her head like a nest, with a metal clip holding it together. Loretta's styling had long left its mark. She looked away then back again, hoping the true reflection of a pretty, young girl would appear, but it didn't change. Slowly, she emerged out to the hallway. There she found Jacob standing against the wall, his arms folded in front of him, his expression showing his annoyance. Her nausea turned to anger.

"I'm the one who's in this state, and you're mad? Well, you know where you can take your anger." She stormed past him and back into the room. He followed her, then slammed the door behind him.

"What in hell's name is the matter with you?"

She rubbed the back of her neck. "I feel sick. I ate something bad. I know I did. Snake or awful squirrel meat." Even the thought of it made her insides flop. "I look ugly! What will Caleb think?"

Jacob stepped toward her. "I'm sorry you're not feeling well. You look fine. A little bedraggled, but ... we all look that way. It's been a rough time."

She felt his arms around her. Sinking into his embrace, she let him lead her to the bed. He sat next to her, rubbing her back. "I told you to take some liquor with food. It kills all the bad stuff."

She was in no mood for 'I told you so.' She huffed and turned away.

"You're beautiful, Jess. You take my breath away every time I look at you." Her mood softened, and her body gave in to his.

"We could both use a hot bath. Did you happen to see one in there?"

"Mmm," she replied.

"Big enough for two?" His handsome face and loving smile soothed her to no end.

She accepted his invitation. Comfort was where she could find it, and right now, it was with him.

The next morning, Will decided to send the family another telegram, telling them they were in Brandon. He left Jacob at the hotel's small café where Jessica joined him.

"Slept in? Will's gone to wire the family."

Jessica took a breath and let it out. Her nausea was strong this morning. "That's good. I don't want to just show up. Your mother would be near hysterics," Jessica mused as she sat down.

He lit a cigarette. "So you've made up your mind?" He blew out the match and threw it on the tin plate in front of him, awaiting her answer.

Jessica was served a cup of warm tea without asking. She looked at him with a smile. "Thank you, Jacob."

"I know you like your tea in the morning."

She took a sip of the sharp, dark drink. The day was cloudy, but not too cold. She felt the air of her home, warmer than up north. After she finished the tea, she swirled the remaining leaves in the cup, then turned it upside down on the saucer and twirled the cup once, twice, thrice. Righting the cup, she looked inside and examined the remains. She wished she had her aunt June's talent for reading tea leaves.

"There's nothing at the bottom of a cup, Jess. You make your own destiny."

She placed the cup on the saucer. "Humph! We both know I have to return to my husband. I can't choose between the two of you. I have to decide which life I want for myself and my future."

"Caleb is not the man you think he is. He may have gone back to the reservation or gone on with his life with someone else. Why shouldn't you do the same ... with me?"

"He's not that way." She adjusted the skirt of her new dress, which was already looking worn. "Is this simply wishful thinking on your part?"

"Yep, I guess it is." He turned to the side of his chair and finished his cigarette while they waited for Will's return.

His body language piqued her curiosity. "So you believe I'll go home to a husband who has abandoned me?" Her body tensed, her eyes misting.

"I hope you don't, to be honest. I'll make something of my life. In time, you will see. I'll be what you want me to be."

Jessica turned to him. "I know."

After a short while, Will was back, ordering a cup of coffee. "Well, the die has been cast. There's no turning back now, cowboys. The man said they should receive it this afternoon. We'll be there tomorrow. I sent it to Burt." He sat down, taking his coffee from the waitress. "Hey, by the way, what did the doc have to say?" Will asked his sister.

"Doctor?" Jacob asked. "What the hell are you wasting good money on a doctor for, when it was just a little food disagreeing with her?"

Jessica ignored him and directed her answer at Will. "He told me to drink water, when I can, and he gave me pills to stop the nausea. I'll be fine."

"All right." Will changed the subject. "Jake and I decided to take you to Burt and June's first. He can take you up to your husband. We don't want to add to Caleb's burden."

"Burden? What burden?"

"Burden of emotions … at seeing you," he fumbled.

She agreed with her brother, feeling the weight in her own heart. She had her own plan, however. Having come so very far, in so many ways, she wanted to go back to the place where it all began. That night and the next, Jessica slept alone. She had to get used to not having Jacob with her.

Chapter Forty-seven

Rail River Acres

*J*essica straightened her back and placed her hands on her thighs, balancing herself on the horse. She dared not touch Jacob's back. The day was cloudy, and mist had formed on the river. It looked different from that day back in May when the sunshine and warmth gave her pleasure to paint by its refreshing, flowered banks. She looked at the figure in front of her. How could she leave him? A final, fleeting thought raced through her mind—*maybe it could work*—then it passed. Caleb waited. Finally, she would be back home, back in her husband's arms, back into the fold of her family. A tear slipped from her eye, and she let it fall down her face.

Cautiously raising her hand, she went to rest it on Jacob's back. Hesitating, she drew it down. They rode in silence. Her extraordinary experience was coming to its conclusion, only to open up a whole new chapter, one as uncertain as the weather itself. She looked at the landscape, wet and green. Fear swept through her. *Do I still have a husband, or has he taken another woman, another life?*

Jacob's hand reached around and found hers. He brought it to his waist and held on to it while they rode. She let her tears fall freely. She had earned the right to grieve.

The two horses with their riders arrived at the banks of the Rail River. The sound of the water finding its way downstream along the green grasses and dormant branches made for a peaceful, winter scene. Jessica had pointed out a path from the dirt road that led them to the place she feared she would never see again. She had one thing to do before reuniting with Caleb.

Will dismounted. Jacob swung his leg over Otis's head and jumped down, then helped Jessica dismount. "You won't have to do that again," she commented as she found the ground. His sad expression didn't make this easier for her. She straightened her dress and coat, still feeling the motion of the horse. Standing alongside the men, she got her legs under her. It had been a long day, and the sun hung low in the sky. The earth beneath spoke as if to welcome her back, and she stooped down to touch its cool dampness. It was late in November and quiet. The birds weren't singing as they had been that May morning. The flowers were asleep, and the woodland was less dense. She stayed touching the ground longer than was comfortable for either man, but she was glad they quietly stood vigil over her.

Her tears dropped to the cool earth as she relived the moment that Blue Heron grabbed her and set her upon his giant horse. She was no longer the young woman he had captured. Her innocence laid buried in the ground, lost to her forever. She rose and turned to her brother, and they exchanged a loving look.

"Sis, let's go to Aunt June's. You don't have to do this alone."

She sighed softly and with resignation shook her head. Then she placed her hand on Jacob's arm. "I have to do this my way. Will, I'll see you both at Aunt June's in a few days. Tell them I am anxious to see them, but I need time with Caleb." She gave her brother a hug and a kiss on the cheek. "And don't you two go off before then," she added with a grin.

"Oh, don't worry about that," Will said. "I'm planting my back side to one of June's kitchen chairs, and that's where you'll find me." The three travelers chuckled through liquid eyes. "Now go and see your husband." He kissed her cheek and went for his horse. She noticed him swipe a tear off his face. "I'll catch up with you down the road, Jake."

She turned to Jacob. He took her hand and asked, "Where is your home?"

"Just over that knoll." Her finger trembled slightly as she pointed to where she was going.

"I'll stay until I see you over it." He gripped her hand. "Jess, are you sure? I know I'm not a safe bet, but that will change. Give me a chance. I promise I'll be a bigger man than I am now. Please, Jess, reconsider."

"Oh, please don't make this any harder for us." She hiccupped with emotion.

His strong arms were around her, and she let herself stay with him for a while longer. Then his lips found hers. She held his kiss, not wanting to be the first to unlock their lips and bring an end to their time together. Releasing herself from him, she touched his damp face. He cleared his throat, and she took a step back. He mounted Otis. It was time for her to walk home.

Climbing over the knoll, she knew she was out of his sight. He would ride back to his parents' home. What will he tell them? She prayed it would be only what they could handle. Her heart ached painfully in her chest, the sadness colliding with her anxiety. When she and Jacob meet in a few days, she will be Caleb's wife. Again, she would tuck their love in a secure place in her heart.

The expansive field laid out before her. She took in the sights and smells of the land she had so longed for. It felt too vast to her now and she quickened her pace, but her courage began to wane and her legs became wobbly. She knelt on the cold grass, surveying the field. Just a little farther, and she would be able to see the house. A chill breeze touched her face, and she thought of their warm stove, her kitchen, her art room, their bed, her chickens, and Suzy the cow. She smiled. It would still be there … he would still be there. There was only one way to find out, and that was to cross this field. Her resolve strengthened, and she continued with great purpose.

Chapter Forty-eight

*P*oking the fire to encourage its flames, Caleb could barely control his anxiety. His wife would be home soon. He cursed Will again for his vagueness. Which direction they were coming from, his telegram did not say. He couldn't work today. He roamed the field and walked along the river, then into the woods and back. He found himself nearly running home when he thought he heard a horse approach. Turned out to be his imagination. Deciding to stay close to the house, he worked his land and took care of the livestock. He loosened some hay in the barn and brushed down Lightfoot. Still, his energy could not be dampened.

The hours ticked by excruciatingly slowly. After a quick meal of bread and cheese, he stepped out onto the porch, tucking his shirt into his pants and straightening his hair back into a queue. Boones came around the house with a low bark, then a louder one. It caught Caleb's attention, and he looked out over the field. "What'd ya see, Boy?" Boones' whole back side moved with his vigorous tail wagging. Caleb spied a figure rising up from the land. As his heart beat wildly, he controlled his reaction. She wouldn't be alone. It must be a lost stranger. Before Caleb could hold Boones back, the dog took off, running into the field. Caleb stepped down and began to walk toward a woman running to him. His throat tightened. He walked faster until he was running himself.

Jessica's heart burst with joy at the sight of her husband. "Caleb!" She tried to cry out to him, but her voice was weak with emotion. Boones ran into her legs, and she knelt down to take in the softness of his fur. She rose and Caleb was upon her. He swept her up in his arms, his strong, loving arms, lifting her off the ground. The land echoed the sound of a man and woman weeping together, reunited.

She was on her feet again. Caleb placed her at arm's reach. "Is it you?" His face was wet and stricken with awe.

With a quivering voice, she could only say, "It's me."

They looked at each other for a while, then embraced again, now with Boones jumping on her, demanding attention.

"Oh Boones, my good boy! How you've grown!" Again, she buried her head into his soft fur, then kissed his forehead, laughing through her tears. He sniffed her and licked her face. Then she was in Caleb's arms again, his voice muffled in her hair. "I never thought I'd feel you again. I thought this day would never come." She could only hold on to him as he curved his tall body to surround her.

"I can't let you go." He wept with a slight laugh. "The spirits returned you. It's a miracle!" She felt him pull her away from him, then he surveyed her from head to toe. "Are you all right? Are you hurt at all? Why are you alone? Where's Will, where's Jacob?"

Jessica heard the questions rush out of him and she was overwhelmed. She looked into his liquid, blue eyes. "I'm well. I wanted them to leave me by the river. They're at Burt and June's." She took a moment to survey her husband. He was as handsome as ever. A little thinner, perhaps, his hair much longer, some white in his goatee, but he looked remarkably well. Maybe too well.

Caleb examined his wife. He had expected her to be dressed in the same clothing he had last seen her in—the hand-sewn smock over the light-blue day dress. The brown, wool coat she wore was dirt-stained and tattered on the hem. Her face was thin and her eyes were a bit sunken, not as bright or lively as he had remembered. They held something else, and he recognized the look of someone having experienced a terrible ordeal. He felt desperate to take it from her.

He ran his hand over his goatee. "Jessica, I'm so sorry, forgive me. I should have gone with you to the river. I … I can't forgive myself." His words were choked with emotion.

Jessica pressed into him. "Don't torture yourself. Let's be happy now. We'll have time to talk later."

Caleb squeezed her slight body until she laughed. He took her hand. "Come on, let's go inside. I have lunch and cider."

Jessica felt faint as she sat down at the kitchen table. She swept her hands over the smooth, wooden surface and placed her head down.

"You're not well, Jess." His hand was on her forehead. "Let me get you that cider."

He took two pretty glasses down from the shelf, hand painted with flowers and golden rims. He poured the beverage into each of them, then handed one to her. She drank it down right away. As she placed the glass on the table, she noticed that the expensive, delicate crystal wasn't anything she had owned in her modest kitchen.

He quickly gave her a refill. "I can't believe you're here, Jessica. The telegram said you'd arrive today, but I … I. …" His shoulders lowered and he shook his head. "I'm in shock, to tell you the truth."

"So am I. It's been a long way home, Caleb. I'm so happy to be back." She began to sob.

He bent over and put his arms around her bony shoulders. She patted his hands. "We'll be back to ourselves soon, won't we?"

"Yes, and the sooner the better."

Jessica touched his beautiful face. Her hand went to her swirling head. "I think I need to lie down."

Caleb immediately stood up and helped her to the bedroom. She entered the room, and a rush of memories flooded over her— the lovely simplicity, the quiet retreat she often dreamed of while she had lain on the ground, hurt and frightened. "It's just as I left it."

She was still wearing her boots and coat, and Caleb helped her remove them. She saw him looking at her dress. "I had to get a new one." His eyes showed his despair, and she had no words to comfort him.

She climbed into the bed and rested her head on the soft pillow. She began to shiver, and Caleb placed a heavy blanket over her. He leaned over and kissed her mouth. She felt his warm lips and wanted more. "Don't go." After reassuring her he'd be by her side, she closed her eyes, inhaled a ragged intake of air, then her body relaxed as she exhaled. She had made it home.

Chapter Forty-nine

*J*essica woke from her nap, and for a moment, she didn't know where she was. Then she smiled as the day's events came rushing back to her. She raised herself to peer out the window above the bed. The forest behind the house seemed innocent enough, but it made her ill at ease. She pushed aside the covers and found her coat. The room was warm with the small, wood burner crackling softly in its hearth, yet she felt chilled.

As soon as she entered the main room, the heat from the large, potbellied stove continued to bring warmth to her. It was a luxury she would never take for granted again. She spied Caleb sitting on the porch. Reluctant to leave the heat, she put on her boots and coat and went outside. He darted up when he saw her. "Did you sleep? How are you feeling? Are you hungry?"

Yawning, she rubbed her neck and stretched her back. "Yes, I did sleep. It was lovely. And I'm starving."

He had put together sliced apples, cold meat from last night's roast, and more bread and cheese.

"This is the most delicious food I've ever tasted." He watched her eat, and her moans both touched him and grieved him. She drank more cider and again examined her glass.

He saw her drag her finger over the topography of the hand-painted flowers. "Where did you get this?" Her tone lacked judgement.

Caleb stopped eating. The glasses were a gift from Jane, and he cursed himself for overlooking such a detail. "From a friend of Sally's." By the look on her face, his answer was inadequate.

He pushed his chair away from the table and brought his napkin to his lips. He paused and gathered his thoughts. "Mrs. Jane Cabot is staying with Ben and Sally. She thought I needed some refinement, I suppose."

Her face was unreadable. "Jane Cabot? I didn't think that type of woman interested you." She gave him no time to respond. "When I return these pretty glasses to her, I'll be sure to thank her for taking care of my husband while I was away."

Taken aback, he felt his defenses mounting. "It was nothing. She didn't take care of me. I mean, not in the way you're thinking. You won't have to return them. I'll just give them to Sally. There's no harm in receiving a gift."

A raise of her shoulder had him feeling helpless. She didn't believe him. "It's fine, Caleb. We've been through a lot. I needed comfort, too."

Now the tide shifted dramatically. "I don't want to know, Jess."

She sighed. "Can we go back, Caleb? To the time before I went down to the river?"

Reaching for her hand, his insides quaked. All he wanted was her—to be with her, to be in her. Nothing else mattered. She smiled, and it released all his guilt and jealousy. For now, he had his life back.

After a few shy moments as they reacquainted themselves with each other, it seemed as if she had never been apart from him. His body felt miraculous to her. She was finally touching him and loving him, and he was loving her back. His desire for her remained as strong as ever, and he released every bit of it as he brought them both to the most intimate moment they had ever experienced together. Catching her breath, she turned and formed herself into his body. They talked softly with one another about the land, the dog, the weather, and his silversmithing, along with her family and her desire to see them. Neither of them brought up her kidnapping or her rescue, even if the room seemed full of anticipation, waiting for a story, waiting for answers.

Jessica rolled over on her back and gave the most satisfied sigh she had ever released from her being. Caleb brought the heavy quilt over them. He gently placed his hand on her belly, slowly moving it over its taut surface. "We'll have to fatten you up." He continued to caress it, and now she took his hand and put it higher as he went for her full breast. He reached down and tasted its sweetness, then he kissed her stomach and went even lower under the covers. Jessica moved nervously, bringing him upward, and he returned to her breast and then to her lips and neck.

She snuggled into him under the warm blankets. He felt strong—perhaps strong enough to weather what she needed to tell him, but not now. He whispered, "I love you." She returned the sentiment as a few tears escaped, running down her face, wetting their flesh.

Chapter Fifty

The next morning, Caleb and Jessica sat in the kitchen as they had each morning before her kidnapping. He drank his coffee, she sipped her tea. The familiar brew of dark leaves never tasted so good.

"I have to see Ben this morning. I'll bring them the good news. They'll want to see you," Caleb said.

Jessica leaned back in her chair, her hands wrapped around the warm cup. "I'll be happy to see them, too." She paused and looked at her husband. "Don't forget to take the glasses with you."

Caleb put down his cup. "Jessica, I formed no attachments while you were away. I feel I can never satisfy you with words, so let my actions speak for me. I will go and tell them the good news. My wife is back, and my life is happy again." He laughed and came to her, leaning down to kiss her mouth. She received his kiss gladly, praying that he would still be as happy after she told him of her condition.

"Tell the Loggins they may come by in a few days."

Jessica rolled her head to relieve the heaviness that sat on her shoulders, the soreness reminding her of her travels. Standing in the middle of the parlor, she felt like a stranger in her own home. With her hands on her hips, she surveyed the room. Boones watched her every move. Her art room called to her. She was afraid to look inside. What was it now? A room touched by Jane Cabot? She would get the whole story from Sally. Perhaps it was just more work space for Caleb, or simply empty, cleared of all signs that she was ever an artist there.

Cautiously, she opened the door. To her surprise, it had remained untouched. He hadn't removed a single thing. The smell of paint and paper filled her nose. She let her eyes fall on one thing, then the next. So familiar was it to her, as if it all had waited so patiently. This room held the passion that hadn't left her. It couldn't be stolen or kidnapped, nor ransomed at any price.

Placing her hand on her chest, she took a breath and let it out. The half-finished painting of a landscape laid on her lap easel. The art supplies she had taken down to the river on that dreadful day sat on a shelf, along with the paper and wooden carrier. *He had retrieved them and placed them here.* Her guts churned. The paint-stained rags. Brushes neatly organized, art books, the rug on the floor, the stool she sat on. She closed her eyes and let the sharp pain of sadness run through her. "Oh, Caleb."

Slowly, she lifted the drawing she had done that fateful day, and without much contemplation, she ripped it into small pieces. She turned to her easel. The oil painting of the land she lived on was near completion. She examined her strokes, the mood of color. This one would hang in their home.

Her mind went back to Blue Heron on the river and the light that exposed his body. The dense forest, the open plains, Medford, the cave. The memories flooded her mind with color, shapes, and mostly, the deep need to paint. She looked at her supplies. She'd have enough to start on one of the blank canvases she had prepared before that day. Her heart beat strong, and she wanted to claim her life again. She closed her eyes and rubbed her chest while humming a quiet tune she learned from the Native People. Her body relaxed and she continued to study the room.

A finished painting neatly wrapped in brown paper and tied with string sat on the floor in the corner. She had intended to give it to Mr. Talbot to bring to the Gate's Gallery in Oakland. She gave a short laugh and picked it up, then gingerly tore the wrapping off, exposing a painting of Nob Hill in San Francisco, with a scene of Chinatown mixed into the background. It was good, in her opinion, and she remembered being pleased at the time she created it. She looked at the signature—J. Lingerhoph. Her hand touched the raised strokes, and she examined the light source as she had done so many times while painting it.

It was a beautiful day in the big city, and she had traveled there with Caleb to shop for his smithing supplies. While he went about his business, she painted. Passersby made pleasant comments on her progress as they briefly stopped to look at her easel. The hotel they stayed at was elegant, and she felt swept off her feet. Caleb had little use for hotels, yet he had chosen a comfortable room for them on Nob Hill. A smile crossed her face, followed by the swell of love and guilt rising deep inside her. Would life ever be that simple again?

Eyeing the signature, she squinted and her lips curled. *Why should he get all the credit?*

She decided then and there to kill off J. Lingerhoph. The pen name no longer suited her. This made her laugh, and she felt the release of so much pent-up emotion. She could laugh again. She could be free to paint as she liked under her own name, Jessica Cantrell. Aloud, she made her vow. "I'll paint the vivid colors of life's experience, my experience!"

She took inventory of her paints, and as she touched each square of color, each brush, each tube of oils, she did so with a rebirth filled with purpose and joy for all she had painted and all she would paint. She turned to another shelf where a small box sat alone. It was the only item not in its original place. Her mind must be mistaken. She took it down, and the lid came off too easily.

Jacob's beads, his letters, her drawing of them by Mary's Pond in Hartford. Why hadn't she burned them all?

She knew the answer, and a sadness rose in her. Touching her belly, she returned the box to the shelf, then the world spun. Closing her eyes, she put a hand to her hot cheek. Her mouth was filled with saliva. She was going to be sick. She ran outside and vomited, a reminder of what she had brought home. It was too soon ... too soon to rediscover her life. Her impatience to make everything right again, to paint the world she had seen and lived through, to put Jacob in his place, and mostly, to bring Caleb fully back to her was overwhelming. She returned to the parlor and sat on her paisley chair. She would need her strength to face her family and Jacob, and most of all, the verdict Caleb would hand to her after she told him she was carrying Jacob's child.

His wife was back, his life whole again. Somehow it felt unreal to Caleb. She rested in their home as he walked over to Ben and Sally's. Wanting to rush back and protect her, he picked up his pace. The two flower-painted glasses clinked together in the sack, and he became aware he might break them. In fact, his instincts told him to chuck them in the woods. He dropped the sack by the side of the trail and pushed it into the brush. He'd take care of that later. Facing Jane made him nervous. He knew he had no reason for it, yet they had developed a friendship and he had to admit he had grown fond of her. Today, his love for his wife filled him like nothing else could or ever would.

Ben and Sally welcomed him with hugs and congratulations, their relief showing. Questions about her health, the circumstances of her disappearance, and when they would be able to see her assaulted him. He raised his hands. "All in good time," he said with a chuckle. In minutes, they were sharing a glass of wine and toasting to her safe return. Jane came down the stairs and joined them.

"I'm very happy for you, Caleb," she said. "It's always such a blessing when our prayers get answered." To Caleb, her voice lacked happiness, and he wondered in her world of prayer if this was truly the outcome she sought. He felt uncomfortable in his own skin.

"Jane is leaving us tomorrow," Sally offered. "We will miss her so very much."

Jane took a glass of wine from Ben. After taking a sip, she smiled at Sally but said nothing.

The awkwardness was palatable, and Caleb was ready to return to his wife. After assuring the Loggins they would see Jessica soon, he left the house. Entering the trail, he heard soft footsteps behind him. He turned around. It was Jane.

"I can't leave without saying a proper good-bye. In private."

Caleb nodded. She came to him and took his arm. "May we walk together for just a minute? One last visit?"

"Jane, I have to get back to Jessica. She's fine, but not completely well."

They walked in silence. He stopped halfway down the trail. "Thank you for your friendship, Jane."

She tipped her head to the side. "It could have been much more, but circumstances have changed. I will remember you with great fondness and wonder what could have been."

He snickered. "What would you have done with this man you have so little in common with? I have a past, I don't attend church, I drink, and I have been known to gamble. Not quite the ideal gentleman for a lady such as yourself."

"And yet, we are friends. My life is more than church going and properness. I'm afraid you'll never see the real me."

He looked down at the beautiful woman eyeing him with a coy expression. Clearing his throat, he brought her back to Earth. "I hope you have a good life and find what you need and want. I ..."

"If you're ever in need of a shoulder to lean on or an ear to listen, please think of me. Here is my address. I'd hate for us to never. ..."

The puff of air escaping his lungs was visible in the cold air. "I'm sorry."

She held her head up high. "No need for apologies. Will you take my address?"

Reluctantly, Caleb accepted the cream-colored, folded piece of paper. A hint of her perfume hit his nose as he unbuttoned his coat and placed it into his shirt pocket.

"Don't expect anything," he said.

"Just knowing you have it makes me feel as if we are still friends." She reached up and kissed his cheek, then turned and walked away.

Watching her disappear around the bend, her skirts rustling against the brush, gave him pause. A second of grief hit him. Then he heard the faint sound of glass muffled in a burlap sack. He closed his eyes, then opened them. Shaking his head, he headed home. Again, the freedom of the trails spoke to him. He vanquished the thought, yet what had Jessica gone through, and how would it affect him, his marriage, and everyone around them? Holding no illusions of the real world, he knew it wasn't going to be a smooth adjustment. His reaction to parting with Jane proved that.

Chapter Fifty-one

*I*t was time to reunite with her family. Jessica looked through her clothes as if they were old friends. For a moment, she indulged in her choices. Yet, the array of dresses, blouses, skirts, and shoes, along with the many accessories she had acquired, began to repel her. The frivolity of it all was obscene. She chose a simple blouse and skirt ensemble. Her dark-maroon waistcoat with the high fur collar and her leather gloves and wool hat would stave off the cool day. With a heavy blanket in the open carriage, she looked forward to the luxury of riding in a proper transport, even if theirs was a second hand one.

Filled with nervous anticipation, she tried to steady her nerves. Waves of nausea swept over her. She was sure the whole clan would be there. She fiddled with her hair in front of the mirror and caught her husband's grave expression as he entered the bedroom. The last pin entered her upswept bun. "Almost ready," she said.

"I have something to tell you, sweetheart."

Her heart skipped a beat. He called her sweetheart—that was a good sign. Jane Cabot was on her way back to San Francisco. *What now?*

Caleb took one of her hands in his own. "There's no easy way to tell you this. Your father passed away some months ago."

Sharply withdrawing her hand, she looked at him in disbelief.

"No, that can't be. No! Oh God, he left without knowing I was safe." She placed her hand to her stomach. She felt as if a furnace had been ignited in her belly. She held on to Caleb for support. He led her to the bed.

He rubbed her back. "I know this is a shock. He was buried alongside his parents in Hartford. We can travel there someday if you want to visit his grave."

"Where is my mother?"

"Your mother decided to let her lawyers close the estate, and the house is up for sale. She arrived here last week and is living with Burt and June. Do you want to wait until tomorrow? It will give you time. You need more time to adjust."

Jessica gripped his hand, her chin trembling. "I need to see my family."

The carriage wheels crunched on the gravel drive as they came around to the front of the yellow bungalow. Jessica was captured by its warm coziness even in the middle of winter. It was like a second home to her where she lived before Caleb, where she found her roots in art, where she healed. She had come through so much since then. How would her family see her now? Her mother waited.

Caleb wished with all his heart he could have stayed behind. Since Burt told him of Thomas's passing, he learned Bethany had left Hartford right after her husband's funeral to come live in Clermont City. It was disappointing news and he hadn't seen her yet. He knew when she laid eyes on him, it wouldn't be with a smile and warm greeting. Along with her, there would be the odd reuniting of his old partners in crime, Will and Jacob. What had he let himself get into? He could have made excuses. Burt would have been happy to come get Jessica and whisk her off to her family. Wasn't the factory always overwrought with orders this close to Christmas? *What the hell was I thinking?* Just then, Jessica placed her hand on his arm. "I don't think I could do this alone, Caleb." The acute need to protect her washed away his previous thoughts.

As he helped Jessica step from the carriage, he spied Bethany from the corner of his eye coming down the walk—alone. She took her daughter in her arms and gently rocked her as they cried together. "Father, he ... he's. ..." He heard his wife cry in muffled tones. He stepped aside to let them have their reunion.

Caleb entered the house. He found Burt and an anxious June, along with Jacob and Will. He was relieved the rest of the family had stayed away. June hurried past him with a handkerchief to her mouth. The three men exchanged looks filled with the past and the unknown of the present.

"Thank you for bringing her back." Caleb offered his hand to Jacob. They shook with equal pressure. He couldn't read the man's face, but then he never could. He offered Will his hand.

Will shook it earnestly with a broad smile. "I guess you're stuck with us now, Caleb."

Burt greeted Caleb with a hearty embrace. "I'm happy for you, son. This is indeed a very happy day for our family. Will tells me you boys met some time ago. I was surprised you hadn't told us yourself."

Caleb felt his worlds folding in on him and he looked around, at a loss for words.

"Some things are better unspoken, Father," Jacob interjected.

Just then, the women came in all flustered and teary-eyed.

"Uncle Burt!" Jessica ran to the giant man and felt his fatherly embrace. She looked up into his eyes. "Caleb told me about Father." Her tears spilled. Burt hugged her again. "I'm very sorry, my dear."

She turned to her brother. Will touched her back. "There was nothing we could do, Jess. Father was his own man."

She looked up at Will. "I know, but I wish I had seen him before—"

"I know, Sis."

Jacob was by her side. "Thomas was a good man. It's a real loss to our family."

Jessica acknowledged Jacob's statement but offered little else. She could barely meet his eyes. She followed the others into the dining room. June stood at the front of the table next to her seated husband. Her emotions poured out as Burt handed her his handkerchief. She fixed her apron and wiped her tears.

Her aunt looked tired. Her face had aged, and the greenish glint in her eyes had dimmed. As if reading her mind, Jacob said, "Mother, for once, sit down and let someone else do the work. Where is your housekeeper?"

"Thank you, Jacob, but I wouldn't think of it. I've looked forward to this for a long time. Hannah is having some well-deserved time off with a friend. She made acquaintances with Mrs. Winsor's maid. Oh, she will be so happy to see you, Jessica."

"I look forward to seeing her, too, but I'm glad to hear she's socializing." With all eyes on her, Jessica surveyed the table. She felt her insides stir. She hadn't seen this much food in a long time. It was an abundance she found hard to take in—a roasted chicken, two chickens to be exact, dishes mounded with root vegetables, and a large bowl of mashed potatoes. The brown gravy came to the top of its server, and a butternut squash soup permeated the air with the scents of cinnamon and cloves. There was no end to the biscuits and butter. She wasn't sure her stomach could hold more than a bite or two. She sipped on some water, aware that she was the center of attention. Lowering her head, she fought to stave off the swelling desire to vomit. She heard her mother saying

248

something about an ordeal and telling her story in her own time. "Mother?"

"I said you will tell your story in your own time, but I pray it wasn't too harsh and you will find discretion in accounting it to your aunt and me."

"Yes, of course," Jessica replied, feeling the world tilt. When June went back into the kitchen, she stood up to help her. The room spun, and the floor was at her cheek. She lay there stunned, her head pounding in her skull.

"Oh, my Lord!" she heard her mother shout. A platter of food hit the wood surface near her head, and Aunt June's feet came into view surrounded by broken ceramic and sweet potatoes.

The strong arms of two men lifted her off the floor, and she saw Caleb and Jacob staring down at her, each with concerned expressions. She put her hand to her head, hoping to stop the whirling motion. Her thoughts went to the time she fell off of Blue Heron's horse and she feared she might be there again. This lovely place with the beautiful food and feeling of safety might all be a dream. Had she escaped? Were she and Jacob together? Had she really walked home from the Rail River into her husband's arms? "Uncle Burt," she murmured as his large hand placed a cool cloth onto her forehead.

"Yes, we're all here. You'll be fine now. We're here." She felt herself falling back into the arms of her husband. Her body was being carried upstairs. The flower ceiling looked down on her.

Jessica woke up with June sitting by her side and the smell of beef broth steaming in a bowl next to the bed. "I think I might be back home right now with Mother downstairs preparing dinner, and Father expected any minute," she said weakly.

June patted her arm. "You are home, my dear, safe and sound. Your mother is getting another cloth for your head. Your good father is looking down at you, knowing what you must have suffered. I know he would be mighty proud of his daughter."

Jessica tried to rise. "I've been selfish, Auntie. I only thought of myself and didn't think how it would affect anyone else, most of all, Caleb."

"You better lie back now and not get all worked up. That's probably what caused your fainting in the first place. I want you to promise me to take good care of yourself. A little selfishness isn't a bad thing, I've come to know."

"Yes, Auntie, I promise. It's good to see you. It always feels like home when you're around. I'm so happy to see Mother here. I know what it must have taken for her to leave Hartford."

Just then, Bethany entered the room and placed the cool, damp cloth on her daughter's forehead. "It did take a lot for me to leave. I couldn't at first, but I'm glad I did. We are all together here."

Jessica touched her mother's hand and squeezed it, hoping her love for family extended to Caleb. "Mother, have you talked with Caleb since you've been here? You must have seen by now what a good man he is."

Bethany stood above her, pressing the damp cloth to her forward. She gave a small huff. Jessica gently removed her hand. "I don't think I need that anymore."

Her mother stood straight, folding her hands in front of her, clutching the cloth. "I must say what I feel, Jessica."

June cleared her throat. "Now, Bethany? Must it be now?"

"Did you bring many things from the house in Hartford?" Jessica cut in, hoping to stave off her mother's disapproval as long as possible. She held her breath.

Her mother pursed her lips. "Caleb and I haven't talked since I arrived. He seemed set on ignoring any of my help." She took a breath and let it out. "I think he isn't suited for you. He should have known better than to let you go off on your own. He told Burt to tell me I wasn't welcome in his home, your home."

"Now, Bethany, that's not the whole story." June turned to Jessica. "He said he would rather not have her visit quite yet."

"I think it's time we consider a different situation for you. I simply can't bear to know you are in that place, that place where. …" Wringing her hands, Bethany turned away.

"Mother, I understand."

Coming back to face her daughter, she perked up and held

Jessica's hand. "You do? Then you'll come to live with me? I'll be purchasing a home of my own soon. Your uncle has shown me some very nice possibilities." She patted her eyes and smiled at June.

"No, Mother. I only said I understood. It must have been just awful for you and the family not knowing if I were dead or alive." She sat up and leaned forward, taking her mother's hand. "But I will not be moving. I will stay with Caleb. I fought hard to get back here. You will never know how much I tried to get away and come home, to *my* home."

Bethany withdrew her hand. "I see." She turned to the door. "I will have to accept the fact that my daughter no longer cares about the emotional welfare of her mother or her family."

Before Jessica had the time to react, her mother was out of the room. She laid back. "Auntie, would you please ask Caleb to come up?"

June stood and smoothed her apron. "Your mother has been very upset by these events. She's not always herself. She was hoping you would be there for her. I tried to tell her that we are all here for her, but she won't listen. She insisted on having you live with her."

Jessica sighed. "Poor Mother." She looked at her aunt and shrugged her shoulders. "There's nothing I can say. Will you talk to her, Auntie?"

"Of course, my dear. Now let me go get your husband. He's sick with worry."

Caleb sat by her side, his hand on her stomach, his blue eyes intensely peering at her.

"I think we should leave as soon as you feel up to the ride home."

"No, I want to stay. I'm feeling better now." The broth was restorative. She felt her life force reenter her body. "Just a little while longer, Caleb."

She rested on the couch downstairs with a warm cup of tea. Her mother and aunt talked in the kitchen, and the men had retreated to the porch. Burt was in his study, most likely retrieving his favorite port wine. Jessica remembered how he loved a glass of it after a hearty meal. She positioned herself to spy on them, but she could only see the back of Will. How she wished she could be a fly on the porch railing. Then she heard Jacob's voice raised in anger. Pulling herself up from the couch, she listened intently, the words of the men coming in and out of reach.

Chapter Fifty-two

$\int$ tepping out with the others, Caleb drew up his collar. The day was getting cool. Will and Jacob's coats were even more tattered than his wife's. What she must have gone through.

"How is she?" Jacob's voice was full of concern.

"She'll be fine. She needs to rest ... at home. Now tell me, how the hell did you find my wife? Where on earth was she?"

Will turned to his brother-in-law and patted him on the back. "This is one hell of a thing, isn't it? Who would have thought, you and I becoming kin? How the hell did this happen?"

His tone was dryer than Caleb expected. He wasn't pleased about the circumstances, either. "Yeah, and here I thought I was well rid of you two. Now answer my questions."

Jacob faced Caleb straight on. "You're not our boss anymore, Cantrell."

"Tell me how you found my wife."

Will stepped up and related the story. In conclusion, he said, "I'm rushing through it for now. Maybe later I can tell you the details. I don't want the women overhearing this."

Caleb cupped his chin and rubbed his whiskers. "So I was closer than I thought. Jesus, I heard about the renegades but had no idea. ..." He shook his head. "So why the gap in time? You could have made that ride in a little over a week."

Jacob leaned on the railing of the porch, his arms folded in front of him. "We had to take her up north with us. Business there we had to tend to. We got her back here as soon as we could."

"Is that so?" Caleb could feel the rivalry between him and Jacob rising from the past. A lifetime ago, he would have taken this man on no matter the challenge. Time suddenly felt squeezed, and the past was now mixed with the present. "Did you know she was my wife?"

"Yes."

Jacob's defiant answer riled Caleb. "You son of a bitch." He came in closer. "I know about you and her."

Will cut in. "Gentlemen, gentlemen. Let's not get into this here. Listen, Caleb, she's back safe and sound. Let it go, both of you!"

Jacob backed away and Caleb relaxed his shoulders. The tension was thick in the air.

"So we ran into Levi in Brandon," Will began. "What's this about a scout? Was Jessica taken as some bargaining chip?"

Caleb glanced at the window. His wife sat on the couch, sipping tea. In a lowered voice, he recounted the meeting with Rex Conrad. "I don't know where he is now. I haven't talked to Jessica about any of this. I'm sure she has plenty to tell me."

"Do you think he hired the Indian to take her?"

Caleb had a hard time reconciling her disappearance with the circumstances of his past.

He scratched his chin. "I think so. Damn, Harper was the only one they took in alive. He spilled his guts for clemency."

Jacob became agitated. "Christ, what do we do now?"

Will stared at the porch floor and Caleb stared at Jacob, shaking his head.

"All right. We do nothing and hope this is the end of it," Will offered. "I doubt they'll send another scout out for us."

"I hope you're right," Caleb said. "It's understood we keep this under our hats?"

The cousins nodded in agreement.

"You don't have to worry about us, Caleb. Jake and I will be clearing out of here pretty darn soon. We've got plans."

"What plans?" Burt asked as he came onto the porch with glasses and the port.

Jacob looked out beyond the porch, his hands on the railing. "Our plans."

"Before you go into all that," Burt began, "I've got something to tell you boys that might change things."

Jacob took the glass of wine from his father. Will sat on the edge of one of the chairs, and Caleb decided to remain standing. He was finding it difficult to compose himself. He wanted to take Jacob aside and get to the real question—what happened on the trails between him and Jessica?

Burt poured the wine. "We set up a reward for the safe return of Jessica, and ... well ... looks as if you've earned that reward." He had Will's and Jacob's attention. "It's a good sum of money, boys. I think you should take a hard look at the advantages this could present. Make something of yourselves, in a proper way."

Jacob turned to Caleb. "I don't need your money."

"Don't worry, it's not my money."

"What?" Will looked hard at Caleb. "You didn't think my sister was worth putting your money up for?"

"Now listen here," Burt chimed in. "It doesn't matter where we came up with it. The point is, you have a great opportunity in front of you. It's time to re-evaluate your positions in life."

Jacob took a sip of wine, then glared at Caleb. "Doesn't matter. It can go back to where it came from. I didn't bring her back for money."

"Jesus," Caleb breathed out.

"Yeah, I have my pride, Cantrell."

"Your poor man's pride will get you nowhere." Caleb softened. It would be of no use to get into it with Jacob. He would just as soon have them leave without the money. Let them earn their way.

Will remained silent as his cousin fought aloud with his conscience. Caleb could see the wheels turning in Will's head.

"Caleb's right, Jacob," Burt implored him. "Like I said, this is a great opportunity for you. We have our family together again. It's truly the work of fate that this happened the way it did."

"Well, Uncle Burt, give us the amount," Will said plainly.

"It's over ten thousand, give or take some." Will gave a long whistle. "It's in the bank earning a little interest, which was Frederick's idea." Burt quickly cleared his throat with the mention of Jessica's ex-husband. Before he could speak further, Jacob was cursing loudly.

Burt grabbed his son's arm. "Settle down, Jake."

Jacob puffed up his chest but said no more.

"Yes, Frederick did contribute half, and if your conscience can't take his money, then at least take the sum Thomas and I put in."

"Five thousand from Freddie, huh?" Will tipped his head. "That's mighty generous of him, but then again, he seems to have a way with a buck." He turned to Jacob. "We'll talk it over. As business partners, we need to discuss this."

Caleb lifted a brow. *Business partners?* "Since your discussions have nothing to do with me, I'll excuse myself and return to my wife." Caleb set down his glass and walked back into the house. He couldn't stand to see the pair's false pride showing like a shiny penny in the rain. They were hungry for the money.

Jacob felt the very opposite. It had everything to do with Caleb. He would now have the means to make Jessica his wife and support her. "Father, Will is right. We need to think about this. Our plans might not be what you want to hear. You may find the money would be better served elsewhere."

"Son, I only ask that you and Will stop the traveling, gambling, and whatever else it is you've been doing to earn your way and settle down into a career that has meaning and integrity." Burt looked sternly at his nephew. "I'll not support your gambling habit, Will, so get that notion out of your mind. I'd rather give the money to charity than to see you throw it away at the tables and on women."

Will sheepishly looked down at his shoes. "Yes, sir."

"Now, then. You're both grown men, and I have little to say as to what you do with your lives, but I do believe that this money gives us—your aunt, Bethany, and me—an opinion as to how it's spent."

"Are you trying to buy me, Father?"

Burt paused. Jacob held his face in check. He had said the wrong thing. "The world has made you into a cynical man, my son, and it's not something I like to see. I suggest you do talk it over. We'll discuss this again in the following days, unless you have to leave us to engage in some important business." Burt left them alone.

Jacob felt the sting of his father's mocking words. "Christ Almighty!" he cursed to no one in particular.

Will sat back in his chair. "It's a fortune, Jake. We could go into San Francisco, get an office, and really make a business out of our trading skills. All these years could've been preparing us for this. We've learned a few things, damn it. Let's make the most of it."

Jacob looked at his glass of port. "I don't know."

"What do you mean you don't know?"

Jacob sat still as Will stepped from the porch and began to pace in front of him.

When he came back, his blue-green eyes were sharp, his tone unwavering. He talked into Jacob's ear. "You and I are going to take all of this goddamn money and go to San Francisco and start ourselves a real business, and you, my friend, are going to let my sister lead her own life."

Jacob rubbed the back of his neck, then reached for a cigarette from his shirt pocket. "That may not be possible given the circumstances."

Will grabbed his arm. "I've never been more serious, Jake, and I don't want to hear about any *circumstances*. This is it. We've come to a crossroads."

Jacob took down his arm and Will released it. The two men faced each other. He slowly went for his pocket again. "I know. Sorry." He lit the rolled cigarette and exhaled the smoke. Will had taken him out of his fantasy. To him she was so close, but his heart again had tricked his mind. He felt empty.

"Are we still partners?" Will asked, "or do I take my share and we go our separate ways? And before you answer that, I have to say … if I'm let loose with all that cash, well, I'm damn afraid it might be the death of me."

"Damn it!" Jacob gave Will a friendly shove. "God, I feel as if I'm *married* to you."

Will laughed out loud. "I promise I'll never ask for a new dress or bonnet."

Jacob cracked a smile. "Go to hell!"

They studied each other and came to the same resolve and forgiveness they had come to know. With a handshake, they had re-established their partnership and friendship.

"Will, I think we have to give Frederick's part of the money to Jess."

Will considered the thought. "Five hundred to her. We'll need the rest if we're going to do this right."

"So we take all of it then?"

Will nodded with a grin.

"I'd like to see the look on Frederick's face when he finds out we got the reward." Jacob smirked.

"Yep, that dignified Englishman might just come undone." Will laughed.

"Serves him right, the bastard. Hiding his money like this, betting she'd never return."

Will began calculating the next move in their newfound circumstance. "We'll deal with Frederick when the time comes." He lifted his glass. "Merry Christmas, Cuz."

Jacob met his glass with a clink. "And a Happy New Year."

Chapter Fifty-three

*C*aleb helped Jessica down from the carriage. "I'll be in as soon as I store the rig."

She went into the house. Reuniting with her family had exhausted her. Fainting embarrassed her and alerted her to the fact that she wasn't as strong as she had hoped to be once back home. Standing in the middle of the room, she began to cry, happy and sad at the same time. Before she could compose herself, Caleb was at her back, his arms wrapped around her shuddering body. He led her to the paisley chair. She could feel his eyes searching her face. "I'm just being emotional. I'll be fine."

"Let's go to bed, sweetheart. It's late and I'm beat."

They lay side by side with their fingers entwined under the covers. She placed her head on his shoulder. Many moments passed, yet she could not sleep. "Are you awake?"

His hand tightened around hers and he whispered, "Do you want to talk about what happened to you?"

The quiet request gave her the feeling he was afraid to upset her. Jessica's heart felt too big for her chest. "Yes, and no."

"I understand, but I'm in the dark here. What have you gone through? What did they do to you? Will told me where they found you. I was close, Jess. I shouldn't have given up searching for you, damn it."

Swallowing the lump in her throat, she slid her hand from his. She lifted her body to rest against the wooden headboard. Crossing her arms over her chest, she began to let the events unfold. "His name is Blue Heron, and he took me from the river that day. He knew you or he knew your name. Rex Conrad told him he was looking for you for some crime and that if they kidnapped me, he and the Indians in the camp would get money from you. If not, he would marry me. No money came and we were married." She stopped to catch her breath and let him absorb her words. She caught a glimpse of his fine features lit by a shaft of the moonlight. His brows were knitted, as if he was trying to solve a problem.

"Was there a marriage ceremony?"

She smirked. "Yes, but it was of no consequence to me. It was silly. I hardly spoke a word."

"It might not have meant much to you, but it did for him, for them."

"For him? For them? Caleb, he kidnapped me! Because of something you did!" Her emotions were unleashed. "What did you do?"

As if coming out of a daze, he looked into her eyes. "Yes, I'm sorry. It was wrong of him."

"Do you know Blue Heron? Is he and the rest of them part of the Klamath people?"

Caleb pinched his lips. "I knew of him and his father, Sam Farrow, but only from a distance. His community was in another part of the reservation. I heard about their split. I didn't think it was possible for them to take anyone." He sat up. "I assume you consummated the union?"

Jessica couldn't believe what she was hearing. "I don't want to talk about any of this for another second." Angry and hurt, she turned away.

He pulled her around. "Come here. I'm so sorry, Jess. I did things I can't take back, but you're safe. I would have given my life to not have this happen. Believe me, I'll never forgive myself."

She leaned into him, wishing away her problems, hoping the

conversation would end and she could go back to re-entering her life. It seemed murky now, and she wasn't sure in what direction to turn. "Rex Conrad is dead. I suppose that's good news for you."

"It is. I can't tell you why, Jess. Tell me more about what you went through."

Sharing her experience at the Indian camp was easy. She told him what it was like to sleep in a hut and what she had learned along with her great need to escape. They talked about the Indians, who wanted a life free of the reservation. When Caleb told her their ultimate fate, she felt a jab of sadness for Lea and From-Wings, Blue Heron, and the rest. Not Mallow. "They will never have the life they once knew," he said. Then Caleb's next question turned her world inside out.

"There is one thing I want to know, Jessica. What was your relationship with Jacob when you traveled together? The fainting, the weak stomach. Are you pregnant?"

Her heart became irregular. She straightened the sheets and blanket. Her pillow felt like a block of lead at her back. She shook it out and fluffed it, then tugged it behind her head. It was inevitable. Somewhere inside her, she thought she could keep her secret and claim Caleb as the father.

"Tell me." His face was rigid.

She felt a side of her emerge, wild and without shame. "I was with him. I found comfort with him."

Coming away from her, he closed his eyes. "Oh God." He rose and put on his clothes, then left the room. She lifted herself out of bed. Wrapping her dressing gown around her waist, she joined her husband in the parlor.

The sound of Boones sleeping, the crackle of a burning log in the stove, the river's flow in the distance. She sat down. Caleb was seated at the edge of his leather chair, staring at the fire flickering behind the glass front of the stove. "I didn't know you felt so strongly about him. I confess I read his letters to you. I saw the drawing. Excuse my intrusion, but I wanted to hold something that was you. I didn't expect to find what I did." His voice held a conviction that undid her. Getting up, he stood and looked down at her. "Go to him, then. Damn it, why did you come back? A telegram would have explained it. I could have gone on with my life, knowing at least you were safe." His eyes filled with angry tears. "I could have gone on with my life, Jessica."

Slowly, she rose and stood before him in such a way as to command his full attention. "Now you listen to me, Caleb Cantrell. I have traveled through suffering heat and biting cold, and rain and mud. I was beaten, and I pulled myself out of the very depths of fear itself, all so I could survive to be with *you*, here in *our* home. I struggled every day to stay alive so we could sit beside each other, to make love again, in *our* bed." She swallowed hard, tasting the hardship. "Yes, I love Jacob, and yes, I laid with him. He asked me to join him, but I came back because I chose to be with you. I love you and I want. ..." She heaved a great sob and sank back into her chair.

"What do you want?" He showed little compassion.

She looked down at her stomach. "I"—she took in a deep breath and let it out between pursed lips—"I want you to be the father."

Caleb's chest trembled. He had missed her so much, he could barely respond to her request. He looked away as the tears ran down his face. Pulling back his hair, he went into the kitchen. A thousand questions ran through his head. Returning to the parlor, he took his seat. "I don't know what to say." His mind went to Jane, and suddenly, he ached for her comfort. He couldn't look at his wife. He was disgusted by his deep hatred of her and Jacob's togetherness. "I can't lose you again, but this is too much." The words choked his throat.

She pressed her lips inward and lowered her head. "We both did things we regret. It was a terrible trial, but we got through it."

"Have we?" He felt betrayed. "What now? What becomes of

this love you and he have? Will I always be wondering? How can I trust you? He saw the hurt in her eyes, but he couldn't back down. "You're asking me to raise another man's child. What the hell does Jacob say to all this?" His anger was at the surface now.

"Jacob doesn't know and he won't ever know."

Spring from his chair, he shouted, "Jesus Christ, Jessica! What have you done?" He went to the vestibule and grabbed his coat.

"Caleb!"

Chapter Fifty-four

*D*ay after excruciating day, she waited. Each night, she slept alone while Caleb slept on a pallet in his workshop. The days were long, even with the light being extinguished early in December.

Today she would visit her mother and aunt. It wasn't time to tell them about the baby—her and Caleb's baby. She calculated it several times, and each time she had the child coming into the world several weeks early. It would have to be. As she brought the carriage down the mountain, she weighed her options. Where would she go if Caleb rejected her? The thought of living with her mother made her sick. Pulling the carriage over to the side of the road, she vomited.

"Jessica, you look pale," her mother said after embracing her. Before Jessica could give an excuse, her mother was on to another topic. "I have news."

Looking from her mother to her aunt, she waited.

"I've bought a house just on the next block," Bethany claimed with satisfaction. "I want you to come take a look. It's big enough for company, if you ever decide to … well, if you want to visit me."

The tears rolled down Jessica's face. "I'd love to see it, and of course I will visit." Noticing the sadness in her mother's eyes, her own grief for the loss of her father emerged. "I know it's hard without him."

"Yes, well, one must carry on." Bethany straightened her shoulders. "And if things change, you will always have a home with me," she said, crossing her arms in front of her skirt. "There, I said it, June. Now let's have tea. I want to know how you and Caleb will be spending Christmas. Will and Jacob are in the city, planning their business, but I'm sure they will make it for the day. We will celebrate family." Bethany looked at June with a smile. "We have our children back."

"Indeed!" June exclaimed as she raised her teacup. "The new year looks bright!" She drank from her cup as if to seal the statement. "Your uncle Burt has given them all the money as they requested, and I think some will go to you and Caleb."

"Auntie, I think you and Uncle should take it back. Don't you need it for your own lives?"

"Tish! We are doing just fine. And as your uncle has said, Frederick owes it to this family for being such a stingy, horrible man."

Jessica smirked. "He didn't call him that, Auntie."

"Well, that's what I say. But let's not dwell on that. I'm so pleased my son and nephew will be close and successful."

The reward money was substantial, Jessica thought, but she worried about Frederick's involvement. He could cause trouble for Will and Jacob. She decided to keep her opinions and concerns to herself. After what she experienced with them, she knew they were hard up for money and a different life. It pleased her to know they would now have the means to change their course. With talk of Jacob, her hand went to her lower belly, hidden by layers of pleated skirt. Every night, she fell asleep cupping the slight protrusion. The protection she felt for her unborn child was overwhelming.

The conversation veered toward the coming holiday season, and the warmth emanating from the two women buoyed Jessica. The sadness of Thomas's passing mixed with the joy of a bright future. She wished to take some of the positive spirit with her. Perhaps she should break the silence with Caleb. After so many days, it had become unbearable. Jacob would be in San Francisco—close but not too near. Somehow, it could work. She would have to bear up during holidays and other occasions when they came together as a family. He was her cousin. Their love would remain, as always, deep inside her heart, and now with their child.

Before dusk, Jessica left her mother and aunt. The visit went well, and they didn't suspect a thing. She managed to keep down the refreshments and turn the conversation around to focus on decorating her mother's home or the Christmas feast her aunt would serve.

Once home, she brought the rig into the barn. Caleb was there, grooming his horse. The light was dim, and he was nearly a shadow. He didn't turn to look at her, and with a huff, she left him alone.

The sky was black and clear with a swath of stars scattered across it. She lit the lamps and stoked the fire. She was not looking forward to another silent meal with him while the turmoil in her churned along with her rising anger. If he wanted her to go away, she would have to accept it, yet the very notion made her want to burst into tears.

Finally, Caleb came inside, and she could hear him remove his coat and hat. He went to the cupboard that held the liquor and poured some brandy into a glass. In one gulp it was gone, and he poured himself another. She glanced up at him. He stood to her left, staring at the fire, his blue eyes hooded, his lips in a tight line. Where was the man who loved her? Was he still there? She sat very still on her red, paisley chair, the one she hoped to grow old in. The fire blazed as hot as the tension in the air.

"I don't like it." His voice was low and hoarse.

"I'm so sorry, Caleb, I. ..."

He brought his hand up to silence her. "I see I have no choice. I don't want to live without you, so ... I'll take things as they are, and God help me, I won't live to regret it." He swallowed his drink, grabbed his coat, and went out to the porch.

It wasn't the loving statement of trust she'd hoped for, but the weight of the world was lifted from her. "Thank you, Caleb," she said softly to his back. She waited a moment before she went to the window. A candle in a silver holder crafted by his very hands sat on the windowsill. She touched it lovingly. It would get lit as soon as the kerosene lamps were lowered and bedtime approached. The cozy glow would softly illuminate their bedroom. Would he come to her tonight or stay away?

Jessica lifted her shawl from the peg and stepped out. She sat on the smooth, cedar bench. The moon was full, bathing the world with white light and scattered shadows. It reminded her of a time when she and Caleb were new and full of promise. He stood just off the porch, his blond hair alight, his body, tall and strong.

He turned to face her. "You must be happy to have both me and Jacob."

She sucked in a breath. "That was cruel."

"But true."

This was not the way she wanted her life to go, yet determination swelled in her and she knew she would make the most of the life ahead of her. With Caleb by her side, she could make this right. "Are we to be a family then?" A shiver ran up her spine. She brought her shawl tighter around her shoulders. He came up on the porch and leaned against the rail, his hands folded across his chest.

"You're asking me to raise another man's child. A family? No, not in the real sense."

"You can adopt him or her, and the child will be yours in name and, hopefully, in your heart."

"I see you have this all figured out. I suppose you had time to think about it. Jacob deliberately kept you to himself, and you went along with it. How can I forgive that?" He turned away from her, his voice nearly lost in the night. "When is the child due?"

Feeling more hurt than any beating she received from Mallow, her chest heaved with emotion. Her voice shaky, she said, "I think July."

"And if I choose to tell Jacob?" His question felt like a threat.

"For the sake of the child, please don't. What will we tell him or her– an innocent child?"

He slapped his hand on the railing, his profile etched in anger. "Goddammit, you should have thought about that before you let your damn lust get the better of you! I assume it was mutual."

"Caleb!" Jessica grabbed his arm, forcing him to face her. "I love this baby. It comes from love, but I choose to be with you. I love you with all my heart."

"All of it? I think not." His sour tone sparked her anger.

"Stop it!" Her words echoed in the stillness of the night.

He slowly turned from her and bowed his head. His words came low. She could hear the sound of them breathing. "I'm sorry."

"Caleb."

"Will I have to share you with him? I don't think I can do that."

"No, you are my husband."

"Life is never what one plans. Because I'm still in love with you, we will stay together and I'll keep your secret." Turning to face her, he looked her in the eye. "But someday, Jessica, it will come out, and you and I will have to deal with the consequences. Nothing happens without consequence."

"I don't see how it will be exposed if only you and I know."

He shook his head. "I hope you're right."

"I promise to keep your secrets also." She knew she had lit a fuse, but she didn't care. She didn't want his pity, only his respect, and for them to be on level ground.

"What?"

"I heard my brother and Jacob talking, though I'm sure they thought I was ignorant of it.

What happened in Colorado, and what had that to do with my kidnapping?"

She had stunned him into silence, her nerves on edge. Did she really want to know?

He fished in his pocket for a cigarette but found none. Scratching his head, he began to speak. "We worked together, Will, Jacob, and me, along with a group of gunrunners." He spoke without looking at her. "There was an incident in Colorado. Jacob saved my life. We had no idea of the ramifications, only that we needed to leave the camp and head out in separate directions. I went to Oregon, and Will and Jacob went south. The scout, Rex Conrad, was hired to look for us and take us back to Colorado… to stand trial. Instead, he was looking to make a buck off the incident and hired the Indians to take you. I guess he thought they could hold you while he came to me for the ransom. He got himself killed instead."

"Stand trial?" He looked at her, his expression was serious, almost cold. A shiver run up her spin. "Keaton. The burned camp. I read an article about it on my trip out west." She brought her hand to her mouth. "Oh God, Caleb. I can't believe you and my brother and Jacob could be a part of that."

"Believe what you want. The truth still remains the same. We never could have imagined that …" His voice cracked and he cleared his throat. "I'd prefer it if you didn't discuss this with Will or Jacob."

"If that's what you want," she said softly.

He turned to her. "Looks like we have another secret between us."

She pursed her lips. "Are we safe?"

"I think so, but I'll always be looking over my shoulder. Let me worry about that." The puff of air escaping his lungs was white in the cold night. "Now I need your forgiveness."

She wasn't sure what to say. Her life had been dramatically altered by the two men she loved, yet their futures would be intertwined forever with hers. "For the baby, I forgive you."

"Sounds like a trade—my forgiveness for yours." He stood closer.

"I don't want to bargain with you. I will raise this child alone if I have to. I can take care of myself." She didn't know why she was being so defiant. Were her survival instincts still in charge?

"Getting yourself back here proves that." He brought her to sit with him on the bench. "I won't ever put you in harm's way again. The honest truth is, I love you, Jessica. That hasn't changed."

She nodded and came to sit closer to him. They found each other's hand and held on tight. The sharp edges of their defenses having been filed down, Jessica felt that her little family's future held more promise than peril. The moonlit landscape, sparkling with dew, captured her attention. She breathed a sigh of relief. This was her home … her heart … her sacred terrain.

THE END

Acknowledgments

I would like to thank everyone who encouraged me to continue with my Traveled Heart series.

It's been such a joy to write.

I also want to thank my team– Julie Christine Johnson for her insightful developmental editing.

Jane Dixon-Smith for her wonderful cover design and great formatting. Joyce Mochrie, my copy-editor and proofreader for her meticulous editing and proofreading. Without these talented ladies I would not have the novel I present to the world today. Thank you so much!

Thank you to my family– my daughters, Star and Heidi, my grand-children, Nathan, Dylan, Miles, Liam and Dalila, my sister Beth and brother Earl, and special thanks to my wonderful husband, Jeff. Your love and support is invaluable.

Thank you to my readers and their feedback. I will always keep you in mind as I continue to write. You are the inspiration that keeps me wanting to put out my very best work for you to enjoy.

I'd like to thank the women who came before me who had the courage to pursue their dreams even when those dreams and desires contradicted the rules and restrictions of society.

Peace and Love,
Veronica

Traveled Hearts

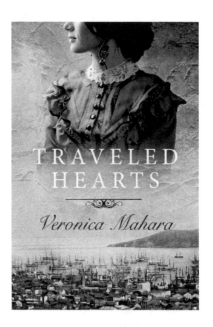

The first in the Traveled Hearts series begins with
a dangerous romance and society's restrictions. Both will
lead Jessica Messing, a budding artist down paths filled
with hardship and discovery in Victorian Age America.

Veronica Mahara is the maiden name of Veronica Stoneman who lives with her husband and two cats surrounded by her family and the beauty of the Pacific Northwest. To find out more about the author and future publications visit: veronicasunmahara.com

CPSIA information can be obtained
at www.ICGtesting.com
Printed in the USA
BVHW041129030121
596871BV00025B/2597